STRICTLY A FAMILY MATTER

STRICTLY A FAMILY MATTER

BASED ON A TRUE LIFE EXPERIENCE

FICTION

RAMON L. QUEZADA

iUniverse, Inc.

New York Lincoln Shanghai

STRICTLY A FAMILY MATTER
BASED ON A TRUE LIFE EXPERIENCE

iUniverse books may be ordered through booksellers or by contacting:

iUniverse
2021 Pine Lake Road, Suite 100
Lincoln, NE 68512
www.iuniverse.com
1-800-Authors (1-800-288-4677)

The names of persons have been changed
in this fictionalized account of the
<u>incidents that occurred</u>.

ISBN: 0-595-33660-4

Printed in the United States of America

DEDICATED TO THE MEMORY

OF MY BROTHER ROMAN,

MY PARENTS,

MY UNCLE GUADALUPE

AND TO

MY AUNTS

CARMEN

AND

CLEOFAS

AND

WE ALSO DO NOT WANT TO EVER FORGET

MY AUNT MARIA

"The laws of meaningful coincidence does connect events and people that are apparently not at all connected in terms of logic."

—Carl Jung

CONTENTS

▼

INTRODUCTION xiii

PROLOGUE 1

PART I

Chapter 1:   A NEW APPROACH 7

Chapter 2:   OLD PHOTOGRAPHS 14

Chapter 3:   MATTER OF URGENCY 20

Chapter 4:   THE INITIAL STEP 29

Chapter 5:   THE INVITATION 36

Chapter 6:   THE CEMETERY DREAM 44

Chapter 7:   NEW INSIGHTS 50

Chapter 8:   VIBRATIONS 58

Chapter 9:   THE INCIDENT 63

PART II

Chapter 10:   UNUSUAL SYMPTONS 73

Chapter 11:   DOCTOR BLOOM 78

Chapter 12:   SEEKING HELP 84

Chapter 13:   SPIRITUAL SUPPRESSION 91

Chapter 14:   A PAST LIFE REGRESSION 98

Chapter 15:   THE GURGLING SEWER 106

Chapter 16:   GOING TO THE SOURCE 112

Chapter 17:   SEVEN SISTERS DREAM 119

Chapter 18:   AN INSPIRATIONAL MOMENT 125

Chapter 19:   THE RESTLESS SPIRIT THEORY 133

Chapter 20:   THE OLD STORY TELLER 141

Chapter 21:   MICHELLE'S MISSION 147

Chapter 22:   LYNN'S STORY 153

Chapter 23:   THE PLAN 160

Chapter 24:   DESPITE THE DEVIL.. 166

Chapter 25:   A CLEAN SPIRIT 172

Chapter 26:   A MOMENT TO REFLECT 178

Chapter 27:   THE GATHERING... 184

Chapter 28:   CRYSTAL TEARS.. 190

Chapter 29:   THANKS FOR THE LOVE....................................... 196

ACKNOWLEDGMENTS

My gratitude to my good friends Jim Bell and Jackie. Also to Jim's daughter Lauri Bell and her good friend Sharon. Many thanks go to Marge Cooney, Ann Maria Sutor, Sharon Noordewier, Susan Pilcher, Alden Hess, Wanda Walker, Bill Chaput, Paula Greevly and to, Alex Baez. Also my thanks go to my devoted supporters Pat Weiss and especially to Beau Gage who edited my final draft. My thanks also go to Margo Smith who typed the Expression of Love letter. Then there is Dorothy Scovil and of course to my very special friends the late Dick Ahearn and the late Kevin Coffey. I especially wish to thank Phyllis Hogpian and Sharon Meyer who willfully shared their investigative psychic knowledge with my family. A very special thanks goes to my good friends Jim and Geri Waelti who never gave up hope. Also want to thank my friend Gonzalo Plasencia.

My love and appreciation to my sister Elena Margarita and my nieces Marta Bozymowski and Elena Luisa Quezada who were also unexpectedly drawn into this unusual phenomenon. I wish to thank my brothers Mike, Carlos and my late brother Roman who gave their support to the family unity gathering and to all my nieces and nephew who also participated in that event.

I also am grateful to my late cousin Margarita Vasquez and especially to my niece, Margarita Vazquez Rosa. In addition I shall never forget the memory of my late Aunt Carmen who taught me the art of old fashion story telling and the real expression of love. I also wish to thank my cousins Angel Rosa and Nacho Herrera for taking the time to try and understand their American cousin.

My heart felt gratitude goes to my late Uncle Guadalupe Quezada who was my family mentor and to his daughter Ludivina who originally stimulated my interest in my Mexican heritage.

A great deal of thanks goes to my dear friend Laurie Nadel who contributed her professional advice and wisdom.

But most importantly special thanks goes to my dear friend Cindi Onefeather Armstrong a/k/a Lois Gleason with whose willingness and dedication helped to make things happen. Without her this story could never be told.

R.Q.

INTRODUCTION

It has often been said that when the student is ready, the teacher will be there. However, there are times when the student needs to be jolted awake from their daydreaming in order to get them to pay attention. This is the case with Armand Seguera who is the student and his teachers are spirit guides from the other side. The materials used in this course are no more than just an open mind and an open heart.

Strictly A Family Matter is about how a young Mexican mother of five goes about spiritually uniting her family forty-three years after passing away and how her youngest son Armand, was chosen to help fulfill her last wishes.

Armand's awakening comes from a series of unexplainable coincidences and a constant flow of vivid dreams. However, he is not alone, because others members of his family have also experienced some of the same dream phenomenon. But, unbeknownst to Armand, there is also another family spirit wanting attention and whose wishes also need to be fulfilled. This complicates matters and so the spirit world decides to provide Armand with a young assistant named Lynn Sullivan.

The story encompasses the exercising of ones intuition plus a variety of metaphysical subjects including love—family love to be exact. It is a spiritual love energy that has no boundaries between those persons living on the physical plane of existence and with those spirits existing on the other side. It is the kind of love energy that transcends time and space and can take you back in time or forward into the future. It is an energy that exists for everyone.

PROLOGUE

▼

JUNE 14, 1925
DURANGO, MEXICO

Situated in the distant foothills of the Sierra Madre Mountains in Mexico's northern State of Durango is the town of Canatlan. Canatlan is the municipality that is responsible for governing all the smaller towns, villages and ranches within its immediate surroundings.

Small shade trees decorate Canatlan's central plaza and directly across the road is the church of San Diego with its two colorful bell towers. On the far side of the plaza is a municipal building and the telephone and telegraph center. The open marketplace is located on a narrow cobblestone thoroughfare that runs through town and on the outskirts are the stockyards, the cemetery, a gas pump and the train station. The rail line connects Canatlan to the City of Durango, the state's capital city, with the same name, thirty-five miles to the south.

A short distance down the road from Canatlan, is the small village of San Jeronimo. Throughout San Jeronimo are rows of one-story windowless pale brown adobe houses. Cows rest in the shade while chicken's strut about pecking for food everywhere. A lone donkey stands motionless under a shade tree and nearby pigs wallow in the mud. Dogs roam about freely on the unpaved dusty streets in search for food. The weather is very hot and dry.

Growing along the banks of the river that passes on the outskirts of the village is a grove of lofty weeping willow trees. Dominating the center of San Jeronimo is a large two-story vacant hacienda. Abandoned by its owners during the Mexican Revolutionary War in 1910, the deserted hacienda stands as a silent monument to a pre-Revolutionary War way of life. Next to the hacienda stands the church of San Jeronimo and where on this fine sunny Sunday afternoon in June, there is a wedding ceremony being preformed. Parked outside, are automobiles, horse-drawn carriages, a saddled horse and a donkey. Inside the church, Rodolfo Seguera and Adelina Rivera are being united in holy matrimony. Adelina looks radiant in her white wedding gown and the tall mustached Rodolfo is also a handsome figure in his dark suit.

Rodolfo's ushers are his two younger brothers Pedro and Victor. A few years ago, Rodolfo had gone north across the border to seek work in Detroit, Michigan. He had now returned specifically in order to marry Adelina.

The bridesmaids are Adelina's two younger sisters, Carmen and Cleofas. Adelina teaches school in San Jeronimo and is the second oldest of six sisters.

As soon as the ceremony is concluded, the lone San Jeronimo's church bell begins to clank announcing another union between a man and a woman. Family and friends begin to stream out of the church and into the bright sunlight. The guests then begin to joyfully shower Adelina and Rodolfo with small handfuls of rice before moving towards the house that is directly across the road. The reception is being held at the home of the Adelina's parents, Luis and Julia Rivera.

Although there is much to be joyful on this fine June day, there is also a cause for sadness, because after the reception Adelina and Rodolfo will be leaving on the evening train to Durango and then on to Cuidad Juarez. From there, the couple will cross the border into El Paso, Texas and then continue their journey to Michigan.

A tall shade tree dominates the center of the Rivera family's exceptionally large courtyard. In one corner, a wooden platform has been especially erected for the dancers and the scene is ablaze with brightly colored decorations. The courtyard has now become alive with music and laughter. The guests eat, drink, sing loudly and dance energetically to the traditional country music and popular Revolutionary War tunes. Children are playing everywhere, while boisterous political rhetoric is prevalent amongst several of the men gathered in one corner of the courtyard.

Then, as the late afternoon sun begins to set behind the mountains and the sky turns to dusk, the faint sound of a train whistle is heard in the distance. This is the signal that the celebration has come to an end and it is time to chauffeur those who are leaving San Jeronimo to the Canatlan train station. Everyone then boards the automobiles and carriages for the short trip.

The gentle sounds of sniffling can be heard throughout the train platform as family and friends begin to embrace and share their final good-byes. Eyes are filled with tears as each member of the Rivera family takes their turn embracing Adelina for one last time. But then, just as Adelina was about to board the train, her mother Julia, presents Adelina with a small elegantly decorated black velvet pouch. The pouch is somewhat heavy for its size, but Adelina knows that it contains a beautiful blue beaded rosary. The rosary beads were made from a precious turquoise gemstone that had belonged to Julia's oldest daughter Maria. Unfortunately, Maria passed away five years earlier. Hence, this particular gift is a symbol of their family's love and devotion to one another and represents the family's hope and dreams that someday soon the family will be reunited.

As soon as the last passenger boards the train, the conductor gives the departure signal and the engineer immediately blows the whistle. Suddenly, the train is jerked from a dead stop that creates a loud screeching sound of heavy metal rubbing against heavy metal. Slowly the train begins to chug away leaving those who are staying to wave goodbye from the platform. At the same time, many of passengers themselves began to wave white handkerchiefs through the open train windows. Within only a few moments the train rounds the bend and slowly fades away into the darkness. But for Rodolfo and Adelina, it is a future that is full of hope and for the many dreams that are yet to be fulfilled.

CHAPTER 1

▼

A NEW APPROACH

After having completed a long overdue trip report, I paused to glance at the office wall clock it read 6:00 PM. It was not unusual for anyone to be working late, except that it was a Friday afternoon in mid-July, so everyone else had already departed for the weekend. Doug Adams, the office manger who routinely worked late, was on vacation. The only other person present in the office was the cleaning lady.

Leaning back in my swivel chair, I decided to relax, so I stretched out my legs and extended them atop the desk. I then placed my hands behind my head, took a deep breath and after closing my eyes, I allowed the air to slowly escape from between my lips. It felt great to relax after having reached the end of a hectic week.

During the summer of 1978, Donaldson Williamson, a large Wall Street stockbrokerage firm was in the process of undergoing an aggressive expansion program. The firm was in the process of opening new branch offices in cities all around the country. I was one of the firm's branch office operations specialists and therefore, I traveled a great deal. My own office was on the fourteenth floor of the Madison Building which is located on Broad Street and only one block from the New York Stock Exchange.

Recently, there hadn't been much time for me to think about what was really on my mind. Two months earlier, I had broken off my engagement with my girl friend Diana English. The breakup had left me somewhat perplexed and now I was beginning to get reflective. The reason for the breakup was simple. Diana was pressuring me to get married, move to the suburbs and have children. Except for the marriage part, none of the other things appealed to me and I had no enthusiasm for changing my life style to that degree. I respected the fact that Diana was thirty-five years old and with only a few more child bearing years. I just wasn't prepared to raise a family.

Suddenly I decided to stop feeling sorry for myself and to go and have a cold beer with my good friend Rick Mulhren. After snapping my briefcase shut, I waved goodnight to the cleaning lady and headed for the elevators. Outside, the weather was the kind of afternoon that one would expect in mid July, it was hot and humid. I immediately crossed the street and entered Maxwell's pub. On Friday afternoons or any afternoon for that matter the bar is always crowded. I scanned the smoke filled room until I spotted Rick chatting with some of our drinking buddies. It took me only a moment before I caught his eye and motioned to him to join me in one of the empty booths. I really wasn't in the mood to socialize with the boys tonight and was hoping that I could have a private conversation with Rick. Rick quickly excused himself from the group to come over and join me.

Rick was also an employee of Donaldson Williams and was the editor of the firm's branch operations procedural manuals. Being involved with the branch procedures meant that we worked very closely. Besides work, Rick was one of my closest friends and confidant. He was extremely perceptive, intuitive and was also inquisitive enough to research subjects that he or anyone around him knew nothing about. Mainly, I enjoyed his company and good humor.

"Hi Rick!" I'm glad I caught up with you. Hope I'm not disturbing you?" I inquired.

"Hi Armand. No, you're not interrupting anything. I was just shooting the bull with some of the guys," Rick replied. "But I was wondering if you had heard the latest rumor?" he added.

"You mean about Doug being promoted?" I answered.

"Yep, that's the one! I think that should make you happy Armand, after all you're next in line to fill Doug's position," Rick exclaimed with some enthusiasm.

"Thanks Rick, but I think that you're just as qualified to fill that job as I am. Besides, I don't want to build up any false hopes in the event that I don't get the job. I'm also aware that the new trend has been for management to begin bringing in so-called experts from the outside," I explained by expressing my skepticism.

"You might be right Armand, except that they just see me as a writer and an editor. You continuously work close with Doug and you're in the decision making process with management," Rick commented. "Believe me when I say that you're exposure in the firm is sufficient enough that it will get you the job."

The waitress arrived with a couple of mugs of beer and placed them on the table. "Why don't you run a tab for us?" Rick suggested to her.

"Sure," the waitress replied with a pleasant smile. Rick and I were no strangers to Maxwell's. We knew the bartenders, waitresses and many of our colleagues hung out in the place. At times, it was sort of an office away from the office and a good place to hear gossip and rumors.

"I know this promotion is important to you, but I also know well enough to know that you've got something else on your mind. You haven't spoken about Diana since your breakup," Rick inquired.

Feeling a bit edgy about what I was going to say, I decided to first take a sip of my beer. I began, "You're absolutely right Rick! I wish Diana hadn't made such a point about wanting to have kids. I know how important it was to her. However, I feel as though I helped to shatter her dreams and it even broke her heart at the same time."

"But I think it also broke your heart a little too," Rick added.

"Rick, I'm no different than anyone else, I want to love and be loved," I said. Now I was getting to the reasons for my wanting to have a private conversation with Rick. Attempting to get my thoughts together, I hesitated for a moment before bringing up the next subject. "I don't know how to say this to you Rick, but I think that I may have a serious problem."

"What kind of a serious problem?" Rick asked, sounding both concerned and a bit confused by my statement. "I don't believe it," he added.

"You see, I may just be using marriage and babies as an excuse. Do you recall when I broke up with Karen about four years ago?"

"Yes, I do. The circumstances behind that breakup were very similar to this one. Karen was also pressuring you to get married and to have children," Rick recalled.

"That's right. As soon as any of the girls I'm dating start talking about marriage, I break-up with them and run from the relationship," I stated.

"Are you telling me that you get cold feet at the thought of getting married?" Rick said, while he was still trying to comprehend the problem. "Good God Armand, I've known you for a long time and I would never have suspected that of you. I know that we've never discussed it, but I just thought you fell out of love with the girls. One thing I do know about you, is that your first marriage left you with a bad taste."

"That's possible, but the answer to your first question, is yes," I sadly admitted.

"Maybe it's just the fear of making a marital commitment," Rick commented. "There are lots of guys out there who don't want to get married. Look at Fred Hanson. How long has Fred been dating Shirley? Eleven years and they're still not married. However, I don't see any of this affecting your work. I continue to see you take on new challenges all the time," Rick added.

Now I was getting closer to my point, so I said, "Rick, I hope you're not going to laugh at what I'm about to tell you."

"Nope, I promise," Rick responded, accompanied by a nod of his head.

"As you know, I'll be forty-four years old next month, and so what I would like to do is to try and get my act together. You know how I'm always rushing around, traveling everywhere and never really stopping to reflect on myself. So what I have in mind is to take some time off, just slow down a little and see if I can figure out what's bothering me," I stated while at the same time looking for a reaction from Rick.

"I hope you're not thinking of going to a head shrink, are you?" Rick quickly interjected.

"Absolutely not," I responded. "I know it's the thing to do these days, but I've always taken enough pride in my ability to handle my own personal problems. There's no reason why I can't do it in this situation. I spoke to Doug just before he left for vacation, and asked him if I could take a week off when he gets back. He said it would be okay, so what I'm thinking of doing is going to Detroit and spending a little time with my family."

"Detroit, why Detroit?" Rick quickly inquired. "I would think that you would want to head for the mountains or a quiet beach for this sort of thing. What do you expect to find in Detroit? You've often told me how you want to go back and visit your family in Mexico. I know that you've been there a few times and this might be a good time for you to go there, if being away from the world is what you're looking for."

I began my explanation; "Not too long ago I read an article in one of those psychology magazines that said reflecting on your childhood can be extremely beneficial and that our behavior as adults is a direct result from our upbringing. Detroit is where I was born and raised. It might help me to gather some insights into my childhood behavior. Usually, I just go there and socialize with my family and friends then leave. This time I plan to make myself more aware of the things around me. Maybe even visit my old grade school and then go out to the playground and walk around there for awhile. There is plenty for me to reminisce about in those schoolyards. Besides, something inside of me is telling me that I should go. I don't know what it is or why, but I think that I should just go and find out. For now, my trip to Mexico can wait."

"I've read about that childhood regression approach. Psychiatrists use it a lot," Rick commented, while he tried to remember something, "Do you recall that about a year ago when we were having cocktails in the lounge at the Ambassador Hotel in Chicago. You told me then that you've always suspected that there was someone or something special out there somewhere in the world just waiting for you to make the connection."

"I remember. So maybe that's the reason I've got to slow down and allow whatever it is to catch up to me. Then whenever it is arrives, I'll know. But for now, I just want to pursue this course of personal understanding the best way that I know how," I said, summing up my thoughts.

"I've watched you tackle some very difficult assignments, so I'm confident that you can handle this one too. Going to Detroit sounds like as good a place as any for you to begin your search for the real Armando Seguera," Rick remarked with a smile and a bit of skepticism in his voice. "Just do me one favor, okay?"

"Sure, what's that?"

"Don't go checking yourself into some monastery."

We both started laughing heartily and raised our beer mugs as a toast to my personal pursuit and to our friendship.

*   *   *   *

One week later, I was flying high above the clouds on my way to Detroit. Flying usually put me in a relaxed frame of mind to do some serious thinking. Now I had an opportunity to reflect. To begin, I was born Armando Seguera, on August 18, 1934. I was the fifth child born to Rodolfo and Adelina Seguera. The big event took place in our family's home on Duluth Street on Detroit's westside.

Shortly after graduating from high school I decided to take a trip to Mexico. The reason for my trip was because I had only seen but a few relatives during my entire childhood. Those who did come were adults and they never stayed for very long.

However, I was aware that there was a large family somewhere living in the State of Durango. This all started in the summer of 1953 when a female cousin from the Seguera side of the family arrived at our home on Duluth Street to stay with us. She was just a few years older than I, and her name was Christina. The purpose for Christina's visit was for her to study English and to seek employment. It was Christina's presence in our home that prompted me to make the trip to Mexico. Christina spent hours filling my head with names and places that I had only heard of in my childhood.

So it was in August of 1954, when I packed up my 1951 Ford and headed for the border all by myself. First, I drove directly to Mexico City, then on to Durango and from there to Los Angeles, the last place I visited. I went wherever I had relatives. The entire trip, which was a very memorable one, lasted about two and a half months.

Shortly after I returned to Detroit I was inducted into the Army where I spent two years in the service of my country. My father passed away while I was still in the service and after my discharge, I found employment in the Detroit branch office of Donaldson Williams. During those years, things were going quite well for me and so I married my girl friend, Bertina Dudansky. Shortly after, we had a son named Joseph. Within three years, we were divorced and within a year, Donaldson Williams transferred me to the firm's home office in New York City. Except for the separation from my son Joseph, the move was the ideal situation for me.

My flight arrived on schedule and waiting for me was my older sister Marcy.

"Hi! How was the flight?" Marcy inquired.

"Good. In fact it was extremely smooth. Just the way I like it," I replied.

While making our way to the parking lot we discussed the weather and the heavy traffic conditions around the airport. Marcy was a rather private person and didn't talk much about herself. She was an administrator for a small insurance company, where she had worked for twenty-five years. Two years ago, her boy friend John passed away suddenly and unexpectedly. John had been a high school music teacher and had taught Marcy how to play the classical piano. Marcy continued to live alone in the Seguera family home on Duluth Street with her faithful dog Sergeant and her cat Tinkerbell.

Duluth was a middle class tree lined residential street. The majority of the wooden framed houses were painted white with each house having a front porch. Almost all the lawns were neatly groomed. However, I could see that the neighborhood was beginning to change somewhat and not for the better.

As soon as Marcy and I got out of the car, I could hear Sergeant's loud barking coming from inside the house. I also couldn't help but notice a group of young men standing in front of the corner grocery store. The young men looked much older than the usual school boys who had hung out there in the past, which included my buddies and me.

"Do those guys cause any trouble around here?" I asked.

"What kind of trouble are you talking about?"

"I don't know, making lots of noise, drunken rowdiness, I suppose," I replied.

"No, the store closes early these days. You won't have any trouble sleeping, if that's what you're worried about. However, they do drive a bit too fast through the neighborhood. Other than that, they don't bother me; I never go to that store. I do all my shopping at the supermarkets in Dearborn."

Over the years, Marcy had taken excellent care of the house. My father, Rodolfo Seguera had bought the house when it was new in 1923. My father, along with his relatives and friends were in the construction business. They, along with my father, had crossed the border into the United States from Mexico during the height of the Mexican Revolutionary War in 1915. Most of the men were skilled carpenters, like my father and the others laborers who were seeking employment and for that reason they made their way to Detroit. Then, in 1925, shortly after my father bought the Duluth Street house, he returned to Mexico to marry his childhood sweetheart, Adelina Rivera.

Returning to Detroit, they immediately proceeded to fulfill their dreams of raising a large family. Hence, it was in April of 1926, when their first son Rodolfo Jr., was born. Then two years later Francisco was born followed a year later by Marcella and the year after that, Ricardo. I was born in August of 1934 and I was the last of the five Seguera children. From what my brothers told me, we were a very happy and close knit family. But then, like a bolt of lightning out of the sky, on October 31, 1936, our mother suddenly died. She was thirty-six years of age. So sadly, eleven years after it had all begun, the dreams of our family had come to an abrupt standstill.

CHAPTER 2

▼

OLD PHOTOGRAPHS

The Duluth Street house is a two-story wooden framed house painted white like the majority of the homes in the neighborhood. The house also has a front porch and so before entering the house, I paused to reminisce about the swing that our dad had hung up on the porch when we were kids. I remember how I sometimes fell off the swing only to have it come back and bump me in the head. It didn't take me long to figure out how to get out of the way.

Upon entering the house, Sergeant who resembled a small Collie without the long pointed nose continued to bark and wag his tail. He had no hesitation about expressing his joy while I vigorously caressed his neck until he calmed down.

After dropping my bags off in the foyer, I headed for the kitchen to get myself a cold beer from the refrigerator. What immediately caught my eye when I entered the dining room was a new shining black baby grand piano. "Hey! That's a nice looking new piano. Does it play as well as it looks?" I asked, humorously.

"Sure," Marcy replied with a cocky smile.

In the other corner was the dining table with a shoebox full of photographs. "What's this?" I inquired. "It looks as though you've been collecting some old family photographs."

"Oh! Ramona has taken an interest in our family's history. She thought the pictures might help her to better understand," Marcy replied.

"Do you mean, Ramona our niece?"

"Yes, so I've been going around the house collecting them. I never realized how many there were," Marcy remarked. "These are the pictures that were not put in any of the albums. In fact, I even found a good number of them that I hadn't seen before." Marcy said, holding up one of the photos.

The photo was that of Aunt Yolanda and Uncle Mateo. In the aftermath of my mother's passing, the five of us, ranging in ages from two to eleven years of age were left without a mother. Many of the relatives, who had originally journeyed to Detroit, had either passed away, returned to Mexico or had moved to Los Angeles. The only remaining relatives living in the Detroit area were my mother's Aunt Yolanda, her husband Uncle Mateo Luna and their son Pablo or Paul as he came to be called. Paul was twenty-one years old at the time and he was confined to a wheelchair with some sort of a muscular deficiency. We also had a bachelor Uncle Willy, who lived somewhere on the eastside. Both Uncle Mateo and Uncle Willy were from the Seguera side of the family and were in fact, my dad's first cousins.

Aunt Yolanda and Uncle Mateo, along with Paul moved into our home the same day that my mother died. Yolanda not only had the responsibility of caring for her invalid son, but also had now taken on the additional burden of caring for the five of us.

The photograph that we were viewing was that of a youthful Aunt Yolanda and Uncle Mateo. It was one of those brown tainted photos taken in the Santiago Studio in Canatlan, Durango. The year was 1914. Since Uncle Mateo had been a Colonel in Pancho Villa's Revolutionary Army, he wearing his uniform. He looked quite handsome and extremely distinguished standing next to the young attractive Yolanda. There was also a picture of Uncle Mateo mounted on a white horse and displaying a rifle.

"Remember how Uncle Mateo used to tell us those wild war stories," I recalled.

"The more he drank, the gorier the stories got," I added.

"That used to upset Yolanda to no end. Then she would yell lies! Lies! Lies!" Marcy said, as she remembered.

There were additional pictures of Yolanda and Mateo also taken in Mexico and El Paso. The last picture of them together was taken in Los Angeles. Sometime in the late 1950's, and shortly after Paul passed away, Yolanda and Mateo moved to Los Angeles to be near Uncle Mateo's sister Belen. Not too long after moving, Yolanda passed away.

Uncle Mateo then retired to Guadalajara, Mexico and he too passed away shortly after.

"Here's a picture when I went to Yolanda's funeral in Los Angeles," Marcy said pointing to the various photos in the box. "That's Belen's son Sam, and next to him is his wife Laura. The other two women are Belen's daughters, Catherine and Elizabeth."

"Where's Uncle Mateo?" I asked.

"Oh, he's the one who took the picture, Marcy replied. "I suppose you know that Aunt Belen died about a year ago," she added. "Didn't you used to visit her during your trips to the west coast?"

"Yes, I did. I used to stop by and say hello to her. After she died, I received a letter from her daughter Catherine. However, after that I lost touch with her son Sam and haven't been in contact with him ever since. Maybe I'll look him up the next time I'm in Los Angeles. You wouldn't happen to have his phone number?" I inquired.

"He's not hard to find, he moved into Belen's house in order to take care of his dad," Marcy remarked.

Picking up another picture, Marcy said, "Here's a picture of Pa and Uncle Victor. That was when Uncle Victor came to visit us in 1951. They certainly resemble one another. They both have mustaches and they're the same height, except that Uncle Victor has blue eyes," Marcy added.

Uncle Victor was my dad's younger brother and he lived in Durango. He had eleven children, Christina being his oldest. Because of the shortage of men during the Second World War, the United States government needed farm laborers to help with the harvesting of crops. That's when the American government created a labor exchange program with the Mexican government that allowed Mexican farm laborers to come into this country to work. Uncle Victor was on such a program and traveled all over the United States. He said that he had been flown into remote farming areas just to pick cucumbers or whatever needed harvesting. The program continued even after the war and when he came to visit us, he was working on a farm in upstate Michigan. This was the first time that we'd met and I was deeply impressed by the way he carried himself.

"Have you heard from Uncle Victor lately?" I asked hesitantly and wondering if he was still alive.

"Yes. He was in Mexico City with one of his daughter's for awhile. We still exchange Christmas cards and the last one came from Durango, so I think he has moved back. I have his new address, if you want it," Marcy commented.

"The last time that I saw Uncle Victor, was in Mexico City. That was several years ago," I remarked. "Could you put a little note in the card and tell him that I send my very best," I added.

Our family came from the State of Durango, which is in the northern part of the country. As we scanned through the photographs many of the names of places were familiar. However, we were having some difficulty identifying many of the subjects and at times we found ourselves just guessing. Even though I'd been to visit these locations, I still could only identify a few of the people. It may have been because these pictures were taken many years ago when all the subjects were very young. Some may have already died. With many dates missing or faded, it was hard to determine the dates. One particular photo showed a group of young women in light-colored dresses and with their hair combed back. The four girls in the front row were sitting on what appeared to be a log bench and the others were standing behind them. They were all facing the camera and appeared as though they were enjoying themselves. Water was visible at the foot of the picture, suggesting that they may have been on an outing. Behind them were some weeping willow trees, which suggested to me that this must be the grove in San Jeronimo. The only person that we could identify was our mother who was giggling in the back row. Since she was one of six sisters, we could only assume that all the sisters were there, we just couldn't identify them. There were several more photos taken all on the same day, all with the same subjects in the same location.

Another photo was that of our mother's mother, Julia Rivera. She was very fair-skinned woman with her white hair combed back. She wore a very stern expression on her face and may have been in her sixties when the photograph was taken. For many years I had seen this same picture in Aunt Yolanda's bedroom. However, I never realized it was my grandmother until I went to Mexico for the first time. By then, all of my grandparents had passed away, so I never had the opportunity to meet any of them.

"Here's one you've never seen before. Look," Marcy held up another photo.

Marcy was absolutely right. The picture was that of our parents dressed for some special occasion. They were standing next to an old style car in front of the Duluth Street house. Pa looked very distinguished wearing a light colored business suit and matching hat. He was holding the car door open while resting one foot on the running board. Ma was leaning against the front fender and was smiling directly into the camera. She was wearing a black shiny flapper dress that was tight fitting. She was also wearing a black hat that was popular at the time. Again, there was no date. But by the make of the Ford, the picture could have been taken sometime during the late 1920's.

Ma looks really great here, doesn't she?" I commented. Besides the usual studio photographs, this was the best snapshot of my mother that I'd ever seen.

"She certainly does. It looks like they're going to some special affair. I suppose they enjoyed themselves like everyone else during those years," Marcy commented.

Another photograph showed our mother standing next to a large shade tree. She was wearing a white long sleeve blouse and a full-length skirt that went down to her ankles. Her black hair was combed back and her expression was that of contentment. Scribbled on the back of the photo were the words, San Jeronimo. Like many of the pictures there was no date, but she may have been around twenty years old.

"Do you remember anything about Ma," I inquired.

"Vaguely, I was seven when she passed away. I know she was always there for us and I remember that she enjoyed laughing. What I seem to remember most, was the way she rationed out things, like candy for instance. It was always considered a big treat just for us to be given a piece of candy. There was always a lot of joking and laughter whenever she cut up the candy into small pieces. I know we were very close as a family and we did lots of things together. I missed her a great deal after she died, I still do," Marcy reflected with sadness.

"Where did you find all these pictures anyway?" I asked.

"I found the one of Ma and Pa standing by the car in Ma's old sewing kit. It was tucked away in the closet. I'd used the kit a couple of times before and never paid much attention to what was at the bottom. I couldn't believe that it was there. I found a few in the steamer stand-up trunks that are stored in the basement storage room. They were tucked away in those small drawers that are used to store jewelry," Marcy pointed out.

"Why did you say Ramona wanted to see these pictures?"

"Well, you know Ramona, she has always taken a personal interest in her Mexican heritage. She's been studying Spanish ever since high school. Now that she's taking some psychology courses in college, she seems to be interested in finding her self-identity. Anyway, why don't you ask her yourself, aren't you having lunch with her on Tuesday?" Marcy commented.

"Self identity," I uttered to myself. "Yes, that's right, I am having lunch with her on Tuesday," I answered, while still thinking about self-identity and wondered if it was the same as self-understanding.

"I'm sure she'll no doubt discuss it with you during your visit. As you know, she can get very enthusiastic about things and wants to share her projects with everyone. She told me that she couldn't wait to talk to you." Marcy commented.

One of the last pictures that I lifted from the shoebox was also taken in my youth. The picture showed me with my boyhood buddies playing baseball in a vacant lot. There was Freddie Bombalski at the bat while Tony Wisnicki was just getting ready to pitch the ball. Butch Polinski looked like he was on first and Little Eddie and I were playing the infield. Then for a moment my mind drifted away to those childhood days and the good times we had playing together.

What was interesting about my family was that the majority of our neighbors were of either Polish or Ukrainian descent. We were the only Mexican-American family living here in this particular community. The Polish children primarily attended the local parochial school while the rest us of attended the local public school. Amongst our friends and at school we were called by our translated Americanized names. My brother Rodolfo was called Rudy. Francisco was known as Frank and Marcella was Marcy. Ricardo was called Rich and I was known as Armand, short for Armando.

While putting the pictures back into the box, I held the picture of my mother and father. I was suddenly struck with the realization that I knew very little about my mother. I was only two years old when she passed away, so I certainly didn't remember anything about her. Other than my father taking us to visit her grave as a child, she remained a total mystery to me. No one ever spoke about her and as far as I was concerned she was just a gravestone with her name engraved. Even my trips to Mexico were not fulfilling in that respect. During my visits, I spent more time with my Uncle Victor's family than with the Rivera side of the family. I had met four of my mother's sisters and although we talked about my mother, I really never got around to discussing her in depth.

This collection of pictures was now beginning to stimulate my curiosity and was still quite puzzled over why the photographs had remained hidden away at the bottom of boxes and small drawers. Certainly, these photos had now become an important part of our family's history. Now all we had to do was to identify everyone.

After placing the last picture in the shoebox, I wondered if my quest for self-understanding went back much further than just playing baseball in empty lots.

CHAPTER 3

▼

MATTER OF
URGENCY

Marcy and I were the first to arrive at Rudy's house in the suburbs of Detroit for a Sunday afternoon barbecue. Marcy went directly into the house with the homemade potato salad that she had brought, while I went around to the back to look for Rudy. As soon as Rudy saw me, he greeted me with, "Hi brother, how are you doing? Long time no see." He then asked, "How are things doing in New York?"

"Everything's fine," I answered. "Hey, the yard looks nicely groomed. I like the way you arranged those flowers and shrubs over by the back fence," I commented.

"Thanks, but it takes a lot of work and I don't really have the time to give the flowers and shrubs the attention they deserve. But, I well have the time after I retire," he remarked.

Then, Rudy's wife Joanne came out of the back door with a couple of beers. "Hi Armand. It's good to see you again. It's been awhile. But I see that you're looking well. Thought you might like something to drink," she said, while handing over the beers.

"Hi, nice to see you again too Joanne and thanks for the beer," I responded. "I was just telling Rudy how great the yard looks," I added.

"Thanks, but your brother did most of the work. How long will you be here?" Joanne asked.

"I'll be here for about a week. I thought I'd spend some time getting reac-quainted with the family. I know that your family has grown and I haven't had the opportunity to spend much time with the kids," I responded.

Rudy was just about ready to retire from one of the big automobile companies where he had worked for thirty some years. He had also served in the Second World War aboard an LST transport ship in the Pacific. Shortly after his discharge he married Joanne and they had seven children, all of them grown now and most of them with families of their own.

"It'll be awhile before the charcoal gets hot enough to begin grilling, so why don't we sit in the shade before the others show up," Rudy suggested.

As soon as we made ourselves comfortable, I opened the conversation, "You know, Rudy, Marcy has a collection of old photographs of Ma and Pa that she found tucked away in different places around the house. Apparently, they've been there for a long time and after all these years Marcy wasn't even aware that they were there. They're really nice pictures of Ma and Pa, not the kind of pictures that should be hidden. In fact, I'm sorry we didn't bring any of them with us. Anyway, do you have any idea why these photos would have been tucked away?" I inquired. I was hoping that Rudy being my oldest brother might provide some insights into the matter.

"No. Not off hand. I can't think of any reason why they would have been hidden," Rudy replied. "Where did you say she found the pictures?" he asked.

"They were in Ma's old sewing kit and in dresser drawers. A few were in those old Stand-up steamer trunks that that Ma and Pa used when they came from Mexico," I responded.

"What do you remember about Ma?" I continued my inquiry.

"What I remember is that she kept a very neat house, almost like a ship. Each of us had chores that we had to perform and no one was allowed to go out until they were done. She also made certain that we finished our homework. One thing that was very important to her was that we spoke Spanish correctly and she gave Frank and I, classes several times a week. She was always telling us that some day we would be meeting our grandparents and she wanted to make certain that we would be able to communicate properly with them." Rudy then stopped and thought for a moment while trying to remember something else. "Another thing that I remember is that she was very active in Our Lady of Guadalupe church which was part of the Mexican community downtown. She contributed a great deal of her time on the weekends. We used to spend a lot of time playing in the church's recreation hall," Rudy remarked. "I guess you don't remember the recreation hall?"

"No, I don't remember the recreation hall," I responded.

Suddenly, we heard a woman's voice from across the yard. She was an attractive auburn haired woman perhaps in her early thirties, "Hi Rudy, where's the rest of the gang?" she asked.

"They haven't got here yet," Rudy replied. "Why don't you come over here and meet my brother Armand."

The woman came into the yard and approached us with one hand extended to greet me with a warm smile. She then introduced herself and said, "Hi, I'm Phyllis Connors and I live next door. My husband Harry should be here in a minute. I understand that you live in New York City. It must be nice to have such a big place at your doorstep."

"It is, but I've been traveling a lot and haven't seen much of it lately," I replied.

Soon, other family members began to arrive, including Ramona with her two children. Ramona was in her late twenties and was Rudy's third oldest child. She immediately took me aside and asked, "Are you still coming for lunch on Tuesday?"

"Certainly, I've been planning on it. Has there been some change?" I asked.

"Good, I'm glad you're coming. I've got something that I think is important that I want to discuss with you," she said as though not wanting anyone else to hear.

Next, my brother Frank and his wife Jennifer arrived with their two daughters, and a short time later, Rich with his wife Debora also arrived. With only a few exceptions the entire Seguera family had now gathered to enjoy a pleasant afternoon. Among the missing was Rudy's second oldest daughter Michelle and my son Joseph, who was no longer living in the Detroit area.

*   *   *   *

The next morning and after Marcy went off to work, I went down the stairs into the basement to conduct my own hidden photo investigation. The sturdy workbench that my father had built many years ago was still intact. Along one wall were the baskets full of clothes and on the far side were the furnace, washtub and washing machine. Next to the washtub was the door to the storage room. I went over, opened the door and went inside. Along one wall were some wooden shelves where some dusty dishes and some vases were stored. Because there was only one small window, there was only a small amount of light filtering into the room. The overhead light was also extremely dim and so I couldn't properly check out the standup steamer trunks the way I wanted. Other items that had belonged to my mother were an old Singer sewing machine and a player piano. It was so dim and dusty that I changed my mind and decided that I would come back at some other time.

It was very pleasant outside, so I decided to take a walk around the neighborhood and check out those schoolyards where I used to play. At the same time, I thought that I might wander over to my niece Michelle's house, which was only a short distance from Marcy's. Michelle was married to Stan and they had two sons. Stan was a stockbroker in the Detroit office of Donaldson Williams, thereby giving us something in common.

Michelle knew more about the family than anyone else, and so over coffee, she proceeded to fill me in with all the latest family gossip. One of her complaints was that the family didn't hug enough. That she didn't remember her parents hugging her when she was a little girl. One of the reasons that she married Stan was because he liked to hug and that she makes it a point to embrace her boys at every opportunity. I had never realized how important a little hugging might mean to some people.

*   *   *   *

Tuesday morning, I was up early and decided to drive out to the Holy Trinity cemetery where both my mother and father were buried.

Beyond the trees that line the entrance into the cemetery is a pond filled with floating water lilies. Then spread out on the grassy knoll on the far side of the pond is a religious cross whose formation is created from a bed of colorful flowers. At the top of the knoll is a large white marble mausoleum, which is an impressive sight from the wooden bridge that crosses the pond, especially in the early morning sunlight.

The trees and shrubs looked well trimmed and there was freshly mowed green grass everywhere. The scene was quiet and serene, except for some bickering birds and a landscaper who was working with an electric saw in the distance. After locating the gravesites and arranging the flowers that I had brought, I knelt to pray.

After a moment, I stood up and began to speak aloud, "Hi, I saw the picture of the two of you standing by that real neat car. You were in front of the house. You both looked exceptionally good and it appeared as though you were going to some special occasion. Anyway, I hope you had a good time wherever you were going. But that's not the reason why I'm here," I then paused for a few seconds,

"Because of the dream," Ramona stressed.

"The dream, what dream?"

"Didn't Aunt Marcy tell you?"

"No, I'm afraid she didn't say anything to me about any dream. Whose dream was it?" I inquired.

"Boy! I don't believe it. If you want to keep a secret, just tell my Aunt Marcy. She'll keep it, even if you don't care if she tells someone," Ramona remarked. Getting back to the subject, "A couple of weeks ago, I had one of those dreams that wakes you up in the middle of the night. I had my heart pounding in my ears, and for some reason it was the kind of dream where one remembers every little detail."

"Okay, I guess I've had a few of those in my lifetime. Can't say that I remember any of them right now," I stated.

"In the dream, I'm standing at the end of a deserted runway at an airport. I think it's deserted because I don't see any airline terminal or any people. In the distance, there are mountains. It looks like the runway is in the middle of a desert, and there is no question in my mind Uncle Armand, but I know it was Durango. I just knew it. Then when I looked around again, I saw this airplane with the passenger door open and the stairs extending to the ground. Coming down the stairs was this Mexican woman with an extremely serious expression. Although she was moving slowly, I knew she was in a hurry to get somewhere. I then said to myself, 'I know this woman,' except that I didn't have her name. Yet her name was on the tip of my tongue. I just couldn't get it out, or say it to myself. Isn't that crazy? When I awoke, I continued to sense that the woman was dealing with a very important family matter. I still feel that way," Ramona completed the telling of her dream. "You've been to the Durango airport, is that the way it looks, deserted?"

"To be perfectly honest, I don't recall paying that much attention. However, the last time I was there, the planes still used portable stairs to allow the passengers to exit," I explained.

"I thought you might be interested in my dream," Ramona remarked.

"Why do you think the airport was in Durango? Have you ever been there?"

"I've been to Durango, except that I took the bus from Mexico City, so I never got out to the airport." Ramona explained. "However, I just know how I felt after I woke up," she added.

"Maybe it just represents some wishful thinking on your part," I suggested.

"Anyway, the dream left me so puzzled and confused that I spoke to Phyllis."

"Phyllis?" I inquired.

"Do you know my Dad's neighbor Phyllis?"

"Yes, I met her the other day at the barbecue."

"I know you don't know this, but she has psychic abilities."

"You mean she can tell fortunes?"

"No, she's not a fortuneteller. It's just that sometimes she picks up vibrations or messages from the other side. They're usually about things that might be influencing our daily lives. She says that my dream might represent a message from a family spirit in Mexico. A spirit who wants desperately to communicate with our family here in Detroit," Ramona explained.

"For one thing, I don't pretend to understand anything about what Phyllis does and I wouldn't let it influence my thinking," I remarked. "Anyway, as I've told you the pictures have renewed my interest in the family and I do plan to take a trip to Mexico. It might not be immediately, but I promise you that I'll follow up on the exchange proposal. Is that okay?" I made my statement.

"You know, I've been afraid to tell people about my dream and that's why I was hoping that Aunt Marcy had told you. My sisters just laugh at me when I tell them," Ramona explained. "By the way, the idea for the exchange program came to me right after having that dream. Isn't that silly? That's when I immediately thought of you and that's why I called you," she added.

Just as I was getting up to leave, Ramona came over and gave me a strong hug and said, "Thank you for listening to me Uncle Armand. I'm glad that you're going to help."

"Well, I've never made so many personal promises in one day in my entire life," I uttered aloud.

"What did you say?" Ramona responded.

"Nothing,.." I shrugged off answering.

"You know something else? Our family doesn't hug enough and I know that's a Mexican custom. Our family in Mexico does it all the time, but for some reason we just don't' seem to do enough around here," Ramona commented.

There was a remark that sounded vaguely familiar. Seems like I just heard that somewhere. The one thing that I didn't tell Ramona was that the Durango airport is in the desert and in the middle of nowhere.

*　　*　　*　　*

For the remainder of the week I continued to visit the various members of my family and to lunch with some of my old school buddies. The following Sunday, I returned to New York with the addresses of my Uncle Victor and my cousin

Sam in my possession. Whether I was any closer to my quest for self-understanding didn't seem to matter.

CHAPTER 4

▼

THE INITIAL STEP

I could've just taken the time off and gone to Mexico, instead, I wanted to combine the trip with one of my assignments to the southwestern part of the country. Doug Adams had been appointed manager of our department when it was originally formed several years ago. At that time, I was given the position of supervisor because of my extensive branch experience. Doug and I worked well together and on occasion we even went out socially. I knew that it would only be a matter of time before Doug would have the right assignment. For the time being and for the last couple of months the majority of my assignments were either on the East Coast or in the Midwest.

Time was elapsing and so I decided to send notes to both my cousin Sam and Uncle Victor. I wanted to notify them of my future intentions, and not be surprised when they heard from me. Within a month, I received a familiar green and red striped envelope. It was postmarked "Durango, Durango, Mexico." I opened the envelope and read the letter:

My Esteemed Nephew Armando,

I trust that this letter finds you and your family in good health, as we are here, thanks be to God.

It would give me and my family great pleasure to receive you and your family into our home. Please notify us of the date and time of your arrival. We will be there to receive you.

Victoriano O. Seguera

In all my travels to Mexico, I had only seen Uncle Victor twice. I saw him once in Mexico City and again in Brawely, California. He was working on a farm in the Imperial Valley. That was in 1954 when I was driving from Durango to Los Angeles. Due to his extensive traveling, Uncle Victor had never been in Durango while I was visiting his family. However, he had since retired and this would be my first opportunity to visit him while his was in his home.

One day in Mid-November, Doug called me into his office and informed me that there was a minor operational problem in the firm's Dallas office that needed to be addressed. I was to get the assignment, but I didn't need to visit the office until after Thanksgiving. This was the opportunity that I had been waiting for, so I immediately phoned an excited Ramona to tell her the news. I also began to write my Uncle Victor, but even before I could finish the letter, Doug informed me that the trip had been temporarily postponed. No reason was given. This time, I phoned a disappointed Ramona. Since I had the vacation time coming to me, I decided to start making my own arrangements. But fate would intervene two days later when Doug called me into his office.

"Armand, I think that I have the trip you've been waiting for," Doug said.

"The Operations Manager in our Los Angles office has a personal emergency and needs to take some time off from work. Since he'll be out of the office for about three weeks, the Office Manager was wondering if we couldn't provide someone to help out for a few weeks. The only problem is that's it's over the Christmas Holiday. How does that sound to you, and does that effect your plans for the holidays?" Doug asked. "Of course you can fly home if you want," he added.

"Great! Doesn't effect my plans at all. I'll be glad to go and then afterwards, I can still follow through with my personal plans. Thanks Doug," I commented.

"Oh yes, there is one other thing. You still have to stop in the Dallas office on the way back. Is that okay?" Doug asked.

"Sure, no problem whatsoever," I replied.

Once again, the news of my trip made a very patient Ramona extremely happy and again I went back to writing my letters. I was also sending a note to my son Joseph who lived in San Francisco.

*   *   *   *

On the eve of my departure, I met Rick at our usual watering hole, Maxwell's.

"Have you heard any news about Doug's promotion?" I inquired.

"No, I thought you may have heard something. My last report is that everything is on hold for the moment. I'm still surprised that someone from management hasn't approached you. I still think that you're going to get the job," Rick stated.

"Thanks for the support Rick, but I have no choice but to wait and see what happens," I answered.

Changing the subject, Rick asked, "How was your date with that attractive accountant? What is her name, Sharon?" he inquired.

"Yes, we had a pleasant dinner and I enjoyed her company very much. We laughed a lot and I'll call her again as soon as I get back from my trip," I commented. "I suppose that I'm not ready to start something that I'm not up to finishing. I have to admit that I'm still not over Diana."

"I know that you're really looking forward to your trip. What are your plans?" Rick asked.

"Nothing too complicated. Of course, I'm looking forward to flying up to San Francisco and spending some time with Joseph. Then, when the job is done I'll fly to Durango and spend about ten days. I look forward to seeing my aunts and my uncle. After that I'll fly to Dallas and complete that assignment," I explained.

"You know, I was just thinking the other day about how you wanted to go back to Detroit and reflect on your childhood. Except that I think that what your dealing with is something cultural," Rick stated.

"Cultural?" I quickly responded.

"It was something that you once told me. You said that you missed having relatives around while you were growing up and how you would have liked to have some cousins your own age to play with you. I also know that you are extremely proud of your heritage and that you feel extremely attached to your relatives in Mexico. Your mother died when you were two and your father died when you were around twenty-one, if I recall. So you didn't receive any of the usual mother-father parenting," Rick explained. "There might be a void in your life that you're trying to satisfy and that might be the self-understanding you are looking for," he added.

"I hadn't looked at it like that Rick, but yes, I suppose you could be right. There is so little information about my parents. That's why I'm looking forward to this trip. Perhaps my aunts and uncle can provide me with some additional insights," I expressed.

"Do you think that you'll have any problems getting someone in your family to visit your niece?" Rick asked.

"None. I think they'll be more than delighted with the idea," I responded.

"Have you given any thought to her dream and that sense of a family urgency that she was talking about?" Rick inquired.

"I thought about it, but I'm not really into premonitions. I'll just have to wait and see," I answered.

That evening, I phoned Ramona. "Hi, I hope you've got your guest room ready?" I joked.

"Sure Uncle Armand. Just send them right up. I'm looking forward to having someone come here. I'm also in a position to pay for all their expenses, including the transportation," Ramona clarified an important detail.

"Other than a school age child are there any other requirements?" I kidded with her. "Oh yeah, have you had any of those strange dreams lately?"

"No. None. But Phyllis continues to tell me that I'm still generating lots of psychic energy. She also says that you've got it too," Ramona informed me.

"I've got what?"

"She said that when she met you this summer, you were also emitting some psychic energy. She said that she's never experienced so many members of one family that are generating so much psychic energy," Ramona stated. "I also still have that sense of urgency and it seems to have intensified," she added.

*   *   *   *

During my visit to California, I was able to fly up to San Francisco and see my son Joseph. He was getting taller and appeared to be quite busy with his school projects, but we made certain to enjoy the time we had together. I also promised to take him to Mexico sometime after he graduated from high school. In Los Angeles, my cousin Sam and his lovely wife Laura invited me over to their home in East Los Angeles for dinner a couple of times. I discovered that Sam was quite a storyteller and he gave me some new information about the family that I hadn't heard before.

One Sunday afternoon, Sam accompanied me to the local cemetery where his mother Belen and our Aunt Yolanda were buried. Driving home from the cemetery, I asked Sam," Have you ever been to Durango?"

"Yes, a number of times," Sam stated. "Once I accompanied my mother there, because she hadn't been to her birthplace for a long time. While we were there, we stopped to visit Uncle Victor and Dolores. At that time, they had only seven children. Now I understand they have eleven."

"I don't know what year you were there, but would have Christina already moved to Detroit?" I asked.

"Yes, she had just recently left for Detroit when we arrived," Sam related. "You know that my wife Laura's family is also from around Canatlan and we went to visit them too. They've since moved to Baja, California," he stated. "My father's side of the family is from the State of Chihuahua and I've been there many times."

"I'll be visiting my uncle in a couple of weeks and I'm not certain what to take them. You wouldn't happen to have some ideas, would you?" I asked.

"When I visit my father's family I take my uncles a couple of bottles of Scotch. Scotch is very expensive in Mexico. And if you want to take the children some toys you can go over to Chinatown or Olvera Street. Both places are not far from your hotel," Sam gave me some very welcomed suggestions.

*   *   *   *

As soon as the plane landed in Durango, it slowly taxied its way to a small glass enclosed terminal. Within minutes, I was out the exit door and standing on the top step of the portable staircase. While taking a moment to enjoy the warm Durango sun, I suddenly remembered Ramona's dream and so I looked out towards the end of the runway. The arid landscape looked deserted. There was absolutely nothing, just small shrubs and cactuses, and standing majestically silent on the horizon were the Sierra Madre Mountains. Surely, Ramona's dream had to have been a coincidence.

Although it had been awhile since I'd seen Uncle Victor, I had no difficulty locating him in the crowd. Standing next to him was his son-in-law Guillermo and hidden behind him were his two small sons. After our traditional embraces we headed out to the parking lot where we climbed into Guillermo's dark blue Ford pickup truck. The two boys jumped into the back with the luggage and some tires.

"It's good to have you here Armando. "How long do you plan to stay?" Victor asked.

"For about a week," I answered.

"Good, there is much to do," Victor remarked, as though he had something on his mind.

In many ways, Durango resembled a cattle town. The majority of the men wore western style clothing with cowboy hats and boots. In the center of a busy traffic circle that we were circumventing, I observed a large bronze statue of a mustached Pancho Villa wearing a wide-brimmed hat and a holstered revolver. He was mounted on a horse that was rearing up on its hind legs while its two front hooves seemed to be reaching for the sky. It was a statue that had been erected since my last visit to Durango.

"That's Pancho Villa," Victor pointed out. He was born and raised here in the state of Durango. When he lived here as a young man, he was a troublemaker and a bandit until he was chased out of the state. When he returned several years later, he came back as a revolutionary general. Now we honor him."

Although I did not know the history, I wondered why Uncle Victor didn't seem too impressed with one of the country's most renowned heroes.

When we arrived at the house, Victor's wife Dolores was waiting for us at the door. She immediately took me by the hand and escorted me into the living room to sit beside her on the couch. Then, acting as though she was going to console me, she asked,

"Why didn't you bring Jose?" she asked about Joseph. "Isn't it time for you to bring your son here to meet the family?"

"Yes, it is, but I promised that I would bring him when he finishes high school," I replied. I was twenty years old when I first met Aunt Dolores. I stayed in the family's Durango home for almost two months in 1954. She treated me like a son and she became my mentor when it came to understanding Mexican customs. I admired her wisdom and the parental guidance that she had given me. She had raised eleven children practically alone and knew how to handle them all individually. I had learned to respect her judgments and I enjoyed the personal attention that she gave me

"You're still not married?" she continued her inquiry.

"No, I'm not," I answered.

"You need a woman Armando," she remarked.

"Well, Aunt Dolores," I started. "In New York City, and where I live we have plenty of laundromats and fast-food restaurants. I can hire a cleaning woman to come in and clean my apartment anytime. It's not that difficult to get things done without a woman. Besides, most of the women in New York City work just like the men do and they don't have time for these things either. We don't get married to have someone take care of our homes anymore. We're much too busy earning a living. When we marry, it's for love, babies or to combine incomes. Sometimes, it's for all three."

"That doesn't sound like a good arrangement to me," Dolores commented. "You need someone to take care of all your needs as a man, not just for cleaning dirty dishes."

CHAPTER 5

▼

THE INVITATION

Then, while we stood around chatting, I presented an appreciative Uncle Victor with one of the bottles of Scotch that I had brought him. This gesture moved Guillermo into action and he immediately obtained some glasses and ice. Aunt Dolores, suddenly shouted from the kitchen, "Only one drink before lunch!" The three of us just smiled while Guillermo poured the drinks.

A few moments later, my cousin Leticia, who was Guillermo's wife, entered the room. Leticia explained that the family was having a New Year's Eve celebration that evening and many of our relatives would be attending. This included cousins from her mother's side of the family as well as our Uncle Pedro's children. Uncle Pedro was also one of my Dad's two brothers and he had died in the early 1940's, leaving six children. All of them lived in the immediate area. Only two of Victor's eleven children had remained living in Durango. All the others had moved to Mexico City a number of years ago, except for Christina.

That evening, the house quickly filled with exuberant children and more Seguera's than I could have ever imagined. We exchanged embraces, toasted to our good health and danced to the music that was blaring from the stereo. It didn't take long for me to get up and dance with my attractive female cousins.

A few of my male cousins were extremely pleased that they had someone with whom they could practice their English. Surprisingly, they knew more English than I would have expected. Then, with each bit of humor, they would share another toast and a hearty one-armed shoulder embrace. The more we drank, the heartier the embraces got. It turned out to be an enjoyable evening to say the least.

Early the next morning, I heard the street vendors making their presence known in the neighborhood. Each had their own unique style for announcing themselves. Outside, I found Victor sweeping the sidewalk. Due to the early January morning chill, Victor's chin was partially hidden by a scarf that he was wearing around his neck.

"Good morning Armando. How did you sleep?" Victor asked.

"Very well, thank you. But I'm afraid I feel a little hung over," I expressed.

Then with an amusing tone in his voice, Victor said, "You'll be over it just as soon as Dolores gives you a cup of her special hangover tea." He then pointed towards the west, "See those clouds hanging over the mountains? It must have snowed in the mountains last night. It feels much colder than usual. But it will warm up as soon as the sun gets higher," Victor commented. "Let's go inside, I think breakfast is ready."

For the remainder of the weekend, Guillermo and Victor drove me around Durango, pointing out points of interest, both historical and current. We toured the central marketplace, the plaza, the train station and the cathedral. Not long ago, Durango had the largest open pit iron mine the world. It originally started as a mountain of iron ore on the edge of the city. But after fifty years of blasting, it had since been depleted into a large hole in the ground.

The following morning, Uncle Victor announced that we were taking a long ride into the country and that I should take an overnight bag with me. He also reminded me to take the toys that I had wanted to distribute to the children. The plan was for us to visit the village of San Panfilo and then Canatlan where my relatives from the Rivera side of the family live. San Panfilo was where the Seguera family had originally settled many years ago. Although I'd been to San Panfilo once before, this was the first time that someone from the Sequera side of the family was going to accompany me.

On the way, we stopped in the front of an old seminary building. "This is the seminary from where they recruited Mateo," Victor stated. "Just as the Revolutionary War was about to begin in 1910, Mateo was studying to be a priest. Then on day, one of the Pancho Villa's recruiting officer's drove up to this seminary and offered a commission to any student who was willing to join the revolutionary army. Mateo wasted no time discarding his robe to join the revolution. You see Pancho Villa needed officers who could read and write. He didn't have many officers who could, including himself."

Continuing our journey north, we passed plowed fields, orchards and cattle grazing on whatever shrubs or bushes which grew along the side of the road. Small trees and cactuses dominated the landscape. Every few miles a small community was visible behind the trees that grew a short distance from the highway. Associated with each community was a church, whose bell towers were visible rising above the trees. These were the same villages that before the revolution were known as haciendas. These were the haciendas that had been owned by wealthy Spanish landowners and who employed a great deal of the population as peasant workers. This method of employment was used to subjugate the masses, thus giving rise to a revolt by the people.

After about an hour, Guillermo slowed down and turned off the main highway onto a dirt road. The truck dipped into a gully before slowly crossing over a rocky, dried-up riverbed. Coming up on the other side was a road sign reading: SAN PANFILO. We entered the deserted-looking village whose streets were covered with a thick layer of dust. Victor directed Guillermo to park near the church and next to a vacant lot that was overrun with weeds.

"This was our home when we lived here," Victor remarked. "Rodolfo, Pedro, and I were all born right here. The reason it looks like it does is because after we sold the property to the church and they tore the house down. The church had intended to build additional classrooms for their school, but so many people had left San Panfilo, it was no longer practical."

"Do we still have any relatives living here?" I asked.

"No one that we've keep in touch with. Everyone else has died or moved away, like our family," Victor replied.

We then walked a few short blocks to the site of a gray colored barren hill where there were only a few small trees and shrubs growing. On the side of the hill was a boarded up entrance to an abandoned mine where an old metal ore cart lay rusting on its side.

Again Victor began to enlighten me on our family's history in San Panfilo. He started, "This is the site of the old silver mine that sustained San Panfilo for a good number of years. The mine was owned and operated by two Americans. The reason the hill is barren is because buried under the dirt is the discarded third and fourth grade silver. Just about every man in San Panfilo worked in the mine at one time or another. Rodolfo was a carpenter and it was his job to shore-up the walls of the mineshafts. Both Mateo and Pedro also worked here. My mother Clara had me delivering food and water to my father and brothers at lunchtime. The mine was closed during the revolution, when I was about nine.

"It was on this very spot that I met Pancho Villa," Victor began, "he came to San Panfilo in 1910 to recruit soldiers for his army and so he gathered all the men of the village right here. This included my father, your father Rudolfo and Pedro. Pancho Villa was aware that he might have enemies amongst the villagers since he had lived in the area when he was a young man known as Dorotero Arango. At that time he was also known as troublemaker and thief. One day he attempted to steal a mule from *Don* Julio the local muleteer. *Don* Julio caught him and then whipped him severely. In fact, *Don* Julio was standing amongst the other men and when Pancho Villa saw him he said that he would offer amnesty to any man who would join his army. Some of the men turned to *Don* Julio and tried to encourage him to accept the offer. *Don* Julio would have no part of Pancho Villa and he remained silent. Not many men did and that is what I remembered."

Victor continued to reminisce about his childhood and even spoke at length about his father Guadalupe. At times, there were tears in his eyes as he gestured towards some object that reminded him of an incident that happened long ago. Many of the stories included my father and I was captivated as I listened to them.

On the way to Canatlan, we passed a small trade school known as La Granja. It was one of the few trade schools in the State of Durango and it was the same school that my father had attended and graduated from years ago.

We then stopped at a small cemetery just outside of Canatlan, to pay our respects to my grandparents. Crumbling all around was the low adobe wall that surrounded the cemetery. There was no grass to be seen anywhere, just dirt and tumbleweed. The gravesites themselves had been arranged haphazardly with no order to what direction they were facing. Many of the wooden crosses that marked the various gravesites were decaying and the crosses themselves were been bent or turned in varying degrees. Most gravesites didn't even display anything to identify the names of the deceased. Very few graves had tombstones. However, Uncle Victor had made certain to provide the members of his immediate family with the proper gravestones.

Continuing on our way, we passed rows upon rows of apple orchards and since it was only January, the trees were bare of fruit. It was then necessary for Guillermo to slow down as we approached the railroad tracks that were just on the outskirts of Canatlan. Driving down the main street we passed the central marketplace, the plaza and the municipal building. Turning onto one of the side streets, we continued for a few blocks before stopping in front of a large white house. Victor got out and knocked on the partially opened door. A young girl holding a broom appeared, "Yes, may I help you?"

"Is *Don Manuel* Contreras at home?" Victor inquired. Manuel had been married to my mother's older sister Consuelo, who passed away several years ago.

"Yes, he is in the patio."

"Please inform him that *Senor* Victor Seguera is here to see him."

"Please follow me *Senor* Seguera."

We followed the girl through the foyer until we reached the courtyard. Sitting in the shade reading a newspaper was Manuel. Manuel was an elderly gentleman with a large white colored handlebar mustache and was wearing a sombrero. He looked very distinguished in his Mexican cowboy attire. As soon as the girl announced the visitor to Manuel, he dropped his newspaper and got up to quickly to greet us. Manuel's smile revealed a set of rust-colored teeth similar to Victor's. The rust color had been created from the high mineral content in the Durango water that the previous generation drank on a regular basis. Today, everyone drank bottled water.

Victor and Manuel greeted one another and began to converse for a few moments before Manuel turned to me and exclaimed aloud, "Armando! It's so very good to see you again. It's been a few years since we saw you last. How is the family in Detroit?"

"Everyone is fine Uncle Manuel." I replied.

Suddenly, a woman came scurrying from the kitchen wiping her hands in her apron, "What's going on Papa? Did I hear someone mention Armando and Detroit?" The woman was my cousin Margarita and she immediately recognized Victor, "Oh, how are you *Don* Victor?"

"I'm fine Margarita. But as you can see I brought Armando with me," he said, gesturing in my direction.

An expression of astonishment came over Margarita and then she exclaimed, "Armando!" We quickly embraced, and then she asked, "How is everyone in Detroit?"

"I live in New York City now, but I keep in close touch with the family and everyone is fine," I explained.

"It's been a few years since you were here last," Margarita remarked. Turning towards Victor she said, "Please *Don* Victor, won't you have a cup of coffee?"

"Yes, that would be fine," Victor replied. "However, I just came to leave Armando here. If he likes, I will be back for him in three days." Victor then took some time to converse with Manuel while Guillermo and I went into the kitchen to join Margarita.

In the meantime, Margarita sent one of the wide-eyed youngsters to inform Tomas, the boy's father that I had arrived. Tomas was Margarita's younger bother and someone closer to my own age. He was also someone that I had spent considerable time with on previous visits. In fact, during my initial visit in 1954, Tomas and I, along with his brother Ernesto and another cousin Carlos had taken a week to go up into the mountains on horseback. It was then that we had sufficient time to get acquainted and to establish our close relationship.

After finishing our coffee, I followed Victor and Guillermo out to the pickup truck and just as they pulled away I heard the sound of another vehicle coming from the opposite direction. It was a dark blue Volkswagen kicking up dust before it stopped directly in front of the house. Painted in white along the side of the car was the word,

"P O L I C I A."

Sitting in the passenger seat was the boy who had gone to deliver the message. When Tomas climbed out of the car he exhibited a broad smile, causing his gold-filled front tooth to glisten in the sunlight. He was wearing a blue denim outfit that exposed the butt of a pearl-handled forty-five revolver from beneath his jacket. The boy, noticing my inquisitive expression, promptly spoke up, "He is my father, Tomas Contreras and he is the Sheriff of Canatlan," he said with pride. "There is nothing to fear."

"It's good to see you again cousin," Tomas remarked. "I hope you plan to stay awhile. I've got to get back to work, but when I get back this evening, we'll sit down and have a long talk. There's a lot of catching up that we have to do."

As soon as Tomas departed, Margarita's husband Roberto arrived. After a brief conversation, Roberto said, "Our daughter Carmela is going to be very happy to see you. Do you remember her?"

"The last time I saw her, she was still a little school girl," I stated.

"She's very interested in the family and wants to meet and know everyone," Roberto commented. "She works in Durango now and stays with relatives while she's there. But on her days off she comes home. In fact, tomorrow is her day off and so she should be arriving home from work around this time."

"How old is she?" I asked.

"She's nineteen years old," Roberto answered.

"What does she do in Durango?"

"She works for the Department of Tourism."

Then, just as Roberto had predicted, Carmela came bursting in the front door like an excited schoolgirl. Before taking time to notice me, she respectfully hugged and kissed her grandfather and her parents. At the same time, she never stopped talking as she attempted to give a detailed report of her work assignments. She spoke so rapidly that I wondered if anyone understood what she was saying. Carmela was an extremely attractive young lady, with large dark eyes, long black hair and a very bright smile. Her enthusiastic energy filled the room and it was obvious that everyone was glad to see her. Finally she stopped directly in front me. She looked at her mother, as though needing help with making the identifying. "Who is this gentleman?" she asked her mother with a curious smile.

"That's Armando Seguera. Don't you remember him?" Margarita remarked.

"Armando Seguera! From Detroit?" Carmela loudly exclaimed, while we shared a warm embrace.

"Yes, I do remember him, but his hair has gotten much whiter," she commented.

"I understand that you work for the Department of Tourism," I stated. "What is it that you do for them," I asked.

"Sometime I greet people at the airport and I show important people around Durango. There's also an American western town that is used as a movie set here. The movie set is just on the outskirts of Durango. You probably passed it on your way here. The movie set was constructed to resemble the town of Los Alamos, New Mexico," Carmela stated, as she paused for a moment to laugh and display a perfect set of white teeth. "What I mean, it resembles Los Alamos in the old days, not today. When the movie production companies come here from California, part of my job is to help them find places for the crew and the actors to stay. John Wayne was one of those actors who used to come here quite often. That was before I started working there."

"Are you required to speak English," I asked.

"Yes, but I don't speak very well," she replied. Carmela then directed her attention towards me, "Now tell us about you Armando. Are you married and do you have children?" she asked.

"No. I'm divorced with a son named Joseph or Jose in Spanish. He lives with his mother in San Francisco," I answered. "I live and work in New York City."

"Please tell me how large is the family in Detroit? I'm very interested in wanting to know everyone," Carmela requested.

"Well, my brother Rodolfo, who is the oldest has seven children," I began.

"Wait! What are their names and do they have children of their own? I do not want to miss anyone," Carmela stated. "Please pardon me, I just need one more moment." Carmela then turned to the girl who had answered the front door earlier, "Juanita, go get me one of your school notebooks and a pencil, so I can record the information that Uncle Armando is going to give me." Within minutes Juanita returned with the notebook. Carmela opened the notebook and prepared to record what I was going to dictate to her. "Okay, who did you say had seven children, Rodolfo? What are their names?" she asked.

"That's correct, Rodolfo is the oldest," I replied. "Then the first one born in his family was Hollicia, and we call her Holly. She was followed by Michelle and then Ramona." Suddenly I hesitated as though forgetting the names of my other nieces and nephews. While Carmela waited patiently for me to give her the other names, I then impulsively blurted out, "Carmela, why don't you go to Detroit and visit the family yourself. That way, you'll not only get to know their names, but you'll get to meet them all personally." My remark even surprised me. Everyone else in the room became silent.

Carmela spoke calmly as though she had not been taken by surprise, "When?"

I then proceeded to extend Ramona's invitation, "As soon as you can make the arrangements. All of your expenses are to be covered by the Seguera family. You would stay at the home of my niece Ramona. Ramona has a large home and has two children and she would be more than happy to have you as her guest. You don't have to reply immediately, perhaps it's something you want to think about and you can make plans after you've had an opportunity to discuss it with your family. I'll give you Ramona's address, so that you can begin to correspond with her. Ramona reads and writes Spanish and you should have no difficulty communicating with her. The trip can even be used to help improve your English."

Carmela, who appeared to be thinking rather seriously, stood up and looked directly at her parents, saying, "Didn't I tell you that I might be going to Detroit sometime soon? No on would believe me."

Both Margarita and Roberto grinned with amusement. My guess was that there had been something going on even before I arrived and that must have been the reason why they also did not appear to be surprised by Camela's reaction.

However, it certainly was not the kind of reaction that I had expected, so I asked, "how did you know you would be going to Detroit Carmela?"

"Because of my dreams," she replied.

Answering in the same confused manner as I once did with Ramona, I exclaimed, "Dreams! What dreams?"

CHAPTER 6

▼

THE CEMETERY DREAM

"Yes," Carmela anxiously began. "For the last few months, I've been having these very unusual dreams." For the children in the room, their eyes rolled as though having already heard the details of these dreams numerous times. Carmela paid little attention to their antics, but she was eager to get on with describing her dreams.

"In the first, dream I'm in a large beautiful cemetery. Why I know it's a cemetery, I'm not certain, because it isn't until the second dream that I begin to notice headstones, trees and green grass everywhere. It looked nothing like the cemeteries we have here in Durango. Then, in the third dream, which was a very quick dream, the cemetery looks the same except that a large white house appears in front of me. But then just last month I had the most unusual dream of them all. I awoke right after the dream and ever since then I've not been able to stop thinking about it. It's left me with a strong feeling that I should do something, but I have no idea what it is that I'm suppose to do."

"So go on with the dream Carmela," I encouraged.

"The dream takes place in a cemetery again," Carmela continued. "It is night time and I can see stars overhead, but the white-house is distinctively visible. Suddenly a bright ball of light emerges from one of the second floor windows and begins to head directly towards me. Then, just as it was about to reach me, it quickly veered upward into the night sky and swiftly moved away in a southerly direction. As soon as I awoke, I knew that I had been in Detroit and that I was also destined to go there. I then asked my mother to write to you. But as you know, we hadn't gotten around to writing, but those strong emotions that accompanied the dream are still with me."

Even as Carmela spoke and used her hand to demonstrate the white ball climbing into the sky, I could sense the emotion in her voice. After pausing for a moment, she seriously asked, "What do you think my dreams mean, Uncle Armando? I'm thinking that the dreams have something to do with my dying in Detroit. That's why I'm confused about honoring your invitation."

"How can you be sure it was Detroit. And how did you know the light was moving south?" I made my usual dream inquiries.

"I can't explain it Uncle Armando. It's just that something told me that it was Detroit and for some reason, I just knew the light was going south," Carmela stood by her explanation.

Next, Carmela left the room for a moment and when she returned she was holding a document. After placing the document on the table, she said, "You see, I've been so convinced that I was going to Detroit that I've already obtained my visa for visiting the United States. After seeing my surprised expression, she turned to her parents and asked them, "Is it okay if I accept Uncle Armando's invitation?" Margarita and Roberto glanced at one another for an instant and then slowly turned back to face Carmela. Together, they nodded their approval in unison. "Uncle Armando, I have been praying very hard for an answer to my dreams and now you've helped to make me a very happy person," Carmela expressed. She then thanked her parents by embracing them and also shared that same expression of affection with me, saying, "You may not understand this, but you see, I believe that it is my destiny to go to Detroit, no matter what happens."

＊   ＊   ＊   ＊

In the morning, Margarita served me a welcomed warm cup of coffee. A few moments later, Carmela came into the kitchen still holding the notebook. She opened the discussion, "Uncle Armando, I couldn't sleep thinking about my going to Detroit, so after church this morning, I phoned the Department of Tourism and spoke with *Senor* Placencia. He is my supervisor, and he said that I have three weeks vacation coming to me this year and that if I want, I could take all three weeks starting this coming Friday."

Again, I was taken by surprise and I exclaimed, "You can begin taking your vacation starting when?"

"At the end of this week," Carmela repeated. "Isn't that wonderful!" she added. Now I can travel with you to the United States," she announced. "After mass this morning, I also spoke to Father Fernandez about our conversation yesterday and he just shrugged his shoulders and said, it just has to be a coincidence."

Next, my cousin Tomas arrived with the car and said he was taking me to visit Aunt Cleofas who lived in San Jeronimo. It only took a few moments before we were on the dirt road leading into town. An old deserted hacienda stood out above all the other buildings. It was the home where a very wealthy Spanish family, the Segovia's had lived prior to the Revolutionary War in 1910. They had been the plantation owners of the San Jeronimo Hacienda. Next to the hacienda was San Jeronimo's church and directly across the street was a home with a very high adobe wall surrounding the property. This had been the home of my grandparents, Luis and Julia Rivera and this was where my Aunt Cleofas lived.

Tomas parked directly in front of the open double arched doorway that led into the courtyard. He also explained to me that Cleofas was getting very old and that her eyesight had become impaired. In the center of the courtyard was a large shade tree. It was the same tree that had appeared in the photograph with my mother so many years ago. The adobe walls were decorated with hanging potted plants and flowers. Also hanging along the wall were birdcages that made the courtyard come alive with color and sound. Sitting beneath the shade tree was Aunt Cleofas and next to her was her husband Juan. Attending to a small group of pre-school aged children nearby was Cleofas's daughter Emilia.

Emilia, who saw us coming, quickly went over to announce to her mother that we had arrived. Cleofas quickly responded by becoming alert, sitting erect and then reaching out to greet us. While I leaned over to embrace Cleofas, she whispered, "I have prayed very hard that someone from the Seguera family would come to see me. You see that it's time. Don't you?"

Without questioning her meaning, I politely agreed, "Yes, I know." I could see that Cleofas had aged and had become quite frail since I had last seen her and from what I was told she could no longer walk. She was seventy years old; however, she appeared to be in control of her faculties and even had a good sense of humor.

"You know," Cleofas began. "Your mother was a school teacher and she taught in the village of Santa Lucia which is just down the road from here. My father Luis worked for the Segovia family. They were the people who owned the hacienda across the street. He was directly responsible for taking care of the large herds of cattle. And when it was necessary, he was responsible for tracking down and capturing the cattle rustlers. Sometimes he was gone up into the hills for days. I was only a little girl, but I had heard many stories. My mother Julia always helped the church to conduct its fiestas including the feast of San Jeronimo, which was held sometime in September. But what I remember most is that my parents loved to have fiestas right here in this very courtyard. My wedding reception was held here, as well as those of all my sisters. In the corner where the children are playing, my father would have a wooden platform built, so that the guests could dance."

While observing the children, I suddenly remembered the toys. Turning to Emilia, I asked her if it would be appropriate for me to distribute the toys to them. Emilia quickly nodded her approval. I opened the bag and began handing out the toys to the bright-eyed children whose faces lit up with excitement.

Since Cleofas was tired and needed to rest, Juan took me for a walk around the town while Tomas returned to work. Strolling towards the cemetery we passed chickens and piglets roaming about the dusty streets. In the cemetery, Juan began pointing out the family plots. Because the gravesites were so poorly marked, many of plots were only identifiable by Juan's memory rather than by any gravestone or cross. Once again, the grave mounds were haphazardly arranged and there was nothing here to suggest that this was the cemetery of Carmela's dreams. I discovered that the people here really didn't need to know where gravesites were located, since in their minds they had stored away vivid memories of those family members who had passed away.

After returning to the house, Emilia approached me and said that one of the mothers wanted to present me with a gift of appreciation for the toy that I had given her son. I turned to see who Emilia was referring to and I saw a proud looking dark olive-skinned woman standing under the archway. She was holding a small bag full of beans. Emilia then whispered to me, "I told the woman that you didn't need the beans, but in order not to offend her, I accepted the gift on your behalf." This was now the second time on this trip that I had been taken by surprise. Noticing my reaction, Emilia stepped forward and took the bag of beans from the woman. Feeling my chest swell up I nodded towards the woman and said, "*Gracias Senora.*" I was deeply moved by this display of gratitude. Here was a woman who owed me nothing, but still chose to express her appreciation by offering me something from her garden.

After dining that evening, Aunt Cleofas with her family sat around the kitchen table to view some old family photographs and to reminisce about the past. Many of the photographs were of my brothers, my sister and me. These were the pictures that my mother had sent Cleofas before she passed away. On the back of each photo and written in my mother's own handwriting were our full names, date of birth and our ages at the time the pictures were taken.

*   *   *   *

Early the next morning, I awoke to the clanking of the church bells. I got out of bed and had breakfast with Cleofas. Afterwards, I walked out and into the courtyard where I saw Juan standing just beyond the open gate. He was talking to two men who were wearing cowboy attire. Juan motioned to me to come over and as I approached them, I recognized the two men as my cousins Ramon and Carlos, the sons of my Aunt Carmen. Directly behind them were three saddled horses. Both my cousins who were about my age immediately greeted me with embraces. Ramon then said, "I know how much you like to ride Armando, so we brought some horses with us. I didn't think you would mind riding over to Sincero. It's only a three kilometers ride going in direction of the mountains." I'd been to my aunt's home before, but I had always driven.

"Of course I don't mind," I replied. "I look forward to riding with you again"

I was extremely glad to see my cousins. Carlos was one of the cousins that I had gone up into the mountains with during my first visit. He knew how much I liked to ride and what a serious student I had been.

Not knowing if I would ever see Cleofas again, I shared a strong embrace with her. There were tears in our eyes when we parted. Then after mounting the beige colored mare, Juan handed me my overnight bag. I then waved goodbye to everyone as we slowly rode away. I didn't realize it until after we began to ride through town, but following behind us was a black floppy eared dog named El Negro. It appeared that El Negro loved to chase chickens and there were plenty of those around to keep him busy.

Within a short time we arrived at a wide stream and a grove of weeping willow trees. Again, I recognized this location from Marcy's collection of photographs. This must have been the spot where the group of young ladies, including my mother had been photographed. To confirm my suspicions, I saw an old log bench on the far bank of the stream. Whether or not it was the same log as in the pictures was difficult to determine. Then, just as we began to cross the stream, I became concerned about El Negro, so I halted my horse.

"Don't worry about El Negro. He's a very good swimmer," Carlos assured me.

I then watched as El Negro swam across the stream by using short jerky motions. Once on the other side, he shook himself off vigorously.

After about a half-hour we came out from behind the trees into a large clearing. Directly ahead, but still in the distance were the mountains. "See those rows of trees over there behind that wall?" Ramon said, while pointing towards some rows of trees whose trunks had been whitewashed. "That is our family's apple orchard," Ramon stated. "Right now the trees are bare and won't give apples until August or early September. That is when we have the harvest and when people from all over Mexico come here to enjoy our festivals. In the meantime, the trees still require lots of work to maintain."

Although I'd been here before, this was my first visit to the orchard. It was well known throughout Mexico that Canatlan was the apple capital of the country.

It was difficult for me not to be thinking about my grandfather Luis. I'm sorry that I had never known him. He had passed away several years before my first visit. But during my ride through this countryside, I couldn't help but wonder how many times my grandfather may have used this trail. This was probably the same trail that he had used when starting out to track down those thieving cattle rustlers. I was aware that my grandfather had a reputation for being good at what he did and that very few rustlers ever got away. In fact, he had been part of a style of living we knew in the United States as the old west and I allowed my imagination to take me back in time. And it gave me a good deal of satisfaction knowing that I was here, crossing the very same ground that my grandfather had once ridden many times before me.

After awhile, the small village of Sincero came into view. Ramon who was leading us, stopped and pointed towards the mountains. "Look! It appears to be an eagle circling above the foothills," He said.

I could see what looked like a large bird circling, but the bird was too far away for me to make a positive identification. I would just have to take Ramon's word. But it was still a magnificent sight with the mountains in the background.

CHAPTER 7

▼

NEW INSIGHTS

The small village of Sincero was made up of about thirty houses, with Aunt Carmen's house being on the outskirts. Her home like many of the others had an adobe brick wall surrounding a small courtyard. A young boy of about eight or nine came running out of the house to help us with the horses. Ramon ushered me into the kitchen where Aunt Carmen was preparing a meal with two younger women. Carmen who was seventy-five year old looked extremely well. Her pure white hair was made up into a braid that hung down her back. She was also fair skinned like her mother had been. After greeting me with an embrace, Carmen went back to the stove while I sat at the kitchen table with a bottle of Coca-Cola that Carlos had opened for me.

Aunt Carmen's kitchen had small tied up bundles of dried herbs hanging in every corner. On her shelves were jars of seeds and dried leaves. It was known throughout the area that Carmen not only acted as a mid-wife, but also helped to cure the sick with her herbal tea remedies. She had even been known to treat bullet wounds. This was a land that for many years had no doctor or medical facilities for miles around not even in Canatlan. Consequently, Carmen had acquired most of her medical knowledge from her mother and from what had been passed down from one generation to the next. Many of the methods that were used to heal the sick had been learned from the Indians. Because of her years of experiences in this remote rural area, Aunt Carmen conveyed a quiet confidence. She was someone who was capable of handling almost any medical emergency should it arise.

The first time that I had seen Carmen was during my initial visit in 1954. She had been riding sidesaddle atop a horse from Sincero to Canatlan. Riding behind her on a donkey was her youngest son Felipe and following along with them was a black dog. That day, she had spoken to me as though we had known one another all our lives.

"We are very happy to see you Armando," Carmen greeted. "I see that your hair has gotten much whiter than before and that you've also grown a mustache. The white hair comes from your Rivera side of the family. Many of us had white hair before we were forty years old. But your height must come from your Seguera side of the family," she added. "How old is your boy and when are you planning on bringing him to Durango? Soon, I hope" she asked.

"Jose is sixteen years old and he is living with his mother in San Francisco. I plan to bring him next year after he graduates from high school," I replied.

"Do you know my sister Flecita's asked for you every time she writes? She would like you to visit her in Salamanca. I believe that's not far from Mexico City," Carmen related. "Maybe you can go there when you come with your son. I will give you her address, maybe you can begin to write to her."

"Flecita, she's your youngest sister, is that right?" I inquired.

"Yes, she's the youngest. She lives with her son Raphael."

"By the way, do you know what Cleofas meant when she said it was time?"

Without interrupting what she was doing, Carmen spoke, "She thinks that it is time for her to die. As soon as they notify me, I'll go over to San Jeronimo and stay with her until the end."

"Is she ill?"

"No, but she thinks it's her time and she's already communicating with the spirits."

"Spirits! What spirits are you talking about?" I quickly responded, trying not to sound too naive.

"Those are the spirits that are waiting for Cleofas to crossover to the other side. Emilia says that she's already heard her muttering Mama's Julia's name in her sleep," Carmen added.

The talk of spirits was not something I had been exposed as a child and I was not familiar with this custom. "I'm not familiar with the spirit world Aunt Carmen and I'm not certain that I believe in them," I stated.

"I'm surprised, but perhaps as you get older, you will," she answered. Carmen spoke of these things as naturally as talking about her cooking. For her, everything seemed to have its place, including the spirits. Changing the subject, she said, "I'm pleased to know that you are taking Carmela to Detroit. It's important that she gets to know our relatives in the United States better. Too much time has passed."

"Because of her cemetery dream, Carmela thinks she may be in some kind of danger if she goes to Detroit," I stated.

"I'm familiar with her dream. She may have experienced a premonition or been given an assignment from the other side," Carmen commented in her usual casual manner.

"An assignment from the other side? Forgive me Aunt Carmen, but I'm afraid that I don't understand all of your customs. What do you mean when you say an assignment from the other side?" I asked again, in a rather puzzled manner this time.

"If you don't know, then it is difficult for me to explain, but sometimes we receive missions from the other side. These missions are sometimes given to us through dreams," she stated. "So watch Carmela very closely and keep your eyes and ears open for anything out of the ordinary."

"I certainly will," I replied.

"However, I do have something here that I think you will understand," Carmen said, as she reached into her apron to bring out an old withered envelope. At the same time, her rosary accidentally fell to the floor and she immediately picked it up. She then handed me the envelope saying, "Armando, we haven't had much opportunity to discuss things in the past, but I recently found this letter and I would like very much to share it with you."

I took the envelope. It was addressed to, *Senora* Julia M. Rivera, Residential Address Known, San Jeronimo, Durango, Mexico. The return address was from my mother on Duluth, Street in Detroit. It was postmarked, June 17, 1936. My mother's penmanship was clear and distinct. The letter read:

To My Beloved Mother,

I hope that this letter finds you and the rest of the family in good health, thanks be to God.

When Rodolfo comes with the children, please take young Rodlofo. He's ten years old years old now and can be a big help to Papa. I would like to see him become a lawyer some day, so that he can become a political leader.

I would like to see Francisco raised by Consuelo. He loves to draw and create things, so I think he should become an artist.

I would like to see Marcella raised by Cleofas. She listens so well. I was thinking she would make a good schoolteacher, like myself.

I would like to see Ricardo raised by Felcita. He has such sympathetic eyes that I think he would be an excellent doctor.

And I would like to see little Armando raised by Carmen. He is so inquisitive about everything, I think he will make a very good historian someday.

I am confident that you and my sisters will raise my children to hold the same strong family values and traditions that you impressed upon me.

Your Loving Daughter,

Adelina Rivera de Seguera

Several moments passed before I spoke, "This letter implies that my mother was aware of her impending death."

"Yes, didn't you know she died of tuberculosis? It was incurable then. Consequently, the Mexican consulate in Detroit would not issue her a visa to leave the United States. She wanted so much to come here and die," Carmen explained.

"I was aware of the tuberculosis and I remember that for a long time we had to be x-rayed every year," I recalled. Going to some clinic in downtown Detroit always scared me and I always put up a big fuss before going. However, what I had just read made perfect sense to me. With so many sisters living in San Jeronimo, why wouldn't she have wanted us to be raised by them.

"I don't see Ofelia's name mentioned here," I asked about one of the other sisters.

"Ofelia was living in Los Angeles at the time," Carmen responded. "She was two years younger than Adelina and sadly enough, she too also died of tuberculosis four months after Adelina, leaving six children of her own. We were expecting your father Rodolfo to bring all of you here so we could raise you, like the letter requested," Carmen spoke sorrowfully. "But then time passed, then years, and after awhile we knew you weren't coming," she added.

"Not too long ago, my sister Marcella found some pictures of my mother and of our family here in Durango. They were pictures that we had never seen before and they made me realize that I knew very little about my mother other than what I've learned during my visits here to Canatlan. Now you've even enlightened me even more. I want to thank you for sharing something that was so dear to my mother's heart," I expressed my own sorrow.

Later that evening, we gathered around the kitchen table. Ramon lit a kerosene lamp that caused the flickering light to cast dancing shadows on the walls and on our faces. Next, Ramon poured each of us a glass of tequila and Carlos rolled cigarettes for himself and Carmen. Then like the family elder that she was, Carmen began telling stories that captivated my imagination. She talked about how close her sisters had been and how much they respected their mother or Mama Julia as they called her. Mama Julia had made certain that they all sang in the San Jeronimo church choir. They were also required to participate in all of the church festivals. I felt like a small boy completely mesmerized by her every word. At times, Carmen used swaying hand gestures to help her describe an incident and other times she would smile at a pleasant memory or frown at an unpleasant one. There were times when the memories were so touching that they brought tears to her eyes.

That evening, while in bed, I wondered how I had overlooked so much of my family's history. I had learned more about my family and my mother in just a few days than I had in my entire lifetime. It wasn't difficult for me to see why my mother would have wanted her children living securely with her sisters. Just knowing that she had been concerned for our future brought me a sense of well being. And what had happened to all those dreams and aspirations she had wanted for her family. What had gone wrong?

Staring out of my bedroom window, I was able to view the spectacular brilliance of the Milky Way in its entire splendor. There was such a multitude of stars that they resembled snowflakes just waiting to make their journey to the earth. I then heard the lone howl of a coyote coming from the direction of the foothills. I was asleep before there was a reply.

In the morning, I heard the crowing of a rooster outside my bedroom window. The odor of fresh tortillas drew me out of bed and towards the smell. Upon entering the kitchen, I saw a small gray owl perched on the back of a chair. At first, it appeared to be a stuffed animal, so inquired, "Is that a toy?"

"Get your animal out here Miguelito!" Carmen shouted to the six-year old boy. Miguelito quickly stopped what he was doing and poked the owl in the belly with his index finger. This caused the owl to quickly open one eye while Miguelito gently picked up his pet owl in his two small hands and ran out the door.

During breakfast, Carmen still had things on her mind and continued from where she left off the previous evening, "You know, Armando, that when your mother and father left here the plan was for the entire Rivera family to again be reunited sometime in the future. We were only waiting for Rodolfo and Adelina to get established in Detroit. As you well know, God intervened. Armando, your mother's letter requested that I raise you." Again, Carmen reached into her apron and brought out another old withered envelope. She then said, "I have now done everything in my power, in the time that God has allowed me, in order for me to fulfill the obligations and the promises that I made to both my mother and my sister Adelina. Here, this is the last letter that we ever received from your mother before she died."

The letter was addressed the same as the first, only the postmark read August 23, 1936. I opened the letter and immediately noticed several dried tearstains. I slowly read what was more of a brief note than a letter. The letter stated how my mother wanted to become and eagle for one day, so she could fly home and embrace her family for one last time. After having read the letter, I walked out into the patio with the letter still in my hand. Miguelito was playing nearby with his friends and El Negro was sleeping in the shade. I went over to the wall and looked out towards the mountains that I had learned to be in awe of ever since I had first seen them. I even scanned the sky looking for the eagle that Ramon had spotted yesterday. But I saw nothing.

I was thinking about my mother's letter. It was more moving than the letter that I read the previous day. In this letter she was almost apologizing to her mother for not being able to come home, so that she could say goodbye to her family. It was her desire that if she could become and eagle for one day, she would fly home so that she could embrace everyone for one last time. The letter had touched me so deeply that some emotional activity that had lain dormant for many years began to stir.

Suddenly, in the background I could hear the revving of an engine from a motor vehicle. Turning to the east I could see a cloud of dust being kicked up like a small dust storm. It was Guillermo's blue Ford pickup. I read the letter one last time.

*   *   *   *

Before leaving Durango, I phoned a surprised, but happy Ramona. I also ordered a wheelchair for Aunt Cleofas. Perhaps she could spend her last days like a queen sitting on her throne. Uncle Victor and Guillermo took me out to the movie lot so I could see where John Wayne had had filmed his western movies.

Friday evening, Carmela and I boarded the overnight bus to Monterrey. In Monterrey we would visit more relatives before flying to Houston. We had been told that it was more practical to cross the Coahuila desert at night, just in case the bus broke down, which it often did. In other words, why stand in the hot sun when you can all huddle together in the chill of the night. As the bus sped across the desert, I couldn't help but notice Carmela silently reciting her rosary.

That night in Monterrey, I awoke in the middle of the night with my eyes wide open. I was perspiring and my heart seemed to be pounding in my ears. I had just experienced one of those lucid dreams that Ramona and Carmela had described. Usually, I didn't remember my dreams, but this time I was remembering every detail. The dream began with me standing on a mountain peak in Durango. The sky was cloudy and I was facing towards the north. In the distance I was able to see a faint white bright light coming directly towards me. As the light grew brighter, I suddenly recognized it as a slow moving passenger jet that was descending and coming in for a landing. As the plane came closer to me, I saw a dark haired Mexican looking woman sitting at one of the passenger windows. I immediately recognized the woman, but I didn't know her name. It was then that the dream ended and I awoke. I was unable to sleep for the rest of the night.

In the morning, I couldn't wait to tell Carmela. As soon as I finished, Carmela didn't hesitate to ask me, "How did you know the woman was Mexican or that you were in Durango? And how did you know you were facing north?"

Confused, I just said passively, "You got me Carmela. I just knew, that's all."

"What do you think your dream means?" Carmela asked, still looking for explanations.

"I don't know," I replied. "My mother's letters were filled with so much emotion; they may have affected me in some way. The woman in the plane may only have been a wishful thought about my mother wanting to fly back to Durango before she died," I attempted the best explanation that I could up with.

"Then what do you think the white light in both our dreams means?"

Then without hesitation and as though someone else had been speaking the words, I blurted out, "It's because my mother is trying to communicate with us!"

"Yes, that is what Aunt Carmen told me. She said that white lights usually represent spirits, so maybe you are right," Carmela commented without her realizing that I had not been in control.

I wasn't listening to Carmela anymore. I remained perplexed for having made a compulsive remark and saying something about my mother. But when I attempted to brush it off as nothing, I had difficulty trying to convince myself.

The next morning, which was Sunday, we flew directly to Houston. After going through customs I rented a car and drove about four hours to Austin. It was around midday when we arrived at my niece Denise's home. Denise's was the daughter of my brother Frank and her husband Gary was stationed at an Air Force base nearby. We spent the remainder of the day with Denise and Gary and in the morning, they drove Carmela and me to the airport.

At the Dallas airport, we had to hurry in order to find Carmela's departure gate. When we arrived at the gate the passengers were already boarding. But then, just as Carmela began to hurry down the ramp, I again loudly uttered a compulsive remark, "Carmela, while you're in Detroit, please make certain that you spend at least one night in the house on Duluth Street, okay?" Again, the words seemed to have a will of their own. Carmela just smiled, turned and then, acting as though she thoroughly understood my instructions, she disappeared down the ramp. There was no time for any additional comments.

▼

CHAPTER 8

VIBRATIONS

After having completed my week's assignment in the Dallas office, I returned to New York. I was anxious to get back into a regular daily routine again. My first day back at the office, Rick informed me that the firm was getting ready to announce the promotions for the year and that his inside source of information had told him that Doug and I were on the list. This meant that Doug would become a Vice-President and move to an office on the administrative floor. In turn, I would become an Assistant Vice-President and move into Doug's old office. At least that was the way things were usually handled at our firm. And since I had no rational explanation for what had happened to me on my trip, I decided not to mention anything to Rick. The truth was, it was not even a conscious decision I just didn't do it. Still lingering with me was this feeling of 'just wait and see.'

I also tried to keep in touch with Ramona and Carmela just to see how things were going. Ramona told me that Carmela was enjoying her visit and that she seemed quite happy. But then, for some reason I got extremely busy and didn't call her for about five days. Then, late one evening Ramona phoned, "Hi Uncle Armand. How are you?"

"I'm fine. How's your houseguest?"

"I don't know if it's the kids getting on my nerves or what, but that feeling of urgency has intensified. But that's not the reason why I'm calling you. Why I'm calling is that there's something really strange going on here," Ramona started.

"What's wrong? Are you having trouble communicating with Carmela?" I asked.

"No. That's not it. We understand one another just fine," Ramona answered. "We've been shopping and sightseeing all over the place. But she is such an attractive girl I do have some minor problems with keeping the boys away. I was wondering if you were familiar with Camela's cemetery dream."

"I certainly am. I hope she hasn't been boring you with the dream. In Canatlan she told anyone who would listen to her," I replied jokingly.

"No, she is not boring me, but I think you're going to appreciate what I'm about to tell you," Ramona begin. "Well, this past Sunday, I took Carmela to the cemetery so we could visit the gravesites of my Seguera grandparents and to pay our respects. But then while were driving through the cemetery, Carmela suddenly yells, 'Hey, this looks like the cemetery in my dreams. Is there a big house around here somewhere?' I told her no, just the administrative building and the mausoleum. She looked really confused. Then, while we're at the gravesites, she kept looking around as though she was going to find the house. Carmela told me that many of the houses in Detroit were similar to the one in her dreams."

"It could just be a coincidence. Lots of cemeteries look alike in this country, so that's not unusual. Even if it was the cemetery what's the connection? Besides it was only a dream," I remarked with my own air of uncertainty.

"Except that's not all," Ramona remarked. "Tonight, which is Wednesday, we went over to the bowling alley to watch my parents bowl. Their neighbors Harry and Phyllis bowl on the same team. You remember them?"

"Yes I do."

"Just as soon as I introduced Phyllis to Carmela, Phyllis gets all excited and says, 'Oh my God! This young lady is sending out all kinds of psychic vibrations and she is on some kind of an important mission.' Phyllis said that she couldn't believe that she was even able to pick up Carmela's vibrations right there inside the crowded bowling alley. I guess that's something unusual."

"Did anything else happen?" I eagerly inquired.

"Yes. Phyllis then asked me if she could do a reading with Carmela tomorrow afternoon. What do you think?" Ramona asked.

I thought for a moment. What kind of a mission could Phyllis be referring too, and weren't they the same words that Aunt Carmen had used? There were lots of reasons for having invited Carmela. The purpose of her visit was to give the girls an opportunity to exchange the family's history and to enhance their knowledge of both cultures. Mainly, it was to expose the entire Detroit Seguera family to their Mexican heritage.

"What does Carmela say?"

"Carmela says there is a great deal of interest in this sort of thing in Mexico. But it's mostly in the small villages and it's kept very confidential. She says that Aunt Carmen knows a lot about the subject. However, since meeting Phyllis tonight, she has developed a strong interest and wants to hear what Phyllis has to say about her cemetery dreams. In case you didn't know, Phyllis conducts readings everyday," Ramona informed me. She also sounded as though she wasn't certain about the reading herself and was just looking for some kind of assurance.

"I must say, Carmela certainly makes things interesting," I commented. "Since I'm totally unfamiliar with how readings are conducted, I have to admit that I'm quite curious about what Phyllis might have to say myself. And if you have confidence in her, I see no harm. What does Carmela say?" I asked.

"Carmela is fine. It's no problem with her."

"Let me know what transpires, okay?" I requested.

∗   ∗   ∗   ∗

The following evening, Ramona phoned again and started right in, "Hi Uncle Armand. I've got a lot to tell you."

"Did Phyllis conduct the reading?"

"She sure did," Ramona responded. "Well, this afternoon Carmela and I went over to Phyllis's and she couldn't wait to start the reading. Anyway, she seemed to be having trouble finding the right room in which to conduct the reading. Apparently, the psychic energy levels in each room are different and it was for that reason we ended up in the kitchen. Of course, I had to act as interpreter and after we got comfortable, Phyllis began the reading. During the reading she told us that she was receiving vibrations through Carmela from the spirit of a young mother. She said that the spirit had a very important message to convey to her family and that the entity was very unhappy and had suffered from severe chest pains prior to passing over to the other side. Phyllis continued to tell us that the entity is unhappy because she wants her family to be united. That she would like to see the family maintains the same values and traditions that had been passed onto her by her mother. That it was very important to her that the family live in complete harmony. It was about this time that Phyllis began to lose the signal. She said that the spirit only wanted to communicate with members of her own kind and stopped sending messages. That's all I can remember. Do you think she was describing my grandmother Seguera?" Ramona inquired.

"I don't know," I answered. "There are many similarities. However, I'm still a bit confused; do you believe in spirits Ramona?" I asked.

"Sure," Ramona answered. "Phyllis says they're all over the place. They only attempt to communicate with their loved ones when they are looking for closure. Phyllis says that this particular spirit is earthbound and that it will remain earthbound until the family unity issue can be resolved. The fact that the spirit is restless means that the spirit is not resting in peace and is seeking help. The spirit may even want to be released from the plane where it exists. I told Phyllis that it sounds like something rather difficult to do if the spirit is over there and we are here. She said that praying for the deceased is a big help."

"How has Carmela been handling all this?" I asked.

"I found it difficult to translate on this subject, but I did my best," Ramona responded. "Carmela said she only knew of two mothers who had died when they were still young. My grandmother and an Aunt Ofelia, was the other. Carmela was disappointed that she didn't get any answers about her dreams. However, she was excited about the reading and started talking incessantly about everything unusual that had happened in her life," Ramona commented.

Since Aunt Carmen was aware of my mother dying of tuberculosis, this information would have been available to Carmela. It wasn't until my recent trip that I learned about the Rivera's family plan to eventually be united in Detroit. However, I was uncertain if it was that kind of unity the spirit was referring too. If Phyllis was mind reading, she was doing it in Spanish. But for the moment, all evidence pointed to the spirit as being that of my mother. I was now even more confused than before and began to realize that I should have paid more attention to Aunt Carmen.

I continued to speak with Ramona for awhile, but before we concluded our conversation, she asked, "What about tomorrow night?"

"Tomorrow night? What about tomorrow night?" I quickly asked.

"We're going over to Aunt Marcy's house. Michelle is going to meet us there," Ramona informed me.

"Haven't you been there already?" I asked curiously. Since two weeks had already passed, I assumed that by now they would have had ample time to visit my sister.

"Yes, we've been there a couple of times, but we're just going over before Carmela leaves. We plan to go through all those old photographs; maybe Carmela can help to identify some of the people. Is there something you need?" Ramona asked.

"No," I answered abruptly with a lie. "Just make certain that you call me again tomorrow night if anything unusual pops up, okay Ramona?" I added, trying to sound nonchalant. What was going through my mind was Aunt Carmen's warning that Carmela might be on a mission and that she should be watched closely. Phyllis had even verified the mission part, but that didn't tell me anything.

*   *   *   *

Having been raised a Roman Catholic, I was taught to believe in eternal life after death. No one said anything about stopping off somewhere along the way to make trouble for your relatives who had remained on the earthly plane. Never having acquired an interest in any supernatural beliefs, I have always remained skeptical. But ever since my passenger jet dream in Monterrey and my two compulsive remarks, I've not been able to reach any practical conclusions. Of course, I also had to take both Ramona's and Carmela's dreams into account and therefore, I was slowly beginning to believe that there might be something to this supernatural phenomenon. Even though the incidents were far beyond my ability to comprehend them, my intuition was still telling me to remain noncommittal. All that I knew at this particular time was that Carmela was supposed to be on a mission of some kind and that tomorrow evening, she would be spending one evening in the house on Duluth Street.

CHAPTER 9

▼

THE INCIDENT

Late the following evening, Ramona phoned with a highly excited pitch in her voice, "Uncle Armand! Uncle Armand! You'll never believe what happened tonight!"

"Hold it! Slow down! Take your time and catch your breath," I interrupted.

Ramona began again, only this time much slower, "It all started right when Aunt Marcy, Michelle, Carmela and I, were looking through those old photographs. Every time Carmela picked up a picture and attempted to identify someone she would begin to tremble. It was obvious that Carmela was embarrassed, so we stopped and Aunt Marcy began serving coffee and cake. Then Aunt Marcy went upstairs and brought down this beautiful old jewelry box that had belonged to my grandmother. I'd never seen it before. One of the items was a beautiful string of pearls along with a number of other attractive looking pieces of jewelry. Naturally, we were all curious, so we began to carefully examine each item. It was as though we had discovered a chest full of lost treasure. Included amongst the items was this beautiful gold ring. Aunt Marcy said it was my grandmother's wedding ring. Carmela immediately took a special interest and picked up the ring to examine it more closely. But then the ring slipped from her hand and rolled onto the table. She quickly picked it up with her right hand and fell back in her chair with a shocked expression. Her hand was tightly clenched and she was pressing it very hard just above her left breast. It scared all of us when she began to tremble again and began gasping for breath. I thought that she might be having an epileptic seizure of some kind. There were tears just streaming down Carmela's face and she looked as though she were in a great deal of emotional pain. To add to the confusion, Sergeant began barking incessantly at Carmela, with no one paying any attention to him, not even to tell him to shut-up. We were so stunned by Carmela's reactions that I was thinking of calling for an ambulance. But suddenly Carmela, still clutching the ring, jumped up from the table and headed directly for the living room in a big hurry. Naturally, we all followed her. I was afraid she might go running out the front door and into the street. But instead, when she reached the foyer, she turned and raced up the stair to the second floor. I was close behind Carmela, with Michelle behind me, followed by Aunt Marcy. In the meantime, Sergeant continued barking somewhere in the background. I thought that maybe Carmela was sick and just needed to get to the bathroom in a hurry. But then when she reached the top of the stairs, she immediately froze. She was in the hallway, directly in front of the back bedroom and that is where she sat down. She then began to stare into the bedroom. It was dark inside the bedroom and the only light that was helping us to see anything came from that dim hall nightlight that Aunt Marcy keeps lit in the evening."

Ramona stopped for a moment, but continued to speak rapidly without slurring her words, "Suddenly, the temperature turned so cold that we all began to shiver. Carmela remained motionless on the floor crying while she continued to stare into the bedroom as though expecting to see something. Now comes the scary part Uncle Armand. Suddenly, a faint white light appeared in the back of the bedroom just above the bed. At first, I thought the glow might be coming from an open window and that was why it was so cold. But then the light began to move towards us and as it did, it grew brighter and brighter, and then it also began to take form. It was an apparition! I couldn't believe my eyes, it was an apparition! Although it never materialized fully as an actual being, it was obvious that it was a woman just a few feet in front of my very eyes. My immediate reaction was that it was the spirit of my grandmother. Then, Carmela started speaking in Spanish, but in some strange sounding baritone voice that didn't seem to be her own. Even though it was still cold, a chill still went up my back and I couldn't get over Carmela's strange sounding voice."

"What was Carmela saying," I asked impatiently.

"Well," Ramona said, trying to get her thought together and still expressing the same emotions from a few hours ago, "I'm trying to remember the order in which Carmela said them. First she said, 'My work is done here. There is nothing more for me to do here anymore. It is time that I return to Mexico to be with my family as I promised. My Mama Julia needs me to help with Cleofas. I want my family to be united and to live in peace and in harmony.' Carmela's strange voice sounded rather determined, even if she didn't sound like she was in control. A lot of what she said was repeated that's why I can remember most everything. There were other things said that I didn't understand. To be honest with you, it happened so fast that I'm surprised that I got any of it right. But even though it was cold, I was feeling a lot of love energy around me. The cold didn't go away until Carmela stopped talking and the spirit moved away into the bedroom. The whole thing from beginning to end lasted about ten minutes."

"Then Michelle asked me, 'Did you see it?' I told her that I did, and that I'm almost certain that it was the spirit of our grandmother. Everything that's happened in the last week seemed to point in that direction. Isn't that right Uncle Armand?'

"Yes, that appears to be right, but go on," I urged, wanting to hear every detail.

"Then Marcy asked, what was it that you saw? I assumed she was just trying to confirm that we had all seen the same thing. Michelle told her that she had seen the apparition of a woman hovering in the doorway of the bedroom," Ramona related.

"What was Carmela doing all this time?" I continued my probe.

"Carmela stopped crying and looked completely stunned," Ramona remarked. "She looked like she was in a state of total disbelief. In my opinion, she had been in some kind of a trance state and had no control over what she had done or said. I believe that she was possessed by my grandmother's spirit. That's the best explanation that I can give you."

"What about Marcy? How did she react?" I asked.

"Aunt Marcy looked as shocked or surprised as Michelle and I. I don't think she could believe what had happened. She appeared to be confused or maybe even somewhat suspicious about the incident. Like 'hey, is this some kind of a joke?' Ramona commented. "All I can tell you is that she didn't say that she had seen the apparition. If she did, she kept it to herself. I do know that none of us wanted to talk about it. Carmela looked really upset, so we said goodnight and we left. All the way home, Carmela never spoke she just sat there staring out the window of the car. I don't even think she was aware that there was a light snow falling and that I had to put the windshield wipers on. She still doesn't want to talk. Right now she's in the bedroom and I'm almost certain that she's praying with her rosary. When I told her that I was calling you, she said that she didn't want to speak to anyone. She just wants to go back to Mexico."

"When is she due to go back?" I asked.

"Saturday," Ramona indicated.

"Saturday, that's tomorrow or today, depending on what time it is," I reacted.

"Try and get Carmela to stay a few more days, so that we can hear her version of the incident. Maybe we can get Phyllis to help us and perhaps conduct another reading," I urged, while still trying to find something that would help me to explain this unusual occurrence.

"I'll try, but I don't think it will do any good. She's in a state of shock," Ramona explained. "Michelle and I have decided that we are not going to mention this to anyone else in the family. And we certainly know that Aunt Marcy won't. What do you think?" Ramona asked.

Nothing like this had ever happened in our family before or at least to my knowledge. I was beginning to wonder why no one wanted to discuss the subject. Being a bit overwhelmed, to say the least, I really didn't know what to say, so I politely agreed, "Sure, okay Ramona. I will need time to think about this and to find a rational explanation anyway."

"I know, so do we all. But do you think that my grandmother's spirit might still be in the house?" Ramona asked.

"I don't know anything about these matters Ramona. But I would say that my mother's spirit has probably returned to Mexico in order to help her sister Cleofas to cross over to the other side," I attempted my first rational metaphysical reply. "I'm assuming that you know that my Aunt Cleofas is dying."

"Yes, Carmela told me. But all I can tell you is that this is one of the most extraordinary experiences of my entire life," Ramona stated, but sounding much calmer. "At least, I now know the meaning of my airport dream and I suppose Carmela should know the meaning of her dreams too. I guess it was my grandmother's time to go home and be with her family, just like the voice said she needed to do. Another thing, you know that feeling of urgency that I had? It gone! I'll talk to you tomorrow after I take Carmela to the airport, okay."

"Sure, but see if Carmela will give you some additional information or insights. I'm eager to get her perception," I requested. "Everything appears to be rather hazy and I'm also overwhelmed at what's transpired. I suppose that I've got a lot to learn," I added. "By the way, there are things about this incident that I neglected to tell you. As soon as I get my thoughts together, I'll call you and fill you in, okay?"

"Okay, and goodnight Uncle Armand, I love you."

"I love you too, and if we were together, I would give you a big hug," I said. "Oh yes one other thing before I hang up. I don't know how to say this, but it appears that we were somehow employed by the spirit world to get Carmela to the Duluth Street house. And if that's the case, we did a good job. Congratulations, we helped my mother to return to her homeland. I just hope Carmela is going to be okay. In the meantime, I plan to talk to Marcy and Michelle tomorrow, goodnight."

This was thoroughly a new experience for me and my mind had been working overtime ever since Monterrey. If I were to follow Phyllis's psychic logic, then everything would make some kind of sense. The unusual series of coincidences pointed to only one thing, the spirit of my mother wanted to return to Mexico. But why did she need Carmela? To leave a message, I suppose. In addition, Mama Julia's name was mentioned during the incident in conjunction with Aunt Celofas's. Another determining factor was that the room in which the spirit appeared had been my parents' bedroom, and no doubt the same room in which my mother suffered with her illness. But for the moment, a feeling of satisfaction had come over me, knowing that I may have helped my mother's spirit to deliver that all-important message to the family.

Early the next morning, I phoned Michelle, who was much more composed than Ramona had been. Michelle immediately inquired, "I thought Ramona and I had agreed to keeping this a secret, why is it that you already know?"

"Carmela was entrusted to me by her parents and, in turn, I entrusted Carmela to Ramona. Consequently, Ramona may have felt a sense of obligation to keep me informed and I'm glad she did," I replied. I then spent a few minutes explaining what I knew about the incident.

It only took a moment for Micelle to begin and I could sense in her voice that the experience was still with her, "I was right next to Carmela when we reached the top of the stairs. That's when I began to feel that chilling cold that Ramona told you about. I was wondering why Carmela was staring into the bedroom, so I began to look inside too," Michelle said, "I then saw this luminous glowing mist hovering in the corner of the bedroom. Then the glowing mist started floating right towards us. As it got closer, I realized that it was a translucent apparition of a woman wearing what looked like a white gown of some kind. I could clearly see her outline and my instincts immediately told me, it was the spirit of my grandmother. I knew this because when I was a little girl, I used to play with my dolls in that room and I always sensed her presence. My sisters never seemed to know what I was talking about."

"Go on Michelle, what else happened?" I urged.

"I don't know if Ramona told you this or not, but there appeared to be a luminous line, like an umbilical cord coming directly from the apparition and leading to Carmela's chest area. As soon as the cord appeared that's when Carmela began talking. Then when she started talking, it frightened me at first. It was such a strange guttural sound, that I was sure Carmela wasn't acting. All the time, Carmela was crying. As you know, I don't speak Spanish and I didn't understand what she was saying, but it sure sounded like what she was saying was packed full of emotion. After Carmela stopped talking, the apparition floated back into the bedroom and the bitter cold dissipated."

"How were you feeling about that time?"

"I don't know how to explain this," Michelle said, looking for the right words to express her feelings. "But it was a beautiful experience for me to be near my grandmother. Even though it was cold and the voice coming through Carmela sounded desperate, there was so much motherly love energy being generated that I began to cry."

"I understand that my sister wasn't certain that she saw anything," I asked.

"I know what she said, but I don't know how she could not have seen the apparition, it was only a few feet away from us," Michelle expressed her opinion. "One other thing, I watched as the spirit floated back into the bedroom. It didn't fade away. It floated out through the back bedroom window. I guess spirits can go through anything," Michelle commented.

Michelle and I continued to talk for awhile longer before concluding our conversation. I thanked her for sharing her version of the incident before saying goodbye. Now I was hesitant about phoning Marcy. My nieces had indicated that Marcy was upset enough, that she might not even want to discuss it with me.

Later that evening, I went ahead and phoned Marcy. I wasn't certain how to begin the conversation, so I began by telling her that I'd already spoken to Ramona and Michelle. Marcy was very composed and quite surprised that I was so well informed and so soon.

"I don't really understand what happened," Marcy began in her noncommittal manner. "Because I'm not certain what I witnessed was really happening. My first reaction was that the girls were playing some sort of a trick. After it got cold, I was sure one of them had opened a window. There is a streetlight from the neighboring street that reflects into that back bedroom, so it was hard for me to tell. You know, I don't believe in spirits and I can't really say that I saw one. But it sure surprised me when Carmela started talking. I do agree with Ramona's translation, but Carmela would have known all that information from her own family, including the names of our relatives. I'm still overwhelmed by the experience and I need more time to think. Besides, I'm too upset to talk about it, even now."

Marcy didn't sound too convinced about there being a spirit. She even suspected that the girls had been playing some kind of a trick. Other than sounding a bit shaken, Marcy remained composed. She was obviously entitled to her personal reasons for being reluctant, and I knew enough not to press her anymore.

*   *   *   *

Interestingly enough my own feelings of 'let's wait and see' had dissipated and gone away. Instead, it had been replaced with a strong urge to fulfill my mother's family unity wish. Since I had also dreamt of the white light, perhaps this was to be my mission, as Aunt Carmen had described. How one went about approaching such an assignment, I had no idea, so I went over to the bookcase and quickly scanned the book titles. There didn't appear to be anything that could provide me with any helpful information. Then, pausing for a moment, I reached for a black hard covered book with gold lettering. I took the book from the shelf and went over to the bed where I flicked on the reading lamp. After climbing into bed, I fluffed up the pillows, sat back and for the first time in my life I began to read the Bible.

PART II

▼

CHAPTER 10

▼

UNUSUAL SYMPTONS

It was a very wet dismal November afternoon in the fall of 1980, when I swung the chair around and began staring out the window. From my corner office, I had an excellent view of the World Trade Center's twin towers. But due to the recent afternoon rain, the upper floors of the towers were obscured behind a moving low bank of clouds. I watched as the mist swiftly drifted by and oddly enough that's exactly what my mind had been doing a lot of lately, just drifting off into a trance like state.

These brief mental lapses had begun shortly after the Duluth Street incident last year. But within the last few months they were beginning to occur more frequently. During these occurrences my mind became completely blank and after shutting out the outside world I would find myself staring off into space. I had also begun to experience some peculiar physical discomforts as well, like a rapid pulse rhythm, which was accompanied by heart palpitations. Then there were those hot flashes and sometimes an occasional buzzing in my ear. There was also this ever-present twinge in my chest just below the left shoulder and although the twinge or ache was not severe, it was annoying.

In addition, my sleep was beginning to be interrupted by dreams, extremely vivid ones. Recently, a number of the dreams had taken place in my family's house on Duluth Street in Detroit. In one dream, I was in the basement where a kitten was playing on the basement floor, when suddenly a dog came running out of the storage room. The dog frightened the kitten so much that it caused the kitten's hair to stand on end and its eyes to pop out of its head in an exaggerated car-toon like manner. Like the passenger jet dream, I awoke startled and not knowing what to think.

In another not so startling dream, I found myself climbing a ladder that extended to the roof of the Duluth Street house. Once on the roof, I begin to adjust a large antenna, so that it was pointing to a satellite far out in space.

An appointment with my personal physician, Doctor Bloom wasn't scheduled for another week, but I was getting anxious to find some answers. Being impa-tient, I decided to visit the Stock Exchange clinic that morning. All I wanted from one of the doctors was to confirm to me that I wasn't imagining these symptoms. While in the clinic's waiting room, I noticed a brochure from a psy-chotherapy-counseling center that had recently opened only two blocks away. Given the stress associated with the brokerage business, I couldn't help but think that it was a good idea to have such a center nearby. Just as I finished reading the brochure, the nurse called my name.

I hurriedly explained each of my symptoms to the examining physician who politely listened without displaying any expression. After the doctor completed his cursory examination, he began to jot down some notes while I finished but-toning my shirt. Then, the doctor glanced at me from over the rim of his glasses and stated that everything appeared normal. The doctor also concurred with me that visiting my personal physician was a wise decision. Despite what the doctor had told me, I was still being bothered by these unusual symptoms. But I guess that I would have to wait until I saw Doctor Bloom.

Suddenly, I heard the secretaries laughing on their way to the elevators and I realized without looking at the clock that it was already five o'clock. Then Ann, my secretary, wearing a yellow raincoat and carrying an umbrella, paused in the doorway.

"Goodnight Armand, have a pleasant evening," Ann stated with a smile.

"Same to you Ann, see you tomorrow," I replied. Ann had been my secretary ever since I was promoted eighteen months ago. She had a lovely personality besides being an efficient secretary.

Next, Rick poked his head into the office and asked, "Is it going to be the health club or are you attending classes at the university tonight?"

"Tonight is club night," I replied.

"Then have a good workout. Wish I was going with you, but I've got to get home tonight," Rick commented.

"Okay, then have a safe trip home," I responded.

"See you tomorrow," Rick said, as he ran off to catch his commuter train to the suburbs in New Jersey.

On Monday and Wednesday evenings, I played racquetball with my friend Kevin Coffey. We played at a health club on Fulton Street, which was not far from the office. On Tuesday and Thursday evenings I attended classes at New York University. Since I was no longer required to travel as frequently, I enrolled in the University's School of Continuing Education. Initially, going to school had not been a problem, but I was beginning to have some difficulty disciplining myself because of the recurring trance states.

After leaving the office, I headed straight for the health club. Kevin was already warming up on the jogging machine when I arrived. I quickly joined him as soon as I changed into my gym outfit. I climbed onto the jogging machine and started running at moderate pace. However, once I was sufficiently warmed up, I was now ready to quicken the pace. In order to make this adjustment I needed to pull the speed control bar back an inch or two. But then just as I reached for the bar with my right hand, a very visible electrical charge came crackling off the end of the bar. The charge arched itself from the top of the control bar to the tip of my middle finger, which was approximately three inches away. Not only was there a loud hissing sound accompanying the charge, but it also caused my body hairs to stand up on end. Simultaneously, my scalp prickled vigorously for an instant. Thinking that I might be getting electrocuted, I quickly withdrew my hand and leaped off the machine. I even noticed a small burn blister on my middle finger.

Then Kevin, who was running on the machine next to mine, yelled, "Hey, what's going on over there? You're causing my body hairs to stand on end."

"Sorry Kevin, there must be something wrong with the machine. Let me ask the attendant if this thing is safe," I remarked, sounding a bit confused. The attendant who was nearby informed me that there is always a certain amount of static electricity on every machine, but none to the degree that I had described. Naturally, I didn't know what to think.

For some unknown reason I had been generating more static electricity than normal. It had been happening at the office whenever I went over to the metal file cabinet or whenever I touched the metal doorknob. Even Ann had noticed the static charges and began kidding with me. At home, static flashes appeared when I went to bed. Sparks would appear from wherever my body touched the sheets, making it appaer as though it were a small fireworks display.

After our racquetball game, Kevin and I took the subway together to Brooklyn where we both lived. I got off the train two stops before Kevin, climbed the subway stairs and started walking towards my apartment building. Then while walking, I noticed that just as I stepped next to one of the lampposts the streetlight up above flickered out. I was perplexed because this was not the first time. It had happened on at least four other occasions. Each time, it was within a three or four block radius of my apartment. I had not even been conscious of the streetlights until they went out. After each incident, I walked about twenty or thirty yards further, stopped, turned and waited to see if the light would come back on again. They never did, and tonight was no exception.

Once inside the apartment, I threw the mail on the desk, kicked off my shoes and plopped myself on the couch. I had studying to do this evening, but I just wanted to rest for a few moments. I lived in the Bay Ridge section of Brooklyn. My apartment was located in a residential neighborhood near where the Verrazano Narrows Bridge connects Brooklyn to Staten Island. Bay Ridge is best known for its large spacious old homes, tree lined streets, churches, restaurants and neighborhood pubs. My apartment was on the sixth floor and I had and unobstructed view of the bridge.

Since I knew so little about the paranormal and spirituality, I began to study these subjects in my spare time. I was trying to locate some reading material that described experiences like the one I had been involved with. Many of my newly discovered metaphysical authors were Jeanne Dixon, Ruth Montgomery and Ambrose Worrall. There was also the famous ghost hunter Hans Holzer. The first book that I had obtained on the subject was "The Sleeping Prophet." This was a book about Edgar Cayce, a psychic in the 1920's and 30's, who prescribed both healing remedies and made predictions while in a trance state.

I had also been reading portions of the Bible each evening at bedtime. I was reading the Bible, not from a religious or historical point of view, but rather from a spiritual one. This meant viewing the philosophies being directed to all beings, both those living on the earthly plane and those existing on the spiritual plane. To my amazement, this particular approach gave me a much broader insight to my own personal understanding of the spirit world. I had been able to locate books about spirits manifesting themselves, but none of them ever explained any of the coincidences that may have led to the occurrences. Some authors theorized that there are spirits who linger close to the earthly plane in order to protect their loved ones and to help them cross over when the their time comes. Those were quite similar to my Aunt Carmen's explanation. Others explained that there were spirits who may be obsessed with some material possession that they may have owned while in the physical world. In these circumstances the spirit would want to remain close to that possession.

There were even times when I was willing to discuss the subject openly with strangers. However, I quickly learned that spiritualism was a topic that most people preferred to avoid. Some would not even discuss the possibility that spirits even existed, while others believed them to be the work of the devil. And I certainly didn't like the idea of associating my mother's spirit with anything demonic. There were also those who had experienced some unusual phenomenon, mainly isolated incidents, but without any clear explanations as to why they occurred. For fear of ridicule most people wouldn't admit to such things and they merely kept their experiences to themselves.

I began to believe that the general fear of spirits came from just plain ignorance. There are certainly plenty of books and movies around depicting that spirits are something to fear. Not being a part of our everyday lives, one can easily be frightened whenever a spirit makes its presence known. I had never seen a spirit and now I wondered how I would have I reacted if I'd been with my sister and nieces on that eventful January evening.

Many things concerning the Duluth Street incident were still bothering me. I began to wonder about the kind of personal relationship that I had with my mother prior to her dying. It was also bothering me to think that my mother's spirit may not be resting in peace because her family was not living in unity or in harmony. Since then, I had given considerable thought to the idea of how I was going to go about uniting my family. Naturally, I'd been procrastinating, because there was still so much to learn. At the same time, I was well aware that my brothers still had not been informed of the incident and they certainly had a right to know. Who told them, didn't really matter, it was more important that they be told. I was completely surprised to learn that Marcy, Ramona and Michelle hadn't leaked a word out about the incident to anyone. How they had managed to keep the incident a secret for so long was beyond my understanding. Then again, I hadn't mentioned any of this to any of my friends either, including Rick. Like others, I was apprehensive and afraid that people would laugh at me.

Whenever I phoned Carmela in Canatlan, she would only say hello to me and refused to discuss the subject. I learned only by accident that Carmela hadn't even said anything to her parents. My cousin Margarita informed me that Carmela had been praying a lot more than usual these days and had been conversing extensively with Father Fernandez. She had also informed me several months ago that our Aunt Cleofas had died. But as far as I was concerned, I still wasn't certain how all of this had affected my own sense of reality.

CHAPTER 11

▼

DOCTOR BLOOM

One Sunday evening, I had another vivid dream that took place in the Duluth Street house. In this particular dream, I'm in the basement again, frantically searching in the crevasses just below the wooden ceiling supports and atop the main cement block foundation. Suddenly, I located a dark brown cigar box. Upon opening the box I discover that inside is a white colored tobacco pouch with a blue emblem. However, I'm unable to read the small lettering that's on the side of the pouch. The bottom of the box suddenly flips open and the pouch slowly floats to the floor. I was jarred awake by the dream and again, I was left with the task of trying to interpret its meaning.

However, I had now reached a stage where I was beginning to think more seriously about sharing my unusual experiences with someone before I went off my rocker. So during my next luncheon with Rick, I decided to confide in him. I carefully chose my words and took my time describing all the details as they related to the Duluth Street incident. Afterwards, Rick gave me that same curious stare that the doctor had given me a few days ago. I also spoke about my unusual symptoms, the electrical charge and the streetlight phenomenon, which had now reached a total of seven. I also explained to him, my recent series of dreams and my visit to the clinic. It was as though I was confessing my deepest secrets. After I completed my story, I sat back and waited for Rick to say something.

"It's a good thing you don't perform on the stage, or you'd be dancing in the dark," Rick's response caused both of us to chuckle. "My guess is that the streetlights were either in a state of malfunction or it was part of their cooling off process, if there is any such thing," Rick commented. "When did you say that you were going to see your doctor?" Rick asked.

"I'm going tonight, right after work," I replied. "You know, I'm just tired of feeling this way. I'm hoping Doctor Bloom can come up with some diagnosis, so he can prescribe something that will relieve me of all these annoying symptoms.

"What do you expect him to find?" Rick inquired.

"I don't know, but I do know that something strange is happening to me and I need to find out before I go crazy. I'm exaggerating of course. Maybe I've just become a hypochondriac. Somehow though, I thought that all these things are connected, including the dreams," I remarked.

"The dreams too," Rick sounded surprised.

"I'm afraid, there are things that happened to me in Mexico that I didn't mention to you before," I remarked. I then watched Rick, as I described each of the events in the sequence that they occurred. Without question, I had Rick's complete attention. Afterwards, I sat back relieved and again waited for Rick's comments. It felt good to have a friend that was such a good listener.

"You've given me far too much information to digest at any one time. This paranormal phenomenon stuff gives me the creeps. Much of what you've told me goes against what I believe," Rick commented.

"I know, but don't you think that I've had a lot of those same beliefs," I added.

"What makes you think there really was a spirit?"

"Mainly because I believe that she was extremely frightened. Carmela was in a strange house with relatives that she hardly knew and she would have done anything to conceal her tears. She would have been much too proud to have allowed that to happen. This indicates to me that she may have lost control of her emotions and that's the reason why she felt so ashamed," I attempted to rationalize my opinion. "Besides, my nieces said they saw the spirit materialize right in front of them."

"But your sister says she wasn't certain that she saw anything other than perhaps a white mist. Isn't that right?" Rick remarked.

"Yes, that's right. But I understand witnesses in these instances don't always see the same thing, if they even see anything at all. Some people do and some people don't," I tried to explain. So yes, it is possible that she didn't see anything," I added.

"Man, Armand!" Rick exclaimed. "Before I can comment on anything, I need some time to think. It looks like we're going to have to spend an entire evening together on just this one subject," Rick said, sounding a bit overwhelmed.

"Whenever you're ready," I answered. "Thanks for listening, I feel better already. Haven't you noticed me staring out my office window lately?" I inquired.

"Yes, a few times, but it didn't appear to be anything out of the ordinary," Rick remarked.

"Well, sometimes my mind just goes blank and takes off by itself. It always happens when I begin thinking about my mother's spirit having been in the house. I immediately go into a stupor of some kind," I said, as I wrapped up my explanation.

Neither of us spoke on our walk back to the office. Then while waiting for the elevator, Rick commented, "I'm really looking forward to our going to the theatre on Friday evening. Aren't you?"

"Yes, I'm going and I'm taking Sharon. Are we meeting at Maxwell's?" I asked.

"I told Mary to meet me there around five o'clock. That should give us plenty of time to get uptown and have dinner before going to the theatre," Rick remarked. "By the way, Mary and I both like Sharon. She seems like a very likable young lady."

*   *   *   *

Doctor Bloom's office was only two blocks from my apartment and going to the doctor was like going to a family gathering. In fact, the doctor belonged to some kind of an association of family doctors. Mrs. Bloom, the receptionist, was the doctor's wife, but everyone called her Mrs. Bee. Besides being the receptionist, she was also the nurse as well as everyone's acting Jewish mother. As soon as I entered the office, Mrs. Bee opened with and influx of inquisitive, but well meaning questions, "How are you today, Mr. Seguera? My, don't we look handsome. Did you have a nice Thanksgiving? And are you planning on seeing your son Joseph for the holidays?"

"No, I'm afraid that I won't be seeing my son for the holidays. But next year he's graduating from high school and I 'm planning on taking him to Mexico," I replied.

"My, isn't that wonderful Mr. Seguera," Mrs. Bee commented. "You do know that Doctor Bloom and I would like to see you find a nice girl and settle down."

"Yes, I know," I replied. Then Mrs. Bee requested the usual urine specimen and arranged for one of the technicians to give me an electrocardiogram.

Doctor Bloom was a short balding man, about sixty-five years of age with a salt-and-pepper mustache. The doctor was extremely polite, considerate and one of the finest people that I had ever met. He believed strongly that a person's physical well being was intimately linked to their psychological state of mind.

I took my time and explained my symptoms to the doctor who gave me that professional glance over the rim of his glasses. I also added the dream activity; the static electricity and my urges to cry which even surprised me when I said it. Then without any expression or comments the doctor proceeded with the examination. While listening to my heart with his stethoscope, there was an "Ahumm, ahumm," coming out of the doctor every few seconds.

"Do you know what heart palpitations are suppose to feel like?" the doctor asked.

"No, not really," I said. "I only know that at times it feels funny in the area around the heart. Why? Is there a problem doctor?" I quickly responded, extremely anxious to hear something—anything!

"Well, after examining your electrocardiogram, the urine analysis and my personal examination, I can find no abnormalities. However, I do find your blood pressure to be slightly elevated. Are you anxious about something? The buzzing in your ears and the static activity are rather unusual. Have you thought about seeing a psychiatrist?" Doctor Bloom commented with his usual personal interest.

"No, should I?" I quickly responded again. I couldn't believe that the doctor hadn't found anything. What had I expected the doctor to find? I really didn't even know. I highly trusted the doctor's opinion and ordinarily would have expected to get a clean bill of health, but now the mystery would continue.

"Don't look so disappointed," Doctor Bloom said with a comforting smile. "Your instincts can't always be right. You should be delighted that we didn't find anything."

"I hope that you don't think that I'm going nuts doctor," I remarked.

"No. But your urges to cry could come from a mild state of depression and the dreams are better handled by those who are qualified to analyze them. Anyway, if you need a referral, I will be glad to give you one," he offered.

Then both the doctor and I began to laugh aloud. Suddenly, there was a knock on the door. "You have other patients waiting to see you doctor!" shouted Mrs. Bee. It felt good to be around caring people, I loved them both.

*   *   *   *

The very next day, Rick and I met for lunch and as soon as I finished discussing my visit to the doctor, Rick quickly interrupted the conversation by saying, "You'll never guess what happened to me last night?" I was driving through my neighborhood when I stopped for a traffic light. While I was waiting for the light to change, I noticed the streetlight above the intersection. I then said to myself, I wonder if Armand were here, would he be able to put that light out. But no sooner did I get the thought out when the light went out. I couldn't believe it, so I checked every streetlight within a two-block radius. I was looking for a power failure of some kind. No luck, that had been the only light affected."

"Don't tell me that I now have eight lights knocked out to my credit. At least, I'm no longer alone in this matter," I said, a bit amused.

Then Rick added, "by the way, streetlights don't shut off in order to cool off."

*   *   *   *

The following Friday afternoon, Rick, Doug and I headed over to Maxwell's. Rick's wife Mary, Doug's wife Christine and Sharon were already there waiting for us. This was the first time we were going out together since we celebrated our promotions last year, included Rick who also made Assistant Vice-President. This evening we were going to see the Broadway show DANCIN' and so after we finished our drinks we took a limousine uptown to dine before going to the theater.

For me, the dancing performances in the show I found to be personally invigorating to watch and found the show to be exceptionally entertaining. Later that evening and after dropping off Sharon, I took the subway back to Brooklyn. During my walk home, I continued to feel a bit energetic from the show, when suddenly I became aware that the streetlamp directly above me went out. After doing my usual pause for a moment, I continued walking, but then when I got only a few yards from the apartment entrance, whamoo! Out went another streetlamp. Two lights in one evening, a new record and neither of the lamps had ever been involved previously.

That night, while getting into bed, I couldn't help but notice that there was more static electricity being generated than usual. Then within a short time after falling asleep, I was wide awake again and sitting up on the edge of the bed. It was another one of those lucid dreams, only this time, I didn't wake up with my heart pounding in my ears. I had been dreaming that my body was airborne high above a snowcapped mountain range. The sky was deep blue and flying next to me was a magnificent looking eagle. In the background, I could hear the faint sound of an Indian's flute playing and enchanting Indian melody. The eagle was gracefully flapping its wings in a smooth rhythm as we were soaring together high above the mountains. Then the eagle turned its head towards me and winked, as though he was telling me that everything was going to be okay. The scene captivated my imagination and gave me a sense of complete serenity and well being. That was the feeling that remained with me even as I awoke. I immediately got out of bed and went over to the window. Perhaps I was expecting to see the eagle flying by outside, but all that was visible were the row of lights strung out along the cables of the bridge. Strangely, I could still faintly hear the flute playing somewhere in the back of my head.

Standing by the window, I was reminded of something that I had read not too long ago. That one of the most desired wishes of a southwestern American Indian tribe, was that while in a state of self-induced drugs, they wanted to view an eagle in flight against the background of a blue sky. For the Indians, it represented the soul in its higher state of consciousness. One of the Indians main spiritual objectives was to experience their souls in a free state, unattached to the physical body.

I was a first-generation Mexican-American, but I was also aware that I was a mestizo. A mestizo is a descendant from mixed European and Native North American Indian blood. I thought that perhaps the evening's performance of DANCIN' had somehow stimulated some ancient wishful desires passed onto me by my Indian ancestors.

Again, I was reminded of my mother's letters and how badly she had wanted to be an eagle for a day. Perhaps the eagle represented her spirit in flight, or was it mine. I was also convinced that Doctor Bloom was right. What was bothering me was not physical, but something that went much further into my psyche.

I had an entire weekend to reflect on the beautiful soaring eagle dream. I also knew that come Monday morning, I would be going to the clinic in order to pick up a copy of that psychotherapy-counseling center brochure that I had seen there.

CHAPTER 12

▼

SEEKING HELP

It wasn't long before a woman with short blond hair and who appeared to be in her late thirties entered the reception room of the counseling center. She was well dressed, about average height, wearing gold rimmed glasses and acted very business like. Then with a warm smile, she extended her hand and introduced herself to me as Diane Evans. After taking a moment to make me feel comfortable, she ushered me into a large consultation room. The room had two large bay windows facing in a southerly direction that filtered in the bright rays of the noonday sun. And since the office was on the eighteenth floor, I could clearly see the Statue of Liberty out in the harbor. Besides a small antique desk, there was a large black leather u-shaped couch that dominated the center of the room. The bookshelves were filled with books and on the walls were several serene lithographs.

I made myself comfortable on the couch while Diane adjusted the Venetian blinds. She then sat directly opposite me in a large stuffed chair of her own. Placed on the coffee table directly in front of me, was an open box of tissues and I wondered if I was going to have to use any of them.

"Okay, Armando, or is it Armand? What do they call you?" She began.

"They call me Armand,"

"Okay, Armand, how can I be of help to you?"

"Well," I began hesitantly. "I'm primarily interested in knowing how I may have related to my mother before she passed away. Since I was only two when she died, I'm also interested in exploring how her death may have affected me emotionally." I was finding this to be difficult, while at the same time I was trying to make myself comfortable enough so that I could say what was really on my mind. "What triggered off my interest in this subject is that my mother's spirit mysteriously appeared to four female members of my family a couple of years ago. Somehow, I played an important role in that particular experience. Now I've become curious enough to seek some deeper insight into that relationship. Her message from the other side was that she wanted her family to be living in a united manner and in harmony. I'm not exactly certain what all that means, but I would very much like to better comprehend her last wish." I kept glancing at Diane, looking for some kind of a reaction, but she remained placid while jotting down some notes. "Oh yes. I'm also suffering from some imaginary symptoms, like a slight pressure on the left side of my chest, just above my heart. On occasion, I experience some rapid pulse beats and what I call heart palpitations. Sometimes, I have hot flashes. I used to have an occasional buzzing sensation in my head, but that's been now replaced with this unusual ringing in my ears. Another unusual activity is that I've been experiencing lots of static electricity lately and sometimes I'll knock out a streetlight or two. That's nine to be exact," I added. "I've also been to see my personal physician who could detect none of the symptoms that I just mentioned, but he did suggest that perhaps I should consult with a psychiatrist." I said with a joking smile. She still did not respond. "There's more. I've also been having lots of dream activity lately. They're the kind of dreams that awaken me with my heart pounding in my ears."

"Dreams," suddenly, Diane reacted. "What kind of dreams did you say you were having?"

"There are so many of them that I can't remember them all." I said. "Many of them deal with my childhood home in Detroit. At times, I find myself in the middle of the basement always searching for something. I appear to be always trying to locate something. But the dream that made me decide to come here was the eagle dream that I had the other night. That's when the flute started playing in my left ear." While Diane listened to me describe my dream in detail, she continued to write even faster than before.

Diane then interrupted and began to give me her general interpretation of dreams, "Basement dreams very often represent something significant from the unconscious. It's also possible that there might be some traumatic childhood experience that needs to be examined closely. These are things that can only be determined through analysis. When we dream, we dream about people and things that can represent certain emotional aspects of ourselves. These may be things that we either like or dislike. The flying eagle was an aspect of yourself that you obviously liked very much. No doubt it is something that comes from your abilities to create and it wants to express itself on a much higher level."

After listening to Diane, I was quite pleased with her approach to the subject. Diane then took time to explain that she was a psychotherapist and not a psychoanalyst. This meant she would need the approval from a licensed resident doctor of psychiatry before she could treat me for any lengthy period of time. Since I was committed to discovering what was bothering me, I told Diane to go ahead and make the appointment.

On my way out the door, Diane inquisitively asked, "Do you feel like something unusual is going to happen?"

"As a matter of fact, I do," I replied, while quickly glancing at Diane who had taken me by surprise. I was impressed with Diane's perception of my situation and I added, "I just don't know what or when."

"From what you've told me, I think you might be psychically charged," Diane commented.

"If I am, it's not the first time," I answered thinking about what Phyllis had once told Ramona about our family being charged. Diane hadn't said much else about anything except the dreams, but that convinced me enough to make me feel like I was doing the right thing.

A few days later, Diane phoned to inform me that my appointment with the psychiatrist, a Doctor Benjamin Lerner, was scheduled for Friday, January 30th at seven o'clock in the evening. She then gave me the doctor's office phone number and address. It wasn't hard to figure out that the doctor's office was located on the upper east side of Manhattan. Then while I jotted down the appointment on my desk calendar, I couldn't help but notice that today's date was January 26th. It was exactly two years ago to the day since the Duluth Street incident had occurred.

*   *   *   *

Friday morning, I awoke feeling exceptionally invigorated and in a mood of high expectation. Meaning, I felt as though something extraordinary was going to happen. In the bathroom, I took a few extra moments to trim my mustache and couldn't help but notice that my hair had been getting extremely gray. For a young man of forty-six, I was beginning to show some age and I had to admit that I was beginning to look a bit more distinguished. Outside, the weather was brisk and so during my walk to the subway, I continued to take deep breaths, filling my lungs with that invigorating fresh January air. It felt great to slowly exhale each breath, somehow knowing that it was going to be an exceptional day.

During the day, I remained in the state of high expectation. I was wondering if perhaps I might receive an unexpected bonus, a promotion or maybe I would hear from and old girlfriend. All day long, I amused myself with Ann and the rest of the office staff. There were even some humorous comments about my enthusiastic behavior. Then again, maybe I was just feeling good because I was following through with the therapy. Seeking help from a psychotherapist, let alone agreeing to see a psychiatrist was a major commitment on my part. Even Rick, couldn't get over that I was even going to see a psychiatrist. We had both been raised to think that we should have enough self-confidence to handle our own personal problems.

That evening, Doctor Lerner wrote quickly as I attempted to tell him everything. Everything that is, but the Duluth Street incident. Otherwise, the session went very well. In concluding the visit, the doctor agreed that it would be in my best interest to continue seeing Diane on a regular basis.

After leaving the doctor's office, the air was still fresh and invigorating, so I decided to walk for awhile. After a short time, I found myself in front of the Wine Press restaurant on First Avenue. Peering through the front window, I noticed a small jazz ensemble playing at the piano bar. Being a jazz fan, I decided to enter and after checking my coat, I went directly to the piano bar. As I approached the bar, I couldn't help but notice an attractive redheaded young lady sitting alone. She appeared to be in her early thirties and since there was an empty stool next to where she was sitting, I sat down next to her. Between selections, the musicians shared their good humor with the young lady, giving me the impression that they were already acquainted. Then after exchanging smiles with the young lady several times, I began to speak with her.

I introduced myself as Armand Seguera and she introduced herself as Lynn Sullivan. Lynn told me that this was her first visit to the Wine Press and that the bass player, who was her friend, had been coaxing her for some time to come and hear the group play. So tonight, she finally decided to come and listen to them. Besides being attractive, Lynn had a pleasant manner and appeared quite confident. Her blue business outfit seemed to match the color of her blue eyes. To my surprise, Lynn worked as a psychotherapist in the evenings at one of the local hospitals. She also did some part time drug counseling in the schools and even had a private practice of her own.

It had only been a week since I visited my first psychotherapist and now to my surprise, I was meeting another therapist. I listened to the music, but I also found

Lynn to be interesting and so I continued to converse with her. At the same time the musicians continued to humor her and kept her chuckling at their private jokes and stage antics. I couldn't help but admire her beautiful smile and the way she laughed. Apparently, Lynn didn't drink alcoholic beverages and that was the reason why she was enjoying a bottle of Perrier Water with a twist of lime. Much of our conversation was about the living conditions in New York City. It had only been two years since Lynn moved to New York from western Pennsylvania and she was now living in the Bronx. During our conversation, I couldn't help but notice that Lynn, on a number of occasions would take her right hand and rub an area below her left shoulder and just above her heart. I assumed that it was just a nervous habit, except that it was the same location as my own imaginary palpitations.

Then, for whatever the reason, which I didn't know, Lynn suddenly asked me, "Armand, if you could describe how you feel this very moment. What would you say?"

"Is this some kind of therapeutic question?"

'No. I'm just curious. How do you feel without taking time to think about it?"

"For one thing, I would say that I'm enjoying being in your company," I responded.

"No. You're still not getting it. Don't you have some inner emotions that you feel? Something personal that you never tell anyone," Lynn urged.

"Well, for one thing, I feel like a young sapling tree that is just getting ready to break through the crust of the earth into the sunlight," I explained. Being amused by the question, I wondered what Lynn wanted to find out about me.

"And when your tree grows big and strong, will you bear good fruit or bad?" Lynn responded with a big smile.

Having just finished reading the Bible not too long ago, I was familiar with what Lynn was referring too. However, I was still curious about her unusual inquiry. But for whatever her reasons, my answer somehow helped to improve the rapport between us.

It was close to midnight when Lynn decided it was time for her to leave and I offered to walk her to the bus stop. While waiting for the bus, Lynn began to comment about our meeting, "I don't know what's going on between us, because, you see, I'm one of those people who doesn't believe in coincidences and so I'm already wondering why we met. I'm not even certain what compelled me to ask you that particular question about the way you feel." Suddenly, the bus could be seen approaching from about a half a block away. "I just don't go around picking up guys. In fact, I don't even go into bars much and I'm not too crazy about guys who drink, but I must say that I've enjoyed meeting you." The bus arrived, but before boarding, Lynn said, "I might be going against my better judgment, but I have this funny feeling that we're going to see each other again." Then with a large grin on her face, Lynn handed me one of her business cards. "Thanks for walking me to the bus, goodnight Armand,"

"Goodnight Lynn, I enjoying meeting you too," I responded.

I watched as the bus pulled away and waved goodbye. I was extremely pleased with our meeting and on my way home I remembered my feelings of anticipation and wondered if Lynn may have been the object of those high expectations. I already knew that I would be phoning Lynn very soon. Walking down the block from the subway station, I tied my old record and knocked out two more streetlights. But before going to bed that evening, my left ear began to ring. It was the signal that I was going to dream. Except that now, I had Diane Evans, my own personal dream-expert to share them with.

*   *   *   *

Diane had arranged the counseling schedule so that I could meet with her every Tuesday afternoon during my lunch hour. When I arrived for my first session, Diane started asking me about my family. I began telling her about my brothers and their families, in addition to talking about my Dad and Marcy. I talked about my Aunt Yolanda, Uncle Mateo and the circumstances surrounding the family's decisions for wanting to make Detroit their home. For the remainder of the session I described the Duluth Street incident. I was anxious to hear Diane's reaction to the story, but when I finished, she only asked, "How do you feel about this experience, Armand?" Diane asked, "Do you really think it happened, the way you described it to me?"

"I wasn't there," I responded. "I'm only giving you a second hand account, which was within about two or three hours after it happened. For now, I only have the word of my two nieces who said they saw the apparition and heard Carmela speaking. My sister isn't certain; she just says that she saw a hazy light. Carmela refuses to talk to anyone about what happened, except to a priest. By the way, Carmela doesn't speak English and Michelle doesn't speak Spanish. That rules out any corroboration between the two of them. All four women did experience the cold chilling air that apparently accompanies spirits. If that's not enough, then there's all those coincidences and the very vivid passenger jet dream that I had in Mexico, that I still have difficulty comprehending. But when you look at the total picture from a spiritual standpoint, everything seems to fit. So I suppose the answer to your question, is yes. I want to believe that it happened. It gives me great comfort t know that my mother's spirit had attempted to communicate with me personally and with other members of her family."

"Do you take drugs Armand?" Diane asked, looking for some kind of relationship.

"No." I quickly answered.

"Have you ever?" Diane continued her inquiry.

"No, I don't use drugs nor have I ever used them. However, I do drink socially," I replied. The session was over and I had now left it for Diane to ponder the questions associated with the mysterious Duluth Street incident.

CHAPTER 13

▼

SPIRITUAL SUPPRESSION

The following week, Lynn and I met at a restaurant on the upper west side of Manhattan. Lynn looked even better than when we first met, but like most first dates, we took time getting acquainted.

During dinner, Lynn remarked, "Armand, you're not the usual Wall Street stereotype salesman that I'm used to meeting."

"That's because I'm not a salesman. I work in the operations end of the business, so I'm not under the same kind of pressure to be selling all the time," I replied. "But I'm still curious why you asked me to describe my emotions the other night," I remarked.

"It was just a general question," Lynn responded. "I'm still not certain why I was even compelled to ask the question. However, I was even more surprised by your answer. It was not what I would have expected," Lynn remarked with a smile.

"Well, you see, a couple of years ago, I had a unique psychic experience," I began my explanation. "Ever since then I've become a seeker of knowledge and enlightenment. Mainly, I'm looking for things that I know nothing about. What I'm expecting to find is the tree of psychic knowledge. A tree that will come forth and give me all the answers I need to satisfy my curiosity. That's why I thought that your remark about the good or bad fruit tree was rather appropriate, since we can learn things from both trees."

"You said something about a psychic experience. Do you want to tell me about it?" Lynn inquired with her own curious tone.

"It's about my mother's spirit which appeared unexpectedly to four female members of my family," I commented.

"A spirit? I'm not surprised. I seem to be attracted to that sort of thing. Please go on," Lynn urged.

I spent the next twenty minutes giving Lynn a brief synopsis of the Duluth Street incident. When I finished, I sat back and waited for Lynn's reaction.

"Have you ever told anyone else this story?" Lynn asked.

"Yes, but only recently. For two years, I was afraid to tell anyone. Now in the last few weeks, I've told two people." I informed Lynn. "Why do you ask?"

"Did they act funny or aloof after you told them?" Lynn inquired.

"Both listeners were very polite. But, I don't think that they had much time to comprehend all the details. It was just that I was getting to a state where I had to start telling someone," I explained.

"What bothers you the most about the story Armand?"

"How do you know something is bothering me?"

"I just know. There is nothing special about my knowing. The fact that you have to talk about it means that there is something still bothering you. There's something you still haven't accepted," Lynn responded.

"Yes there is," I confessed. "Had this been an isolated incident, I would have no difficulty. If it was just between my mother's spirit and I, I could write that off as my being a little wacky. However, that was not the case. You see, there were a number of other people involved here and then there are all those coincidences. How could all of us have been influenced simultaneously?" I attempted to explain my dilemma.

"Maybe your mother's spirit had help," Lynn commented.

"Help? What kind of help?"

"Angels or some spirit guides."

"Angels or spirit guides?"

"Any number of them may have helped to orchestrate this whole thing. Certainly your mother was an earthbound spirit and she still may be for that matter. She's stuck on the earth plane and just can't go running off to other parts of the world. That's where the angels come into play and they would have helped her," Lynn explained.

"Lynn, I'm having a hard enough time trying to comprehend the existence of spirits. Now you're talking about angels and spirit guides!" I said, sounding confused.

"I know that most people don't even acknowledge the existence of spirits and wouldn't even discuss the subject seriously," Lynn began. "They either make a joke of the whole matter or they just write it off as the devil and that's all there is to it," Lynn added. "When I was a little girl back on my family's farm in Pennsylvania, my bothers and sisters used to tease me whenever I spoke to those invisible beings. I could see these beings and they all looked natural to me. What I didn't know was that my brothers and sisters couldn't see them. Everyone thought that I was a little weird, including my mother. She finally took me to see a medicine man that lived on a nearby Indian reservation. I remember that they addressed the medicine man as Grandfather. The medicine man said that at the time of my birth, I had received a great gift from the spirit world. That the spirits had given me the ability to help release disturbed spirits from the earthbound plane of existence. These are the spirits that are trapped between heaven and earth and need to be relieved from their personal turmoil. 'You have the ability to help these spirits to move on,' he said. Of course, at the time, I had no idea what he was talking about. Neither did my mother. But, to make a long story short, up until this day spirits constantly try to communicate with me. They all seem to be in some kind of pain and crying out for help, but I'm too frightened to have anything to do with them." Lynn paused again for a moment and then asked me with an inquisitive smile, "You aren't an angel from the other side, sent here to try and recruit me into helping you to release some old disturbed spirit from the earthbound plane, are you?"

"What!" I said, being taken by surprise. "You must be kidding," I replied with a mischievous smile of my own. "I've never been accused of being an angel. And that's for certain," I added, while looking directly into Lynn's eyes.

"You know that there are angels who can materialize themselves into human beings," Lynn stated. "As I've told you before, I don't believe in coincidences and I'm still curious as to why we met. I question everything and wonder if our meeting was really a coincidence. Your story is full of them," Lynn clarified her point. "You see, I'm on guard against the spirit world and anyone else who might be trying to get me to do something that I'm really frightened to do."

"You mean that you've never used the gift that the medicine man said was given to you by the spirit world?" I asked, with a bit of skepticism, because I wasn't at all certain how you would go about releasing a spirit from the earthbound plane. However, since I had been reading a great deal about these sorts of things lately, I wasn't totally unfamiliar with the subject.

"That's right!"

"If it's a gift then what is there to be frightened about?"

"I don't know, I just am," Lynn answered, as though she didn't want to discuss the subject any longer.

After dinner we took a short walk before heading for our respective subways. On my way home I couldn't get over how I was able to speak openly with Lynn about things that were so personal to me. I also continued to wonder if she had been the object of my high expectation.

But again during dinner, I had noticed that Lynn on occasion had used her right hand to gently rub her breast just above the heart.

*   *   *   *

Diane Evans started the next session by asking, "What were the names of your parents?" I then took time to describe my relationship with my father, Aunt Yolanda and Uncle Mateo. She then asked, "Did you father ever speak about your mother to you?"

"I think that my father was greatly affected by my mother's death because he never talked to any of us about her. For that matter, neither did anyone else. It was though she never existed. Once a year, my father took all of us to the cemetery so that we could pay our respects. Except that our visits were always silent, hardly a word was spoken. All we did was stand there and stare at her name on the tombstone. As I grew older, I thought that shutting out a family's past was a Mexican custom. That was, until I went to Mexico," I stated. "It wasn't until recently that my sister found pictures of my mother hidden away at the bottom of dresser drawers and in some old luggage. Who put them there, why they were there, we have no idea. I must admit that for most of my life, my mother had remained a mystery to me until I went to Mexico. It was in Mexico that I learned more about who she was during her youth," I continued to explain.

"Have you ever mourned your mother's death?" Diane asked.

"No," Diane's question caught me by complete surprise. "I d never felt any emotions in the regard," I responded.

"Don't you ever feel like crying?" Diane quickly questioned.

"Come to think of it Diane, that's also something that's been happening to me lately! I didn't mention it before, but for the last few months, there have been times when I've had this urge to just let go and start crying," I explained.

"And do you ever let go and cry?" Diane inquired.

"No. Because I can't relate the urges to anything, except to my lapses into those semi-hypnotic states. Besides I was taught that boys aren't supposed to cry," I said as though defending some old childhood belief.

Diane's next observation was, "There's also another possibility here, Armand. You could be ailing from the after-forty syndrome. That means you still haven't achieved all those things that you've dreamed about doing in your lifetime. After all, you have been reflecting on your childhood a lot lately. That could be contributing to feelings of depression. It's not so uncommon, you know. But then again, you could be suffering from a case of creative and spiritual suppression."

"What do you mean by creative and spiritual suppression?" I quickly responded.

"Creative and spiritual suppression is when your inner-self is being deprived of freely expressing itself through your God-given talents," Diane explained. "Your goal may be only to release those suppressed desires or emotions. It means that you may just want to be more productive in something other than what you're currently doing."

"But I've got a good job," I replied, a bit indignant.

"But it's possible that the creative part of you wants to express itself even more, and that your real needs are not being fulfilled," Diane commented.

After leaving the center, I couldn't get the thought of spiritual suppression out of my mind and I took longer than usual before going back to my office.

*   *   *   *

A few days later, I met Lynn again for dinner and after, we took a walk. I learned that Lynn was the sixth oldest of eleven children. Her father had passed away several years ago, but her mother was still living in western Pennsylvania. Lynn had a master's degree in the Science of Counseling. The degree qualified her to provide counseling services to drug patients at the hospital and to conduct a drug prevention program at a high school in the Bronx. In her private practice, she helped her clients with past life regression. Past life regression was something that I was not familiar with, although I had read about it in one of the books about Edgar Cayce.

Another of Lynn's areas of expertise was dream analysis. She explained that dreams could only be properly interpreted by working closely with an individual, and that emotional and spiritual growth varies with each person. Since each of us is a unique individual, the dream symbols for one person may not necessarily have the same interpretation for another. That maintaining a dream logbook was a good way of examining the repetitiveness of certain recurring themes that can help to find their meaning. Mostly, her philosophical opinions were a combination of her education, practical working knowledge and her own paranormal experiences.

I thought that keeping a record of dreams was a good idea. But as for reincarnation, it was still something new to me and I hadn't formulated any strong opinions on the subject. However, I do have to admit to having had strong deja-vu experiences. Deja-vu is a state in which a person may have a strong sense of having previously been in a place or in a situation that they're certain that they've never been.

My own deja-vu experiences began shortly after I moved to New York. They occurred whenever I visited older sections of the city that for years had virtually remained unchanged. One of those sections was on the lower east side. Deja-vu would occur whenever I looked at an old warehouse or while looking down a block lined with tenement apartments. The experience would only last for a few seconds and I was never able to recreate the same deja-vu conditions by placing myself back in those same locations. Whether deja-vu is the dredging up of memories from some previous lifetime, is only conjecture. For now, I was merely keeping an open mind.

One evening, when Lynn and I were strolling through Greenwich Village, we passed a streetlight that suddenly went out. Lynn gave me a peculiar look, even though I had warned her that it might happen. Lynn then explained how my electrical energy might be the same as the streetlight, which could cause the light to short out. Her explanation was better than any other that I had come up with.

One Saturday afternoon, Lynn asked if I would accompany her to a party that evening. The party was being held in a loft apartment in the SoHo section of Manhattan. The host Bernie was a super electronic technician of some kind, and his loft was filled with all kinds of sophisticated electronic devices. There were speakers in every corner. Since Lynn and I were the first guests to arrive, Bernie asked if we would like to see a video of his recent Amazon River excursion. It sounded like something interesting to do until more guests arrived, so we agreed.

In order to make the viewing private, Bernie handed each of us a set of headphones that were plugged into a large television monitor. Lynn and I placed the headphones on our heads and then while we crossed our legs to make ourselves more comfortable on the floor, our heads accidentally touched. Suddenly, there was that familiar sound of crackling static. It was coming from our hair and just like at the health club, I could feel my scalp tingle. At the same time, the television tube flashed brightly like a strobe light. The color on the television monitor scrambled into black and white squares. However, within seconds the picture came back to normal. Bernie got real excited and being the professional that he was, quickly tried to locate the problem.

Lynn was now getting the idea of what I had been going through. I couldn't explain it. Apparently Bernie couldn't explain this one either. He soon gave up his quest with an "I don't know what could've happened. All the equipment checked out this morning. Nothing like that ever happened before." Lynn and I just looked at one another and avoided bumping our heads again.

CHAPTER 14

▼

A PAST LIFE
REGRESSION

The following Tuesday, the therapy session started with my asking Diane, "What did you mean, when you said that I may still have to mourn my mother's death?"

"It means that your grief for your mother may be lying dormant and that you still haven't experienced the total loss of her," Diane began explaining. "A person grieving for a loved one can be extremely emotional. Depending upon the ages of the children, the death of a mother would affect them all differently. Since you were only two when your mother died, you would have been totally dependent upon her. My guess would be that you felt hurt, angry, disappointed and you probably suffered from strong feelings of rejection and abandonment. Your ability to express emotional pain verbally would have been limited. This means that you would have expressed yourself through your behavior. You no doubt went about trying to find someone that could take your mother's place. This could have been frustrating for you and by repressing any of these emotions; you would have had to create some very strong irrational beliefs. They would be the kind of emotional beliefs that gave you protection and that would help you to survive until this very day. And since there was no other way that you could have properly comprehended the situation, most of your frustration would have expressed itself in the form of anger."

"Come to think of it, I do recall having had some very angry moments in my childhood," I remarked.

"A child of two has everything going for them and can feel very secure and powerful," Diane continued. "Losing that power would make them mighty angry. My guess is that you may have had your temper tantrums and as you grew older, you displaced your anger and incorporated it into your personality. It may not appear that way, but it reflects in the way you handle your disappointments and rejections. But there is no reason to be distressed Armand. Behind all that anger are tears, and behind those tears, is all that love your mother passed onto you, and that's the relationship you had with her. Don't you think that your mother knew that she was going to leave you kids? In the 1930's, people who contacted tuberculosis had a pretty good idea that their chances of dying were very high. Didn't you tell me that she had written letters to her mother just prior to her death? I'm certain that she would have wanted you kids to be raised by her sisters. It makes a lot of sense to me. Think about it Armand! What does a mother do with her children when she knows that she's going to leave them? For one thing, she begins to make plans for them and then gives them all the love that she can muster from the bottom of her heart and more. She hugs and kisses them again and again. I'm certain that she would have given you all last minute instructions for how you should conduct your lives, after she was gone. You said that you hadn't thought about her during your life, but now her appearance has touched some distant memory of her. What we can do during these sessions is to try and get in touch with those forgotten childhood emotions that you shared with your mother. Perhaps then, those repressed tears will come forth for you. It's the only way you're going to get rid of the sadness, Armand."

"Good God Diane, I don't feel like I'm suffering from any depression or sadness," I stated.

"But what about those symptoms that you're described to me," Diane commented. "First, there are those hypnotic states, the urges to cry and the recurring basement dreams. And we still haven't begun to discuss the meaning of those dreams. All this unusual activity is trying to tell you something, and that's the reason you're here Armand," Diane stressed her point.

I felt stupefied after leaving Diane's office. She had overwhelmed me with a multitude of thoughts that I had never even considered. How does a mother go about preparing her children for the inevitable, I asked myself. Again, I sensed a strong surge of emotion trying to work its way to the surface. Perhaps Diane was right about my wanting to shed tears. Suddenly, my chest began to twinge and I placed my hand above my heart. It was the same area that I had watched Lynn massage, and I promised myself that I would ask her the time next we met.

*   *   *   *

A few days later, I learned that Rick had been doing his own research on the paranormal and had begun to share some interesting insights. Rick had taken the approach that dealing with spirits was not a good idea. That more harm than good could come from attempting such an encounter. Diane had remained neutral on the subject. But I was certain that she was just being careful not to influence me with her opinions.

Lynn, on the other hand, was convinced that the spirits did play some important role in our lives, but only from those spirits that were in someway related to us.

In the days that followed, I attempted to somehow have Lynn fit into my daily routine. On school nights, sometimes Lynn would come to Greenwich Village and meet me after class in one of the university coffee shops. On Friday evenings, I would go uptown and wait for Lynn outside the hospital. Sundays, we would meet in Manhattan and weather permitting we would take long walks around the city or Central Park.

Even though our lives were very different, there was no question that we enjoyed being with one another. Holding hands while we walked had now become commonplace and saying goodbye when parting was no longer limited to just a quick kiss on the cheek. We now took time to embrace firmly and kissed like lovers who didn't want to part.

It was only a matter of time before I got around to inviting Lynn to my apartment for a weekend. Lynn accepted the invitation and the following Friday evening we traveled to my apartment in Brooklyn. After arriving in my neighborhood, we stopped to pick up some Chinese carryout food and while walking to the apartment, we knocked out two streetlights.

After eating our meal, I threw some pillows on the living room floor and turned out all the lights. The streetlights outside offered a reasonable amount of subdued lighting in the apartment as it passed through the windows. Then tuning in on some soft mood music on the stereo, Lynn and I made ourselves comfortable on the living room floor. Lying close to one another, we hurriedly reached out for one another and began caressing and kissing. I was surprised to find that Lynn's body temperature was not only warm, but it was hot and I made the assumption that Lynn was an extremely passionate person. At least, so I thought. Lynn was lying on her back when I reached over with my right hand to embrace her. Then when my hand was about two inches above Lynn's heart a very strong charge of static electricity came crackling and hissing off of the fingers of my right hand. This was the same type of charge that I had experienced at the health club. Only this was no jogging machine. The charge seemed to concentrate itself at a spot directly above Lynn's heart and just below her shoulder. I quickly withdrew my hand. A faint blue charge flickered in an extremely eerie manner for only a second. Lynn, who had her head turned to one side with her eyes closed, may not have seen the charge.

Being totally unaware of what had happened, my immediate concern was for Lynn. Without any comments being made, Lynn laid quietly staring upwards towards the ceiling. I waited for her to inquire about the strange sounds and the flickering blue light, but instead, she began muttering in an unusual manner. Wanting to hear what Lynn was saying more clearly, I placed my ear closer to her lips.

"I feel very strange Armand," Lynn whispered. "I'm afraid to let go."

"Let go?" I questioned, not knowing Lynn's meaning.

"Please help me to let go Armand," Lynn whispered in a low seductive sounding voice. Then she said, "You are the only person who can help me to let go."

Without further fear of another shock, I reached over and began to massage Lynn's neck. This time, there was no charge, but Lynn's body was still quite hot. I then began to speak to her in a soothing manner. "Relax Lynn," I said. There's no need for you to be afraid. Go ahead and let go Lynn, let go! It's okay for you to let go!" I repeated several times. I was still puzzled about the charge and of course for Lynn who was acting as though she was in a daze over the incident. Her hot body temperature also made me uncomfortable and I wondered if she might be seriously ill and if I should be calling for an ambulance.

Next, Lynn quickly sat up, but continued to stare straight ahead and in the faint light of the apartment I could see tears glimmering on her face. Suddenly, Lynn took her clinched right hand and placed it above her heart. Simultaneously, she began to sob quietly in an unusual ghostly manner, but within minutes that awful mournful crying began to get louder and louder.

This was crazy! I began to let my imagination get the better of me. Who was this woman anyway? Maybe this was some kind of witchcraft ritual that I'd gotten sucked into performing. Was she really a weirdo like her family had proclaimed her to be? I began to imagine the neighbors gathering in the hallway listening at my door. And what if they called the cops, what would I tell them? 'Oh no, officer, we're just rehearsing a play.' I even took it a step further, what was I going to tell the judge, my friends and my family? All these images were having their effect on me, but they faded into the background, as the heavy throbbing of my own heart seemed to drown out all my thoughts. Was I having a heart attack? Helplessly, I listened to Lynn and wondered when all this awful wailing was going to stop.

After several minutes, Lynn stopped crying. My heartbeat then returned to normal and I began to relax a little when it appeared that Lynn was beginning to regain her composure.

"Do you have any tissues, Armand?" Lynn calmly asked. "I could also use a glass of water." Lynn's calmness and directness took me by surprise. I reached over and handed her a box of tissues. Then while Lynn wiped her eyes and blew her nose, I went into the kitchen for the water. While testing the water temperature under the faucet with my right hand, I detected a burn blister on the tip of my middle finger, 'what the hell,' I remarked.

Lynn quickly drank the water and immediately requested another. Again, I hurried to the kitchen. All the while, I could hear Lynn still sniffling in the living room. Lynn sat quietly on the floor holding her third glass of water in one hand and a tissue in the other. Sounding more subdued she said, "You helped to heal me. You see, I told you that you we're an angel."

"I did what? I exclaimed.

"You just helped me to overcome something that's been bothering me for most of my life," she responded.

"Obviously, I don't know what you're referring too. Would you please explain? I asked. "You just scared the hell out of me and I almost called for an ambulance."

"Well, ever since I can remember, I've been annoyed by this pressure pain just above my heart. Doctors could never figure out what it was. Then, during my metaphysical studies, I realized that it might be past-life related. You see, it was an issue that I had brought with me into this life from a previous lifetime. The pain has always been present, to some degree. But the night that we met at the Wine Press, the pain or the pressure began to intensify. For some reason, I thought that you might be associated with my past-life. That's why I became a bit suspicious about our meeting. I don't know what you did, but the annoying pain has disappeared. Thank you," Lynn said with a tearful smile.

"That's strange because I was going to ask you about that tonight," I began to explain. "I've been wondering why you were always massaging your shoulder. But for some strange reason, I just kept forgetting. You see, for the last few months, I've been having this annoying twinge just above my heart too. It was in the same spot as yours," I explained while placing my hand above my heart. Tonight, while you were moaning, my twinge also intensified, and my own heart started pounding heavily. I thought for a moment that I might be having a heart attack. Right now, it feels as though my own annoying pain has left me too."

"Yes, I felt the pain leave my body," Lynn stated. "Did you say I was moaning?"

"Yes, and also crying loudly in a very weird manner too."

"I don't recall. You'll have to take minute and tell me about it," Lynn requested. "But do you see what I mean about your helping me. Whether you know it or not, you are an angel," Lynn said affectionately. "By the way, what was that funny hissing sound and what flickered?"

"It was static electricity Lynn. It came from the fingers of my right hand to a spot above your heart." I explained. "Look, I've even got a blister to prove it," I said, as I displayed my hand to Lynn. We then put on the lights so that Lynn could examine herself. She pulled back her blouse exposing her bare left shoulder and I could see a faint red burn mark. Being cautious, I administered some ointment. This entire matter was extremely bazaar and I was still having a great deal of difficulty comprehending why the static charge had been generated in the first place, so I inquired again, "I'm sorry Lynn, but I still don't know what I did that was so remarkable to have helped you."

"For the last few years," Lynn started to explain, "I've been seeing my own past-life therapist. What I've discovered through a long series of hypnotic regressions is that in my previous life I had been a young wife to a nobleman. The nobleman was the lord of a castle. One day, my nobleman went off to fight in some distant land. Waiting for his return had been unbearable for me and I developed a pain around my heart. I then heard through the grapevine that my lord had taken a new wife. Being heartbroken, in great pain and full of self-pity, I decided to take drugs in order to relieve my pain. Being warned not too, I went ahead anyway. I guess that I took an excessive amount of drugs and as a result I died from an overdose. You see, the emotional pain that I've been suffering from came from my heartbreak, self-pity and remorse. And since I didn't face up to those issues in that lifetime, I've had to endure them in this lifetime. Consequently, I've had to overcome those old issues from my past-life, so that my spirit is free to continue growing in this lifetime. My therapist has been trying to help me get in touch with those repressed past-life emotions. We had a number of regression exercises, but none of them were as successful as tonight," Lynn remarked with the same degree of enthusiasm as before. "Tonight, you used the laying of the hands method," she added.

"I still don't know what you're referring to Lynn. What in the world happened while you were moaning and crying?" I asked, being even more determined to get an answer than I was before.

Lynn continued with her explanation, "Well, in order for me to resolve my issue, I needed to go back and touch upon my previous lifetime. At the end of that particular lifetime, my soul did not linger near the body to grieve for myself or to show appreciation for the body that had served me. The electrical charge that you administered gave my soul the energy it required to go back into time and space, so that I could return to that previous existence. In other words, as you massaged my neck and repeated 'let go, let go,' my soul slowly began to separate from my physical body. It was as though your voice had hypnotized me. At first, I didn't know what was happening. As my soul began to rise, I could see that I was still attached to my body, by a silver umbilical cord. I was reluctant to go, but I was being drawn. Being unfamiliar with this sort of an astral projection experience, I hesitated and looked back. I could see my body on the floor with you next to my physical body. It was strange viewing my body from that dimension. Then I saw your soul, standing there waving at me and encouraging me to 'go on!' With your assurance that you would protect my physical body, I let my soul go with the flow of energy that was tugging at me. Then my soul began to quickly rise up into the darkness where there were millions of bright stars. I had no knowledge of where my soul was journeying. Almost instantaneously, I arrived at a castle and floated right into an empty room. Laid out on a bier was the body of a young woman dressed in black. Praying next the body was another woman in black. Suddenly, I recognized the body on the bier, it was I! When I saw myself laid out, I let out a moan. I wanted to leave, but some unseen force was holding me back. So while I hovered over the body, I said a prayerful goodbye and was immediately freed from whatever forces had been holding me. I then followed the umbilical cord back to my physical body."

There were still tears in Lynn's eyes, when she said, "You see Armand. I forgot to show appreciation for the body that had served me. Thank you, for helping me to return to that moment in time." Lynn looked at me and then gently kissed me on the lips, "Please try to understand Armand. I didn't plan any of this. I didn't have any more control over what happened here tonight than you did."

Concerned over the amount of heat that Lynn's body had been generating earlier, I reached over to touch her arm. Her body temperature was now normal. My evening with Lynn was to have been one full of love making, but now we would be up late with an in-depth discussion about what had transpired here this evening. Still being totally confused, I went into the kitchen to get some sodas.

Lynn, who followed me into the kitchen, leaned up against the frame of the doorway and said in a self-assuring manner, "You see Armand I told you that our meeting wasn't a coincidence."

CHAPTER 15

▼

THE GURGLING SEWER

After having breakfast that following Saturday morning, we put on our jackets and decided to go for a long walk. The weather was brisk and sunny as we walked the two blocks to the Shore Promenade. The promenade is a five-mile pedestrian walkway that runs parallel with the coastline of New York Bay on one side and the heavily traveled Belt Parkway on the other side. The walkway is tree lined and wide enough to be shared by both bikers and pedestrians. It was Lynn's first visit to the bayside area of Brooklyn, so we took time to sightsee and admire the downtown Manhattan skyline and the Statue of Liberty. Directly across the bay is Staten Island and we could see ferryboats coming and going from their berths. Looking south there is a magnificent view of the Verrazano Bridge and beyond the bridge is the Atlantic Ocean.

The main topic of discussion was Lynn's regression experience. I was familiar with the reincarnation theories, but last night's experience left me with more questions than answers. Basically, the concept of reincarnation is a simple one. It follows that your soul has lived in other physical bodies in the past and will no doubt live in other bodies in the future. In essence, the soul never dies and exists forever. The object of these recurring lifetimes is to improve the quality of your soul so that it never has to return to another physical body here on earth again. One of these qualities is for the soul to remain free from any abusive or obsessive wants demanded by the physical body. Once a soul remains liberated from these earthly desires, it is then free to move on towards a more heavenly plane of existence. How last night's incident applied to this theory I had no idea. Since I hadn't seen anything unusual during Lynn's crying attack I can only assume that her astral projection experience may have been more of an inward journey one rather than an outward one.

During our walk, Lynn expressed how refreshing it was to have someone with whom she could share her unusual life experiences. "You know Armand," Lynn began. "I didn't mention this last night, but the issue that I've been dealing with in this lifetime, is a mistrust of men. You see I have a great deal of difficulty trusting men, mainly in my relationships. It's the reason why I began to go to therapy. And since I died of a drug overdose in that particular lifetime, I believe that's the reason I don't drink any alcoholic beverages. I don't even like to take medication." Lynn stopped walking and went over to the rail so she could study the water below. "A past life regression should only be attempted when the subjects emotional problems cannot be pinpointed to their present lifetime. Like mine," Lynn stated. "Regressions should usually be conducted by a qualified therapist. My therapist uses hypnosis, but apparently that wasn't enough in my case, but you knew what to do."

"I wish you wouldn't continue to infer that I knew what I was doing Lynn, when I didn't," I expressed. "However, I do plan to go through my material and see if I can find the book about healers who have used that technique. Except that I'm certain it was used for physical illnesses and not for propelling disturbed souls back into time and space."

"On some level, you know exactly what you are doing and on some other level, we were being guided," Lynn responded. Besides, I still think you're an angel in disguise," she said with an affectionate grin

Later that evening, we dined at a local restaurant with Kevin, my racquetball partner. It was already dark when we left the restaurant and started back to the apartment. On the way back, we walked down one of the local streets where in the middle of the block there is a dead-end for automobiles. However, there's a ten-foot wide pedestrian stairway that goes up sixty steps to the street level above. We were just about to climb the stairs when the streetlight at the bottom of the stairs suddenly went out. We glanced at one another and we began laughing aloud. I then took Lynn's hand and together we hurried up the darkened stairway, two at a time. After reaching the top, we took a moment to embrace.

While getting into bed that evening, I noticed the absence of static electricity. I was also aware that my imaginary heart palpitations and annoying twinge were no longer present. I suppose that I had healed myself too. However, my left ear was ringing and I could faintly hear the Indian flute. Lynn said it was my Indian guide from the other side trying to communicate with me. But, whatever the cause, I knew that the ringing in my ear meant that I was going to dream.

Then without apprehension, I was able to caress Lynn's body without fear of a static charge. Our mutual yearning had finally arrived and so we methodically immersed our naked bodies together into a state of ecstasy. Afterwards, we continued to cuddle and talked until we fell asleep. Not long after, I was sitting up in bed with my heart pounding in my ears. Lynn, who had also been awakened, asked with concern, "What's the matter Armand? Did you have a bad dream? Are you okay?"

"I just had another one of those lucid dreams and you were in it," I explained, while I tried to sort out the details. "Let's see," I began. "First, it started with this long white staircase that extended up into a beautiful blue sky and all around were these beautiful white clouds. The stairs had two separate landings, including one at the very top and on the side of each landing were wooden doorframes. On display within each frame were large rectangular gold tablets that were engraved with images of Our Lady of Guadalupe. I remember standing at the foot of the staircase and staring upwards. My immediate intentions were to begin climbing the stairs, but before starting, I hesitated for an instant. I then turned and saw you standing directly behind me and so I extended my hand as though inviting you to join me in the climb. Then, just as you took my hand, the dream ended."

Lynn immediately remarked, "With your staircase having two landings, it seems to resemble the one we walked up tonight. Your dream is certainly an extremely unusual one filled with a great deal of meaning. I know that I've heard of her, but who is Our Lady of Guadalupe?"

"Our Lady of Guadalupe was an apparition that appeared to an Indian peasant named Juan Diego, in 1531," I explained. "The incident took place on a hill in Mexico. The apparition proclaimed herself to be the Blessed Mother and she miraculously imprinted her imagine on Juan's apron. Today, she is the most patronized religious figure in all of Mexico and Juan's apron is on display at the Basilica in Mexico City. I'm certain that you've seen the pictures of her many times," I informed Lynn.

"That was a very significant dream Armand. I think you're going to have an extremely enlightening experience," Lynn stated. "It also looks like I might be going along with you," Lynn remarked humorously.

Sunday morning, we took another long walk along the promenade. We discussed our philosophies about life and death and we also shared our dreams and aspirations as well as our successes and disappointments. We also spent time discussing the staircase dream. Later that afternoon, I prepared a spaghetti dinner that included some warmed garlic bread. Lynn lit the dinner candles and even enjoyed a glass of red wine. Because both of us had to get up early the next day, we went to bed at a reasonable hour.

That night, it was the droning melodious sound of an Indian flute that was faintly playing in my ear. Under the sheets, we simultaneously reached for one another before proceeding to embrace and make love. Afterwards, we talked before falling off to sleep.

It wasn't long before I was sitting up in bed with my heart throbbing. This time, I was perspiring. Again, Lynn was awake and asking what was the matter. The first words that I uttered, were, "I feel frightened! It was another basement dream," I began. "The details are extremely vivid in my mind and the emotions that accompanied the dream hadn't been as pleasant as some of my others dreams."

"Go ahead Armand. Tell me about your dream," Lynn urged.

"My sister's basement was arranged just exactly as it looks today. Only it was completely empty. No shelves, no benches, no clothes hanging, only the washtub. The dream started with me descending the stairs with you following right along behind me. The basement floor was flooded with murky sewer water as though the drain was plugged. In my left hand, I was clutching a Bible and in my other hand, I was carrying a kerosene lantern. Then, just before reaching the murky water, I stopped and began swinging the lantern back and forth. At the same time, I began to demand in a very distinct voice that the sewer water leave in the name of 'Jesus Christ.' I repeated this several times with a great deal of authority. The murky water then began to react as though responding to my command and it began to recede. It started to recede from the far corner of the basement. That's where the washtub and the entrance to the storage room are located. As I continued to speak, the water began to gurgle as though it were speaking to me. That's when I awoke. I felt like I just performed an exorcism."

Lynn immediately offered her opinion, "It's possible that it is something that happened during your childhood. You my have had some kind of traumatic experience in that basement. I know that you've already had similar dreams with similar themes. Maybe it happened while your mother was washing clothes and the dirty water was draining from the washing machine. Then perhaps she had to leave for a moment and left you alone with the water draining all around you. Being left alone with the gurgling water may have been very traumatic for you. Using the kerosene lamp was just a way for you to get rid of your fears. You did tell me once about a frightened kitten in one of your other dreams, didn't you? That dream could have also had something to do with that same childhood experience."

I quickly interrupted and began presenting Lynn with my own theory. "That's really good Lynn. I would've never put that together," I remarked. "But if you recall. I also had a dream about finding a brown cigar box in the basement too. I forgot about this, but as a kid in grammar school, I used to keep my marbles in an old brown cigar box. I kept the box on one of the basement shelves. Perhaps it's still in the basement. So if there were something from my childhood that needs to be confronted, wouldn't it be in my best interest to go there? I know that there are things that belonged to my parents that are still stored there. Just as the psychic energy from my mother's ring affected Carmela, there could also be some psychic vibrations from my childhood still present. It's also possible that one of those items could stimulate that certain something in my unconscious and I could resolve this problem or issue as you call it. As far as I'm concerned that's the only practical approach, I can think of doing. What do you think?"

"No one really knows what could happen, but I suppose it's worth trying," Lynn replied, while she tried to comprehend my plan.

"I also think that you should accompany me," I stated, "especially now that you've started to appear in my dreams. It's also possible that my mother's spirit is still hanging around and that she might have some more messages for our family. Besides, we've spent hours discussing the subject and I wouldn't like to see you miss out on anything. What do you think?" I again asked enthusiastically.

With an expression of complete surprise, Lynn replied, "I don't know. But I think that I'd like to go. I've never been to Detroit before and I've never gone to look for a spirit before either. That would be a switch for me" Lynn remarked. "When do we go?"

"I'm not certain, but I think that I'd like to go over the three-day Easter weekend that's coming," I recommended.

"Okay, that's sounds good to me," Lynn responded with some reservation.

"Good! Then tomorrow, I'll call my niece Michelle and see if she can help us locate a place to stay," I commented.

In the morning, I awoke to find that Lynn had already left for work. On the desk was a handwritten note:

My Dearest Angel,

I enjoyed spending the weekend with you. You're the only other person I've ever known who has had more unusual things happen to them than I've had.

Love Lynn

That afternoon, I phoned Michelle to inform her of my planned visit and that I would be bringing Lynn Sullivan, my new girl friend. Michelle and Stan lived and owned a large house with four separate family units. I was hoping that one of the units might be vacant. I made no explanation to Michelle about my reasons for coming or why I wasn't staying at Marcy's.

*   *   *   *

Tuesday afternoon, I went to my usual therapy session. We were still discussing my early childhood and as I spoke about my early years, Diane continued to take her notes. The hour was almost up and I still hadn't told Diane about the past life regression experience or the gurgling sewer dream. I abruptly stopped talking about my childhood and quickly took a moment to tell Diane about the gurgling sewer dream.

Diane, then commented, "You know that the gurgling water may represent those repressed childhood tears that you've been holding back for so long. Perhaps it's because there is so much emotional pain associated with those tears. In the dream you're demanding that the tears go back. That's what the exorcism ritual is all about. You don't want to face up to the crying experience. As you once told me, you've had the tendency to hold back your tears, something to do with being a man. Isn't that right?"

Before leaving, I told Diane about my plans for going to Detroit.

Diane then asked, "Why do you have to take Lynn with you?"

"Well, I think it would be a good idea if she was with me, just in case the spirits of my parents are still around," I answered.

Diane didn't appear to be impressed with my idea and merely said, "You shouldn't be fooling around with that stuff." There were no further comments.

CHAPTER 16

▼

GOING TO THE SOURCE

The week following the regression experience, I couldn't wait to fill Rick in on the mysterious static charge and Lynn's mournful crying session. As always, Rick gave me his complete attention. After hearing me describe all the intricate details, Rick leaned forward to express his concern, "I think you should be very careful, my friend.

"Lynn could belong to some kind of cult that knows how to manipulate people into performing some very unorthodox rituals." Pausing for a moment, he continued, "You know, I don't believe in reincarnation. When it's over it's over. Dust to dust and ashes to ashes and that's it. Then wherever the soul goes according to our religious beliefs, it isn't coming back into this world."

"I don't think there is anything for me to worry about Rick. After the incident, Lynn appeared to be perfectly normal. She said that she felt fine and that her annoying ache had left her chest. By the way, that included my twinge too," I commented. "By the way, there's also something else that's been happening ever since I met Lynn. It happened again over the weekend."

"What happened?" Rick asked, still trying to comprehend my first experience.

"As you know, Lynn and I do a lot of walking," I began. "I don't know if you're aware of it or not, but nowadays a lot of churches don't use the old style church bells anymore. Instead, they use prerecorded electronic chimes or bells.

Well anyway, the first time this particular thing happened was a couple of weeks ago while we were walking around Manhattan. It happened one evening when we were passing a small church, when suddenly the electronic chimes started coming through the speakers. I stopped to check the time and it was 9:22 PM. That seemed to be an odd time for the church to be sounding its chimes, so we looked at each other and went up the stairs to see if the church was open. It wasn't. We then looked in every window, trying to find a light or person. Our immediate reaction was that the chimes were being tested and that they were no doubt being controlled from somewhere within the office of the church. However, the office was closed and it was dark inside. We didn't think anything of it, until this weekend when it happened again. It happened just as we were directly in front of a church in my neighborhood. I immediately checked my watch and it read 8:37 PM. Aren't church bells or chimes supposed to go off on the hour? Again, there were no lights in the church or in the office building next door."

"Armand, I can't keep up with you now. I just finish reading on one subject and you present me with something entirely new," Rick responded with some confusion. "Did you go to the church administrators the next day and make an inquiry?" Rick questioned. "Maybe the church clock mechanisms were out of sync."

"Actually no, I didn't." I answered. "When we didn't see any lights or anyone around, we assumed the church was closed. It certainly seemed like an odd hour to be testing chimes, don't you think?" I expressed.

"What does Lynn say?" Rick asked.

"She says, it's the angels showing their approval for our being together. She also says I'm supposed to be a healer of some kind," I replied.

"Angels! That's nuts! I know that you're starting to like this girl, but I think that you ought to think twice before you get in too deep," Rick expressed. "She sounds like a lot of trouble to me. Next, you're going to tell me that you've even knocked out some streetlights together," he added.

"As a matter of fact, we have. At least four of them," I responded.

"All this paranormal stuff is confusing," Rick stated. "Most of what I've been reading is strictly theory. There seems to be no proof that any of these unusual things have really occurred. But I still think that you should stop seeing Lynn," Rick said, again expressing his concern.

I hesitated a moment before adding, "I'm going to take Lynn to Detroit."

"What?"

"I'm going to rely on my intuition, for this one. Something tells me that there's nothing wrong with Lynn," I remarked. "Look at it this way, I was charged with static electricity a couple of months before I even met her. Then, over the weekend, I zap her with the charge, right? And now, I'm no longer generating static like I was before and Lynn's feels better and I feel better. Except for the charge, the church bells and the streetlights, everything else seems very natural. We never seem to stop talking and we both have a lot of things to say to one another. Besides, I have a number of reasons for taking Lynn with me to Detroit."

"What are those reasons?" Rick asked.

"Well, I'm trying to get a handle on those recurring basement dreams, especially that gurgling sewer dream that I had over the weekend. Lynn also appeared in that dream and that's why I've decided to take her with me. I'm also convinced that Lynn has some natural psychic abilities that she's been afraid to use. Maybe she can pick up some vibrations from my parents," I explained.

"Armand, I think that you're beginning to believe in this psychic stuff."

*   *   *   *

It didn't take long for the Easter weekend to roll around and before I knew it, Lynn and I were on our way to Detroit. Michelle was waiting for us upon our arrival and once inside the car, I immediately informed Michelle about the purpose of our visit.

Michelle immediately remarked, "That's funny, because for the last few months I've been having some unusual dreams about that basement too. Just like yours, I seem to be looking for something that I'm never able to find. Anyway, you'll have your chance later the family is getting together at Aunt Marcy's tomorrow night."

The following evening, my brothers, their wives and a large majority of the Seguera family gathered at Marcy's. I introduced Lynn to everyone before I took her by the hand and quietly led her into the basement. Once in the basement, I went over to the shelves where some of my father's old tools were still stored. I touched everything; especially those things that I thought may have been there since my childhood. No long lost cigar-box could be located atop the cement foundation blocks. In the far corner, were the washtub, the washing machine and the clothes-dryer. I also wanted to inspect the basement windows. Marcy had told me that while she was at work, the house had been broken into a number of times in the last few years. The first robbery had occurred just two days after my mother's appearance. On the last occasion the burglars had entered the house through the basement window that was just above the washtub. Rudy had nailed some temporary boards over the window, but the other windows appeared to be secured.

Next, I opened the door to the storage room and went inside while Lynn waited outside near the washtub. I began placing my hands on the old sewing machine, the player piano and the old travel stand-up luggage. There was very little light in the storage room, so I didn't stay long. After I came out, Lynn and I stood for a moment in front of the storage room without speaking. This had been the corner that was always prevalent in my dreams. My assumption being that this was the spot where my mother had spent a good deal of her time washing clothes. If that were true, then perhaps her psychic energy may still be present. I pointed to the drain. It was in the very spot as it appeared in the gurgling sewer dream.

The basement tour complete, we went upstairs. However, just as we reached the top and entered the kitchen, Sergeant began barking incessantly at Lynn. This was unusual because he hadn't paid any attention to her before. Marcy could not get him to stop. She even had difficulty getting him into the backyard and she had no explanation for his sudden change in behavior. I recognized Lynn's embarrassment, so I quickly took her by the hand again and we up the stairs to the second floor.

Once we were upstairs we went from room to room, leaving the room where the apparition had appeared as the last place to inspect. Then, when we did enter the last room something unusual occurred that brought us to a sudden halt. The blanket on the bed was moving by itself. Lynn took hold of my arm while we watched in astonishment. Suddenly, a black and white cat's head emerged from beneath the blanket. It was Tinkerbell, whose sleep we had rudely interrupted and who was in no mood for visitors, so he quickly leaped onto the floor and scooted out the door. Regaining our composure, Lynn slowly walked around the room trying to be sensitive to whatever vibrations might be present. I still wasn't certain what to expect and remained on the alert for anything out of the ordinary. Secretly, I may have been hoping that my mother's spirit might still be present. Lynn then sat on the edge of the bed and began meditating. After a short time, she said, "This room is clean of spirits." Disappointed, we returned to the party.

Later that evening, we returned to Michelle's house and the apartment that she so graciously allowed us to use. Within minutes, Michelle and Ramona arrived at the door with a fresh pot of coffee. This was the first time that Michelle, Ramona and I had been together in over two years. The sisters couldn't wait to begin telling their eyewitness accounts of the Duluth Street incident. The memory of the experience was still very vivid in their minds. They were both so excited that they continually interrupted one another. Lynn and I sat quietly across from the girls listening to their every word. After they finished describing the incident, Ramona immediately asked, "When are you going to tell the rest of the family, Uncle Armand?"

I was taken by surprise because I wasn't aware that they had been waiting anxiously for me to be the one to inform the family. "It will be very soon. Please be patient for just awhile longer," I responded to the inquiry.

The discussion continued while Lynn and I asked a number of probing questions. It was a matter of trying to understand the incident in every detail.

Since it was time for Ramona to leave, she got up and excused herself. Then while heading for the door she handed me a cassette tape.

"What's this?" I asked.

"It's the recording that Phyllis made during the psychic reading with Carmela," Ramona quickly answered.

"You're kidding!" I responded. "I wasn't aware that Phyllis had even recorded the session."

"Well, she did," Ramona remarked.

I thanked Ramona and gladly accepted the tape. I then placed the cassette inside my suitcase with the intent of listening to it sometime later.

The following morning was Easter Sunday and we had been invited to have breakfast with Marcy. During breakfast, Marcy told us how she thought the girls were trying to play some kind of trick on her during the evening of the manifestation. Even when she felt the cold chill, she thought that one of the girls had opened a window for effect. She really hadn't any idea to whom or what Carmela was supposed to be talking too. If it was a family spirit, it could have been any number of relatives who had lived and died in that house. The only indications to Marcy that it might be a relative were the familiar names that Carmela was spouting out in her strange voice. Marcy remembered that immediately afterwards, everyone appeared to be overwhelmed and that's when the girls decided to leave. She also recalled that it wasn't until after the incident that Tinkerbell began to go into that room.

After breakfast, Lynn and I went for a short walk around the neighborhood. I wanted to show her where I used to play during my childhood. But again, I couldn't help but notice the boys who were hanging out in front of the grocery store across the street. They certainly looked like they were above school age and I wondered if they were the one's breaking into Marcy's house.

Later that afternoon, Marcy, Lynn and I went over to Rudy's house for Easter dinner. Sometime after dinner, Joanne mentioned that the club that she was associated with had become interested in the metaphysical. In fact, the club had invited a few mediums to demonstrate their psychic abilities. One medium had the ability to contact and release unwanted spirits from a home. Apparently, the few séances that Joanne had attended were extremely interesting and considered successful.

Joanne said that any family with spirits in their home could easily hire a medium through any one of the psychic associations registered in the state.

Lynn and I listened to Joanne with a great deal of interest. I had wondered about attempting to communicate with the spirits of my parents. However, I was only interested in communicating with their spirits and not with their removal. This is what I had hoped to determine by bringing Lynn with me. But for the moment there was nothing to indicate that that would be necessary.

*   *   *   *

On our way back to New York, Lynn mentioned how much she enjoyed meeting my family, even though Sergeant's barking had made her feel a bit uncomfortable.

After we arrived at the airport, Lynn went straight home to her apartment in the Bronx and I went directly home to Brooklyn. I was satisfied with having confronted my dream problem right at the source. However, I awoke the next morning feeling extremely depressed. The depression stayed with me all day at work and even after playing racquetball with Kevin. On the way home, I knocked out another streetlight, but didn't hang around to see if it would come back on again.

Going to bed that evening, I could hear the faint melodious sound of the Indian flute playing in my left ear again. It didn't take long for me to be dreaming about the basement once again. In this particular dream, I was descending the basement stairs by myself this time. The basement was brightly lit up. When I reached the bottom step, I was compelled to turn towards my left and I saw Lynn standing naked directly in front of the washtub. She was looking at me as though she had something important to say. At the same time, her right arm was extended and pointing towards the storage room. On the floor next to her was a large desk lamp with a brilliantly lit white light shining from where the bulb would normally be placed. Lynn suddenly began to waver and appeared as though she were about to faint. Suddenly she began to slump towards the floor and as she did she continued to point towards the storage room. Just then, a jet spray of hot steaming water came bursting through the top of the lamp and thrusting the white light up into the ceiling. I quickly ran to Lynn's aid. At this point, I awoke with this extremely uncomfortable feeling throughout my body. What stood out most in my mind was the bright light. It resembled the white light that appeared in my passenger jet dream.

In the morning, as I was recording the dream into my dream notebook, I was aware that I was sill feeling depressed. I then picked up the phone and dialed Lynn's number, hoping that I would catch her before she left for work.

"Good morning. I'm surprised to hear from you so early," Lynn remarked.

"I don't know how to tell you this, but I thought that after going to Detroit I would have resolved my basement dream problem. Well, I'm sorry to inform you, it didn't. Last night, I had another dream and it was just as vivid as all the others," I informed Lynn. Then without much hesitation, I took a moment to describe the dream.

When I finished, Lynn said, "You said that I was standing by the washtub. Well that's the same spot where I got stung!"

"Stung? What do you mean by stung?" I quickly asked.

"If you recall," Lynn began. "While you were inside the storage room, I was standing outside by the washtub. Well, that's when I felt a sudden cold chill go up my spine. I thought that there might have been a draft coming through the boarded up window. I didn't say anything to you before, but I've been feeling very depressed ever since."

CHAPTER 17

▼

SEVEN SISTERS DREAM

Concerned about our states of depression, Lynn and I decided to meet after my classes that evening to discuss the situation. But before that, I had my lunchtime appointment with Diane. Diane opened the session by bringing up the gurgling sewer dream and how she was certain that the receding water represented my repressed tears. I then gave her a brief report about my trip to Detroit. "And were you able to contact any family spirits" Diane inquired.

"No, nothing unusual happened, except that my sister's dog Sergeant embarrassed Lynn by incessantly barking at her for about five minutes," I responded. "However, that night, I did have another basement dream." I then took a few moments to describe the dream.

"You know Armand, I think that that jet spray of water bursting through the top of the lamp means you're much closer to shedding those repressed tears," Diane stated.

"What?" I answered sounding a bit dumfounded. I didn't know why Diane was so eager to have me cry. Perhaps after one of her clients let's go of their pent-up emotions they feel much better and that makes Diane feel as though she has done her job. My crying urges usually occurred just after experiencing one of my trance-light states or stupor as I sometimes refer to them. That's when my mind seems to stop functioning and I stare off into space for a moment. The trance like states usually occurred when I was studying or when I was looking out the office window. They are frequent and annoying to the degree that they leave me wondering where my mind went. Then for a few moments, I well up inside and then without producing any tears I feel as though I want to cry. I never do.

"As you can see, we've plenty of tissues around here," Diane commented.

*   *   *   *

Later that evening, Lynn and I went directly to my apartment and ordered a pizza before making ourselves comfortable. Lynn kicked off her shoes and curled up on the couch while I sat on the floor. "Do you remember when we talked about how recurring dreams may be the result of some repressed memory?" Lynn asked.

"You mean, like something that may have happened to me while my mother was still alive and that I can't remember on a conscious level. And that whatever it is, is now attempting to emerge from my unconscious mind to my conscious mind," I theorized. "It's even possible that my trance-like stages and my urges to cry may even play some important role in that process."

"That's right, but let me add something else to that. Maybe your mother said to you 'look Armando. I'm placing this very special item right here, and when you're grown up, you'll remember its location.' That could be the reason why you're having dreams where you're looking for something. Don't forget that your mother would have been under the impression that the family was going to Mexico. That means, she would have put the item in a place where it would be going along with the family," Lynn added.

"Like inside one of those old stand-up travel trunks," I commented. "I suppose it could have been something of a personal nature, like a farewell letter to all her children. After reading the letters that she had written to her mother in San Jeronimo, I can see her doing something like that," I stated.

"You did have a dream about a cigar box, maybe the item had been placed inside a box or something similar," Lynn contributed her thoughts.

"Obviously, the dream patterns are trying to tell me that the item is in the basement. In the last dream you were pointing towards the storage room, so that's a possible clue. Lynn, we couldn't have been more than a few feet from the item, maybe even inches. And that's the same place you got stung," I added.

"I like what you are saying Armand, but let's not forget about our depression," Lynn brought up the subject again.

"I think I'm depressed because I missed an opportunity to find the item and you're depressed for the very same reason," I tried to summarize.

"What are you thinking of doing?" Lynn asked.

"Remember that Michelle also told us that she had been dreaming about trying to find something in her basement dreams too. Maybe, I can get her to checkout those old stand-up trunks. That's where my sister found some of those old family photographs a few years ago. I'm beginning to think that my mother may have begun to pack those trunks with things that were intended to go to Mexico. However, over the years my Aunt Yolanda may have removed some of those items and may in fact, have overlooked some things. You know I feel as though we're close to resolving this issue. Finding that lost item may play some kind of role with whatever I have to tell my brothers about her appearance," I remarked.

"Why are you taking it upon yourself to tell them?" Lynn inquired. "Why couldn't it be one of your nieces?"

"Because I'm determined to fulfill my mother's last wish to unite the family and this just might be my best opportunity to accomplish that mission," I responded. "So I need that item whatever it is to help me back up my account of the incident."

It was getting late by the time Lynn and I summarized our thoughts. But even after turning out the lights we couldn't stop talking. I was personally pleased with the results of our evening's discussion and was quite certain that I was closer to resolving my dream issue. Our brainstorming session had given me a sufficient number of ideas to help me plan my next move.

That night, I went to bed without my ear ringing and without hearing the flute however, sometime in the early morning hours, I was awakened. Not by a dream, but by Lynn. She was softly calling my name, "Armand, Armand!" There was a great deal of excitement in her voice as she urgently called my name, a bit louder each time, "Armand, Armand! How many sisters did you say were in your mother's family?"

With my sleep being interrupted, I was still a little groggy. This was a switch usually it was me who was disturbing Lynn's sleep. Naturally, I was wondering why Lynn had awakened me with such an unusual question. You know, I'm certain that I had already told her. "What's going on Lynn?" I inquired, while still half asleep.

"You're not going to believe this, but I just had the most unusual dream of my life. It was like watching a movie. I thought it might be about your mother's family because the dream involved seven Mexican sisters. And don't ask me how I knew they were Mexican, you know the answer to that," Lynn commented. "My heart is still pounding and I'm really thirsty, could you please get me a glass of water.

"Sure," I said, while getting out of bed and going into the kitchen. When I returned, Lynn was sitting up in the bed. "To answer your question, there were six sisters," I responded to Lynn's question. "What kind of dream did you say you had again?" I inquired.

Before speaking Lynn took a couple sips of water and then took a deep breath, "Well, the dream appears to have taken place in Mexico, just around the turn of the century. There were these beautiful mountains in the background and small adobe buildings all around. You were also in the dream and there was this very wise looking old gray haired gentleman wearing a large sombrero. He took me by the hand and ushered you and I to a spot beneath a shade tree. Inviting us to sit down, he then said, 'This event can only be seen once a year.' Directly in front of us was this large wooden platform that resembled a stage. In the center of the platform were two chairs and a table. And then towering over the platform in the back was this huge tree. The dream is about the oldest of the seven sisters. She loves her family, but being in her late teens she was now old enough to marry. However, for all her life, she has had difficulty establishing a rapport with men. In the meantime, her parents have been making arrangements for her to begin receiving male callers. They are hoping that one of these callers will select her to be a bride. There is an air of excitement as the younger sister's help to prepare her to receive the first gentleman caller. Sitting nearby and watching the festivities are the parents of the seven sisters."

Again, Lynn hinted for another glass of water. Eager to hear the rest of the dream, I returned within minutes. "Go ahead Lynn. Continue," I urged.

There was a brief pause while Lynn took time to satisfy her thirst. She then continued with the telling of the dream, "The first suitor to call at the house was a tall handsome gentleman with a mustache. In one hand he was holding a wide brimmed hat. He was wearing a dark suit and a white wrinkled shirt without the collar. The suitor enters from the right and strides to the center of the stage. There he stops to greet the parents with a polite smile and a nod of his head. Then the oldest daughter steps onto the stage from the left and she walks up to the suitor and politely greets him. She is quite confident that he will choose her to be his wife. They then sit at the table to begin their discussion. However, something terrible went wrong during the discussion and she becomes angry. The suitor remains calm and begins apologizing to her. At the same time, he reaches into his coat pocket and withdraws a beautifully colored turquoise stone. Extending his arm, he offers this precious looking stone to the sister. Hurt with disappointment, she quickly snatches the stone from the suitor's hand and with tears in her eyes, she runs off to the back of the stage. Sitting alone at the base of the tree, she begins to stare sorrowfully at the beautifully colored stone. The suitor leaves the stage and goes off to find another woman to be his wife. There is a wedding, but it is only a big blur. All the time, our attention is focused on the sulking girl in the background next to the tree. Heartbroken, full of self-pity and remorse, she remains clutching the stone next to her heart. Although, she is still young and beautiful, she becomes despondent and eventually dies. At the end of the dream, the old wise man walks onto the stage and walks directly towards us. He then addresses us by saying, 'The remorse issue will remain with the girl until she learns how it can be resolved.' Turning, he walked away and then quickly disappeared. That is when I awoke."

Lynn took another drink of water while she waited for my response. I glanced at her several times without saying a word and then laidback down on the bed. My new knowledge about dreams had taught me to keep an open mind and not to dispel these experiences lightly. I wondered if this might be one of those rituals that Rick had warned me to be on the lookout for. It was hard for me to believe that Lynn could have had such a detailed dream. None of my dreams ever ran that long. And if it was my family, why was she dreaming about them anyway?

"What's on your mind Armand?" Lynn asked inquisitively. "How many sisters did you say your mother had?"

Getting back up, I replied, "To the best of knowledge there were six of them. Six," I repeated. Only this time, I said it in a manner as though I also wanted to reassure myself. "Let's see. The oldest was my Aunt Consuelo. She died about ten years ago. Then there was my mother Adelina. Next was my Aunt Ofelia and she also died. Then there is Aunt Carmen and Cleofas, whose name was mentioned in the Duluth Street incident and who died shortly after. The youngest is Flecita. That makes six. I'm really confused, because I don't know how you could have a dream with so many intricate personal details. You seem to know what was going on in this girls head," I remarked.

"Armand, as you've already learned from your nieces dreams and your own vivid dreams, you just know," Lynn responded with a self-assuring smile.

I was well aware that trying to interpret such a dream was going to take hours, days, even weeks, but for the moment I was still tired and a little confused. In the meantime, Lynn got out of bed and went over to the desk to begin recording the dream into her dream logbook.

Not really knowing where to begin, I asked, "Lynn, are you sure this isn't another one of your past life regression experiences?"

"If it was a past life regression, it wasn't mine," Lynn quickly answered. "Secondly, I didn't recognize myself and I didn't wake up crying like I usually do. Armand, the stone in the dream was beautiful. I know that the Indians revered turquoise as an object that had mystical powers." Lynn then paused for a few minutes and said, "You know, an idea came to me just as I was coming out of that dream. Would you like to hear it?"

"Sure, go ahead. I'm listening."

Lynn then took her time presenting her theory, "Could that stone have possibly belonged to your mother? And could that stone be the lost childhood family heirloom that we spent the entire evening talking about last night?"

CHAPTER 18

▼

AN INSPIRATIONAL MOMENT

In the morning, I awoke to find that Lynn had already left for work. On my desk was a handwritten note:

My Dearest Angel,

That was some dream I had last night. Hope to see you on Friday so we can take advantage of the evening and go over the dream thoroughly. I'm still feeling a bit depressed. Hope you're feeling better.

Talk to you later.

Love Lynn

*   *   *   *

That day at the office, Ann asked what was bothering me. I told her that it was nothing and that is would soon pass. But no matter what I did, I wasn't able to shake off the depression. Attending classes that evening didn't seem to help either. Then, just before going to bed that night my left ear began to ring and I knew that I was going to dream. Shortly after falling off to sleep the name Maria began to pop up. The name was in letters on a highway billboard and also as a newspaper headline. It also appeared on a slow moving stock market ticker tape. The tape read Maria, Maria, Maria as it passed in front of me. There was even a neon light that kept flashing Maria, Maria, Maria right in the middle of Time Square.

In the morning, I awoke with the name Maria still on my mind. I immediately associated the name with a song from the "West Side Story" a famous Broadway production and one that I greatly admired. The "Maria" number was one of my favorite selections. But before leaving the apartment that morning, I went over to the desk and scribbled the name Maria all over the next blank page in my dream log book. Then that day at the office I began to sing 'Maria, Maria, Maria' under my breath.

"Sounds like you're feeling better," Ann inquired.

"I don't know what it is, but I dreamt about the name Maria last night. I don't know any girls named Maria, do I?" I asked without expecting an answer.

*   *   *   *

Friday evening, Lynn and I met for dinner and after we went directly to my apartment. Naturally, our topic of discussion was the dream of the seven sisters. Lynn said that remorse and depression were synonymous. It was an emotion that she could definitely relate to and that it was the same emotion that the older sister was experiencing in the dream. Lynn even hinted that perhaps I should call Mexico in order to verify the number of sisters in my mother's family.

We continued the conversation well into the evening, but just before going to bed, I suggested that we listen to Phyllis's cassette of Carmela's psychic reading. This very important recording had been in my possession for over a week and I couldn't get over how I had completely forgotten about it.

At the beginning of the tape, Phyllis is attempting to locate the most receptive area to conduct the reading. Afterwards, finding their way into the kitchen, Phyllis began by stating that the vibrations coming through Carmela were from a very sorrowful female spirit entity. And that the spirit was that of a young mother who had suffered a great deal with chest pains prior to her passing. The spirit was disturbed because her family was not living up to the traditions that had been passed onto them and that it was her desire to see her family living in harmony and unity. The message was repeated a number of times before the reading ended. The reading ended, mainly because the spirit only wanted to communicate with members of her family.

Afterwards, I told Lynn that I was beginning to feel more depressed than before and that I now had a very strong compulsion to communicate with my family. Lynn then listened while I described a number of ideas that I had for approaching my brothers on this matter. It was important for me to make certain that family unity be included in whatever approach that I used. However, what my mother's spirit meant by unity was still a big question, and one that I had been pondering for over two years. I would first arrange to hold a family gathering and I would just tell them everything. I then thought that I would distribute copies of the Carmela's psychic reading tape to them. Naturally, they would each draw their own conclusions and how they would react was up to them. The most important issue here is that they be told. Hopefully by then I will have located that mysterious family heirloom.

That night, we continued to discuss the family unity gathering until we fell off to sleep. Then sometime during the early morning hours, I was awakened by Lynn who was gently calling my name, "Armand, Armand, what's wrong? Why are you crying?"

After opening my eyes, I realized that my face was full of tears and that apparently I had been sobbing aloud in my sleep. "I just had a very emotional dream," I remarked. "All that I could see was my brother Rudy's face and he was mourning our mother's death and he was crying. I've never seen so many tears; they were just flowing down his face."

"What emotions are you experiencing right now?" Lynn inquired.

"I'm feeling extremely sad," I replied. "Listening to that tape last night must have affected me somehow. The image of my brother crying is still very strong and now I feel as though there is something that I must do."

"Like what?"

"I don't know, but I feel as though I've got to get out of here and get some air," I informed her. Getting out of bed, I got dressed and quickly left the apartment. The air was fresh and invigorating as I headed for the bay. When I reached the promenade, I could see the rays from the early morning sunrise just beginning to appear at the top of the Verrazano Bridge. Out in the bay were some anchored freighters, a ferryboat and some flying seagulls, otherwise there was no one else around. I began to walk towards the bridge when suddenly I was struck with a flood of inspirational thoughts and emotions. Then while I tried to organize these thought in my head, I quickly returned to the apartment. Being careful not to disturb Lynn, I went directly to my desk, took out a yellow legal size writing pad and began writing. My thoughts seemed to be flowing from somewhere deep within my being and they were causing me to well up and cry. In fact, I was sobbing again. Sobbing like I hadn't done since childhood and I was using up my tissues.

Within minutes, Lynn was up and inquiring, "What are you doing and why are you still crying?"

"I'm composing a letter to my family," I said. "It's about my perception of the Duluth Street incident and my personal interpretation as to why it occurred. "These thoughts started coming to me while I was walking down by the shore. I was afraid that I might forget them, so I hurried back here in order to get them down on paper."

"You look and sound like you're real involved," Lynn commented.

"I think that Diane is going to be surprised and a little disappointed," I remarked.

"Why is that?"

"Because, I think she wanted to witness my crying and secondly, because I think she wanted me to use her tissues," I said, chuckling a little.

I continued to edit what I had written, while Lynn went into the kitchen to prepare breakfast. She then listened carefully while I began reading the letter aloud. The letter was filled with a great deal of emotion and revealed many of my most personal thoughts. At the conclusion, I knew in my heart that I would never have the courage to read or even distribute such a personal letter to my family. Stapling the pages together I placed the letter in the back of the desk drawer.

"I agree the letter is very personal and it seems to say everything you want, so I don't know why you're putting it away," Lynn stated. "I think what you've written is very inspiring and very beautiful."

"Well, maybe I'll bring it out in a few years and read it again," I remarked. "At least my state of depression has begun to subside."

Later that morning, Lynn had things to do at home so she went back to the Bronx. I had to catch up on my homework, so I spent the rest of the day studying. Later that afternoon I went over to Pipen's pub and had a few beers with my friend Kevin. I then returned to my apartment and read for awhile before going to bed. My left ear was ringing and I knew that I was going to dream. Sometime in the middle of the night I began to dream. In this dream I found myself standing in front of a small leafless tree. The branches that extended in all directions were bare. Then, there was a male voice that said, 'this is the family! It is the most powerful source of love in the universe!' Suddenly, the tree sprouted straight up before me. Simultaneously, each branch on the tree grew in proportion to their relative size with new smaller branches appearing everywhere. The tree grew so tall that I lost sight of the top branches and I could even feel the roots of the tree expanding right below the earth where I was standing. I also sensed the nourishment for this rapid growth came directly from the love energy that flowed from its very roots and right though the trunk of the tree. My second impression was that the entire tree was totally dependent upon its ability to reach out as a unified force. That the family love energy being generated came only from the unity of the family and that the growth of the tree was limitless.

Like a lot of my other dreams, I awoke startled and my first thought was that 'we are all connected.' It had been another emotional dream. I was so accustomed to having Lynn nearby that I missed her when she wasn't around. The emotions that I experienced in the dream were those associated with family unity. I now knew the meaning of my mother's message. It was a simple one; she wanted the family to be united spiritually.

Not wanting to disturb Lynn, I decided to wait until morning to call her. However, when I finally did call, she was still asleep, so I apologized to her before explaining my growing tree dream.

"Looks like your wish about a tree sprouting is coming true," Lynn remarked.

"What?"

"Don't you remember when we first met at the Wine Press and I asked you how you felt," Lynn reminded me. "You said that you felt like a young sapling tree waiting to break through the crust of the earth, so that you could begin growing. Don't' you remember?"

"Well, then it looks like the whole family is going to be growing along with me," I replied.

✳   ✳   ✳   ✳

Monday morning, I left early for the office, and just as I came up the subway stairs, I heard Rick calling my name. It was Rick's first day back to work from an out-of-town business trip. We hadn't seen one another in a couple of weeks.

"Hi Armand, I just happened to be passing when I saw you," Rick said.

"Hi Rick, how was the trip? A productive one, I hope," I commented.

"All went very well," Rick commented, "how about stopping at Maxwell's for a cup of coffee. I've got something that I have to tell you."

"Sure we've got time," I concurred.

Inside Maxwell's we sat down and ordered a couple of cups of coffee. "Okay, what's happening?" I asked.

"You know that I've been gone for a couple of weeks, so when I got home, I decided to take Mary out to dinner Saturday night. We went to one of our favorite restaurants in Rumson, not far from the house. Then after leaving the restaurant we walked to the car that was parked on one of the side streets. Then just as we were passing this church the chimes starting sounding off. I didn't think anything of it until I checked the time. It was 10:39."

"Okay, what did you do?"

"Just like you told me with your own experience, we could find no lights on inside the church. It was hard to tell if the church even had an office, but we walked around the whole church anyway looking for an entrance. Finding no lights on, we started to walk away when all of a sudden I stopped and turned around to take a last look at the church when I saw a faint blue light glowing in the belfry. I asked Mary if she could see the light. She said that she could see the light and that it looked like someone might be up there turning on the chimes. Armand, I now know how you felt when you came out with that compulsive remark at the Dallas Airport. Because, I said compulsively to Mary, 'It's an angel.' So Mary says, 'you're nuts, let's get out of here.' I can't get over it, every time I doubt you and your weird experiences I somehow manage to repeat the same phenomenon."

That same afternoon, Rick and I attended a meeting in Doug's office. One of the recommendations made during the meeting was that I should make a trip to visit the firm's Los Angeles office. I hadn't been out to the West Coast lately and I looked forward to making the trip. The trip was scheduled for the following week.

*   *   *   *

The following day was Tuesday and time for another visit with Diane. With each visit, I was beginning to feel more comfortable. There was one exception however, I had sensed some professional jealousy on Diane's part whenever I mentioned Lynn's name. I had detected it when I attempted to present our theories about the missing heirloom. Diane remained convinced that my basement dreams represented my repressed emotions and she wasn't too happy about anyone tampering with her theories. She also didn't seem too comfortable when I told her that I was taking Lynn to Detroit. However, after describing my recent crying and growing tree dreams, she appeared rather pleased for having made the prediction that I needed to cry.

"Armand, I believe that your crying represents a major emotional breakthrough for you," Diane began. "I believe that you will now begin to view your personal life much differently. You've allowed yourself to let go and cry and you discovered that it's okay to show emotions. The tree growing to that height represents both your emotional and spiritual growth. It's too soon to tell, but you may have broken through that spiritual suppression barrier we spoke about earlier."

"What about that remark made in the growing tree dream?" I asked. "The one where the voice said, this is the family, the most powerful source of love in the universe?"

"You are obviously very deeply attached to your family and you received love from your parents while they were still alive," Diane stated. "It's a powerful force that has been passed onto you and now it's your job to help carry that love forward. It's not only for this generation, but to the next one too. You should be aware that when the tree shot up like it did that it was extending its spiritual love to those spirits in your family who had already passed on before and to those spirits yet to be born."

"Yet to be born," I exclaimed.

"Yes, didn't you say that you could feel the roots of the tree moving beneath your feet?"

*   *   *   *

Oddly enough, my dream activity started about seven months ago, which was about the same time as the ringing or buzzing in my ears started. The flute playing didn't begin until the night of the flying eagle dream. But ever since the ringing began, I'd been averaging at least one clear and concise dream per night and I've had little difficulty remembering any of them. I've only been awakened by about half of them. However, it is when I hear both the ringing in my ears and the flute playing before going to bed that I'm almost certain to experience an emotional dream. An emotional dream is the kind of dream that awakens me from my sleep with my heart pounding in my ears, like the gurgling sewer dream. Quite often, I make a weak attempt to express the emotion that I've just associated with the dream by speaking a word or phrase aloud. Naturally, none of the words or phrases that I utter when I'm still half a sleep ever makes any recognizable sense to me. Many of my dreams have taken place in or around the Duluth Street house, mainly in the basement. The most interesting thing about my basement dreams is that the arrangement of the basement is exactly as it actually appears. This includes furnace, the washtub, storage room and the drain. Very rarely has the arrangement been distorted and the basement it is always well lit up. Trying to interpret these dreams had become difficult and time consuming. Between all my activities, I've had very little time. I've done most of my dream analysis on the subway while going to work in the morning and have made hundreds of notes. In fact, the dream logbook that I started after meeting Lynn was almost full. Having Diane, Lynn and Rick to share some of my emotional dreams with has been a big help. However, it is impossible for me to explain them all and so I limit myself to sharing only the more significant ones. Diane says that the ringing in my ears might be Tinnitus and that I should check with my doctor. However, Lynn and I both knew that Tinnitus wasn't my problem.

CHAPTER 19

▼

THE RESTLESS SPIRIT THEORY

Saturday evening, Lynn and I met at a Mexican restaurant in Greenwich Village. We agreed to avoid discussing anything pertaining to our paranormal activities. Instead, we just wanted to relax in a pleasant atmosphere while at the same time enjoying a good meal. Adding to our pleasure was a strolling guitarist who played many of the traditional Latin and Mexican romantic melodies.

As soon as we left the restaurant, we headed straight for the subway. To our surprise, we didn't knock out any streetlights, even while walking near my apartment. Once we got home, my left ear began to ring, indicating that I would be dreaming again that evening. Beneath the sheets, Lynn and I again shared our affection in a passionate embrace. Afterwards we nestled in each other's arms and chatted for awhile before falling off to sleep. Not long after, I was in dreamland again and when the dream ended, I was awake and sitting up in bed. Lynn, who seemed to be always attentive whenever I awoke from an unsettling dream, was by my side and making her usual inquiries, "What's wrong Armand? Did you have another one of those vivid dreams?'

"Yes, but it wasn't an upsetting one," I replied. "It was just another Maria dream. In this dream, I'm sitting at a piano turning the pages of some sheet music. However, the only words that were visible on each sheet were the name

Maria. I could hear a melody in the background and it wasn't from West Side Story. It sounded like a romantic ballad."

"Didn't the guitarist play a tune called, "Maria Elena," last night?" Lynn recalled. "Perhaps that's what triggered your dream," she added.

The next morning, Lynn and I went out for our usual walk along the promenade. I then informed Lynn that my trance like states and those urges to cry were no longer occurring. This also included my state of depression. They had all apparently dissipated after I had released those repressed tears that Diane so often referred to. We then discussed the missing heirloom and if I should go back to Detroit and conduct an all out search. The other option was for me to approach Michelle and ask for her help. Again, Lynn asked me if I had verified the number of sister's in my mother's family. I hadn't done anything, so after I returned to the apartment, I immediately picked up the phone and called Marcy. Like me, Marcy was only familiar with the fact that there were six sisters. Then, in her usual nonchalant manner, Marcy informed me that her house had been broken into again.

"When did this happen," I quickly asked.

"Oh! It happened while I was at work on the Monday, right after Easter Sunday," Marcy replied.

"How did they break-in?" I inquired.

"They came in through the storage room window and while they were there they ransacked the room. What could they have been looking for?" Marcy questioned.

"I think that you should get Rudy to secure all those basement windows," I suggested. "What did they take from the house?"

"They didn't find much to steal," Marcy stated. "They've already taken everything of value from their previous break-ins. There is nothing of significant value for them to take since I've already put my important jewelry away in a safe deposit box. I still haven't repurchased a new stereo. It looks like whoever's breaking into the house is merely amusing themselves, because they usually leave a few empty beer cans lying around along with some unfinished joints. However, they did rustle through the cheap jewelry and then ended up taking a small portable radio. The police haven't been much help. They think it might be one of the boys from across the street. The boys see me come and go all the time and are quite familiar with my schedule."

"What about Sergeant? Doesn't he do anything?"

"No, he apparently doesn't know how to go about scaring the burglars away," Marcy said. "I don't know what's wrong he certainly doesn't hesitate when it comes to barking at strangers."

"Well, maybe you could use a new watchdog," I offered my opinion.

After saying goodbye to Marcy, I slowly hung up the phone. The break-ins were still very much on my mind and I knew that Lynn, who had overheard my conversation, no doubt was wondering what I was thinking. We've communicated so well since we first met that I was almost certain that she already knew, so I said, "Lynn the house has been broken into again. This time they came in though storage room window and it was only two days after you and I were in the basement."

"I hope that you're not thinking what I think you are," Lynn questioned with some reservation.

"Lynn, do you remember when we tried to figure out what may have caused our states of depression?" I asked.

"Yes, I remember."

"I didn't think it was important at the time, but we did overlook one small detail," I stated.

"What's that?" Lynn asked curiously, as though already knowing the answer.

"After we came up the stairs from the basement, Sergeant started barking at you incessantly, right?" I emphasized.

"Yes, I certainly remember that, how could I forget," Lynn answered. "I also haven't forgotten that the night Carmela was taken over by the spirit, Sergeant also started barking at her, right," Lynn stated with a deeply concerned expression on her face.

"That's right and so I don't think we're dealing with some old lost family heirloom anymore. I think we have a restless spirit on our hands," I exclaimed.

"I know, it's the very thing that I've been afraid of," Lynn responded with a great deal of apprehension. "It's the very thing that I hoped we could avoid."

Lynn and I then sat silently staring at one another. How we had arrived at our conclusion had not been based on any clear or logical explanation. It had been purely an intuitive one combined with a few facts.

"I'm curious how you arrived at your conclusion?" Lynn asked.

"Well," I began. "The first robbery took place the Monday following the appearance of my mother's apparition. They gained entry through the back door. Then, sometime during the summer of that same year, Marcy had invited the family over for a Sunday barbecue. The very next day, which was also Monday, the house was robbed again. That time they came in through the dining room window. Marcy suspected the boys across the street, but without any witnesses the police were unable to help. The third, fourth and fifth break-ins also took place on Mondays and always after Marcy had done some family entertaining over the weekend. It wasn't until the fifth robbery that they broke-in through the basement window," I explained. "For the sixth break-in they came in through the storage room window and began to look for something in that room. Not only that, but again, it was a Monday, and again after Marcy had had the family over with you and I having been there too. Plus many of my basement dreams take place somewhere near or around the storage room. It's also near the same spot where you got stung."

"Whoa, Armand that's pretty good, but I still don't get the connection to the boys," Lynn inquired.

"I'm not saying that there isn't something of value down there, but I think there's a spirit sending out psychic vibrations in the form of dreams. They're being sent to me, Michelle, maybe to the boys across the street or even to someone living in the neighborhood," I remarked. "We now know that there is something or some spirit trying to get my attention. We also now know that the spirit's energy is activated after it has been simulated by family gatherings and that is why the house gets broken into on Mondays. It is almost as though the spirit is crying out, 'here I am.' If the spirit can influence my dreams then it can also influence the boys' dreams too," I theorized.

"Armand, I'm quite overwhelmed by the thought that what's happening might be the result of a spirit sending out psychic vibrations. But I also can't say that I hadn't thought about the possibility," Lynn explained. "I'm having a hard time accepting that conclusion. Do you have any ideas, who the spirit might be?"

"I'm not certain, but since our family was the first to live in the house, I'm assuming that it is a relative. Maybe it's my father or any number of the family members who died while living in that house. Some died before I was born," I answered. "Maybe it's my mother's spirit.'

"I doubt that it would be your mother's spirit, didn't she have some family business to attend to in Mexico?" Lynn reminded me while she thought of another approach to take. "Do you think the house may have been built over some old Indian burial ground?" Lynn questioned in an unconvincing manner.

"I know nothing about the prior history of the land, but it is something to keep in mind," I quickly responded. "I'd like to go over our spirit theories again. Maybe we can pin this thing down and then we can decide what we're going to do next."

Lynn and I had spent many hours discussing our theories regarding the spirit world. These theories came from a variety of sources: such as books, popular religious beliefs, as well as various cultural superstitions and if course, hearsay. Since the Duluth Street incident and the past life regression experience played such and important role in all of this, we were able to incorporate a few theories and conjectures of our own.

According to our theory, there are three levels of existence. They are known as the physical, the mental and the spiritual. At the time of death, when the spirit abandons the physical body, the mental state continues to accompany the spirit. The theory holds that the spirit never dies, but continues journeying infinitely throughout time and space. The desire for spiritual growth is continuous, but excels as soon as the spirit leaves the body. However, the spirit cannot even begin the journey unless it is free of all its earthly obsessions or desires. Therefore, they maybe temporarily trapped between the earthly plane of existence and the higher spiritual planes of existence.

A large majority of these obsessive issues are generally negative in nature and will continue to hold a spirit earthbound until the spirit can come to some positive realization or enlightenment about them. Many earthbound spirits find themselves in a dilemma, because they yearn for spiritual growth and yet they don't want to leave the familiarity of their obsessive desires.

Emotional issues that are negatively charged may include such things as; anger, hate, fear, guilt, self-pity, remorse, addictions and possessiveness of physical objects. Positive issues come from deeply loving relationships with another person that includes the love and devotion for a family or a group of people.

It is assumed that an earthbound spirit spends all its time seeking to improve the quality of its soul for further spiritual growth. However, it may still need to overcome one final obstacle and that obstacle is the complete understanding of its earthbound issues. Consequently, it may need to re-experience its earthly issue for one last time in order to shed the final fragments of its unfinished business. It is at this time that the spirit may seek the cooperation and understanding of an earthly person or entity, such as a relative or medium, in order to help it to make this transition. Trying to get the attention from a relative living in the physical world is not an easy task and may require the spirit to use some unusual methods to make its presence known, and this is when it becomes restless. A restless spirit is usually lonely, insecure, in need of recognition and attention. We are assuming that this is something difficult for it to do, as we might see it anyway. But if the spirit is to get its messages across to whomever it is trying to communicate with, it must use whatever means it has at its disposal.

I knew that trying to determine the identity of the spirit was one thing, but trying to decipher what was being communicated was something else. More importantly, what were we going to do when we found the answers to the questions. I had already made up my mind not to tell Marcy that she had an unwelcome guest residing in her house. I would just wait until we could substantiate our theories.

"What are we going to do Armand?" Lynn asked curiously.

"I don't really know," was my immediate response. "Maybe we could approach some experts in the field and see how we go about handling these matters. I'm certain that restless earthbound spirits are not uncommon after all they're as much a part of the cycle of existence as we are. Many cultures around the world revere their deceased ancestors and have ritualistic methods for attempting to communicate with them."

*   *   *   *

Before going to bed that night, my ears began to ring at an annoying high pitch. Then, within a short time after falling asleep, I was awake and sitting up in bed. Like before, Lynn was also up and making her inquiries. Without hesitation I blurted out, "spiritual pollution! Lots of pollution! It's terrible! The earth looks as though it was hidden under a thick cloud of sadness," I uttered while still being half-asleep.

"Hey! Slow down Armand," Lynn said. "What kind of pollution are you talking about?"

"When the dream started, I was way out in outer-space looking back at the earth," I began my explanation. "The sun was behind me and the earth appeared to be blanketed with one huge spiral cloud. It looked like a giant hurricane, except that the cloud was a dull looking gray with a strange yellowish tint. I was wondering why the cloud looked so shadowy when the sun was shining on it so brightly. Then I began to slowly float towards the earth and as I came closer, I noticed that the huge cloud formation was breaking up into smaller spiral cloud formations. The closer I got the formations began to breakup, but continued to multiply into smaller spirals. First, there were hundreds of them and then there were thousands. They remained motionless and looked extremely sad to me. I suddenly realized that what I was viewing was millions of earthbound souls, each represented by a spiral cloud. These were the souls who were still struggling to resolve their negative issues. I was certain that the shadowy clouds not only represented their sadness but their tears as well. These were the repressed tears that they needed to let go of, so they could flow like raindrops. There was no question in my mind, but that the gray clouds were polluting the spiritual space above the earth. The pollution was so thick that I realized that the new spirits would have difficulty crossing over to the other side. I wanted to do something, but I felt helpless way out there in outer space. That's when I awoke."

"You certainly have some interesting dreams Armand," Lynn commented. "It's amazing how your dream is so closely related to your restless spirit theory that we discussed last night. You must have been deeply moved by the subject."

"You know, I once read about a man who had a near death experience after having been stabbed to death," I began. "Then when his soul began to cross over to the other side, he was met by his deceased brother who told him that he had to go back because there wasn't enough room. Don't you think that if there was enough space for new spirits, it would certainly be up there, so why the spiritual pollution? I don't know."

*　　　*　　　*　　　*

Early the next morning, I found Lynn sitting at my desk with her dream log open and sipping on a cup of tea. "What are you doing, logging in another dream?" I asked.

Lynn calmly said, "No, but this morning, I got up early and decided to study the log. Did you know that the oldest sister from the seven sister's dream fits the criterion for our restless spirit theory? The girl was extremely despondent and sad. She had died of a broken heart and in an extreme state of remorse and she died before she could fulfill her wishes. Not only that there's also the turquoise colored gemstone. A stone that she cherished because it represented her love for a man. It also represented a material obsession." I nodded in agreement. "At the end of the dream, the wise man says that her issue of remorsefulness would remain with her until she could learn how to resolve that issue. All this makes her our number one suspect for being our restless spirit."

"Are you telling me that our dreams are not only directing us to where the spirit is residing, but they are also telling us what issues the spirit is dealing with?" I remarked with astonishment.

"Sure. Why not," Lynn answered. "I believe we're not only picking up the identification of the spirit, but the name as well."

"How is that?"

"Armand, you've already had two dreams about the name Maria," Lynn quickly replied. "I'm so convinced that the seven sisters dream is the clue to our knowing the identity of the spirit. I also think that we shouldn't give up on the missing heirloom either," Lynn commented.

"If that's the case then we have to beat whoever is breaking into the house," I stated. "They must be having dreams that are telling them that there is something of value in the storage room. Let's hope my sister doesn't have any more gatherings until we can find the object."

"Would you do me a favor and call your relatives in Mexico," Lynn asked. "We've got to know if there really may have been seven sisters."

"Lynn, I will call as soon as I get back from Los Angeles, I promise that I'll phone my cousin Margarita in Canatlan. I'm certain that she'll confirm that there were only six sisters," I said with confidence.

"When are you leaving?"

I'm leaving Tuesday afternoon and I'll be in Los Angeles until Friday, then I fly up to see Joseph in San Francisco on Saturday," I explained. "Then I'll fly back to New York from San Francisco on Sunday. Will you meet me at the airport when I get back?"

"Sure, it would be a pleasure, just let me know when you're arriving and at what airport," Lynn said with an affectionate smile.

CHAPTER 20

▼

THE OLD STORY TELLER

After finishing my assignment early on Friday afternoon, I took off and headed for my Cousin Sam's house in East Los Angeles. When I arrived, Sam was waving to me from behind the backyard fence. There were about a half dozen children playing in the yard as well as a group of adults who were relaxing beneath a shade tree. Sam and Laura greeted me with embraces before introducing me to the other guests. At the same time, Sam handed me a can of beer as I made myself comfortable in one of the lawn chairs. Then while enjoying my visit, I happened to look over and notice an elderly gentleman sitting in an old wooden rocking chair on the back porch. He had a large white handlebar mustache, a head of gray hair and his salt and pepper beard was unshaven. Both of his dark leathery hands were resting atop a makeshift old wooden cane. He looked very old and was staring out into space far beyond any of the yards in the neighborhood.

Laura immediately noticed my curiosity, and said, "That's my Uncle Juan Salido. He lives in Mexico for part of the year and he also comes to visit us for a few months. He's almost ninety years old and is in relatively good health for his age."

Shortly after, Sam came over to me and said, "Hey cousin, Juan got very excited when I told him that your family was from San Jeronimo in Durango. You know that Laura's family is also from that same region and Juan used to live in San Jeronimo. He also used to know your grandparents, including your mother and says that he would like very much to speak with you."

Getting up from my chair, I went over to meet Juan and as I approached him, I couldn't help but notice a sense of history about him. The same kind of history that I'd sensed many times with the elderly relatives that I'd met in Mexico. When Juan smiled to greet me, I immediately recognized his stained lower teeth that he had acquired from drinking the heavily concentrated mineral water in Durango. Juan had rich blue eyes, even though he looked more like and old Indian. It was obvious that he was happy to see me and we wasted no time getting acquainted.

"I'm very pleased to meet you Armando," Juan said. "I was very young at the time, but I used take buckets of water to the workers at the San Panfilo silver mines. Your father Rodolfo was a carpenter there and his job was to shore-up the mineshafts."

"I remember that he was an educated man and enjoyed reading a lot. Then he left Mexico for awhile before returning so he could marry Adelina Rivera. Of course, everyone was very sad when Rodolfo and Adelina left San Jeronimo for the United States."

There was more, "Your Grandfather *Don* Luis Rivera was well known for his excellent horsemanship and his abilities for handling large herds of cattle. He was also and excellent marksman. I once saw him draw his pistol and shoot a thrown tin can out of the air at about twenty paces. He was best known for his innate skill for tracking down rustlers. As a lawman he was very much respected by everyone including the rustlers. Before the revolution, *Don* Luis had been a ranch foreman for a very wealthy Spanish family, the Segovia's. The Segovia's owned the San Jeronimo hacienda, which included a great deal of land and a large herd of cattle."

I then took a few moments to update Juan on all of my aunts and informed him as to who had died and who was still alive. I then mentioned that my Aunt Carmen was living in the little village of Sincero.

This bit of information triggered something else off in Juan's mind and he picked up the conversation, "The Rivera sisters were all very attractive. *Don* Luis and *Donna* Julia were always throwing *fiestas* just to show them off. Their daughter Maria was the most beautiful of them all and she's the one that I remember the most. She was much older than I, but for a long time I was a secret admirer of hers. It was a shame that she died at such a young age."

At this point, I couldn't help but interrupt, "Excuse me Juan, there must be some mistake. Perhaps you've confused Maria with some other family. My grandparents didn't have a daughter named Maria. I've always been under the impression that there were only six sisters in the Rivera family."

"No! No! No!" Juan expressed emphatically while waving his extended right finger back and forth while his head followed the same motion. "No mistake. There were seven sisters when I knew the family. Maria was the oldest, even older than Adelina. As a matter of fact, she was even older than Consuelo, if I remember her name correctly. That would make her the oldest."

I was speechless. This was more than I had expected in this brief conversation. I had no choice but to respect Juan's recollection. My next impulse was for me to get up and phone Lynn, but I was much too eager to hear what else Juan had to say.

"Maria was very beautiful," Juan continued. "She had a magnificent voice and she loved to sing and dance. In fact, she used to sing hymns in the church and she always sang at the *fiestas*. I will always remember her beautiful smile and how she loved to laugh. Men used to fight over her. Unfortunately, she was afflicted with some strange illness that would make her very weak. She would remain in bed for days at a time. Then something happened to her and she began to spend a great deal of time silently praying in the church."

Juan paused for a moment before continuing, "There was a time when everyone thought she was going to marry a fine young man named Alberto. Alberto was the son of *Don* Fredrico, a muleteer who was a very good friend of your grandfather, *Don* Luis. But for some unknown reason Alberto became betrothed to another woman instead. Everyone was under the impression that Alberto may have wanted a much healthier woman to bear his children. Not long after that, Maria took extremely ill. No one could identify her strange illness. In those days, there were no doctors out in the ranch country." I waited while Juan twisted his mustache between his thick dark fingers. "People said it was because Maria was emotionally despondent over Alberto's betrothal to this other woman. Apparently, Maria had been deeply in love with Alberto and may even have been suffering from a broken heart. All this time, Maria was very sad and withdrawn. Then Alberto joined the revolutionary army and not too long after, he was killed in the Battle of Zacatecas. Witnesses at the battle said that Alberto took his horse and lariat and then roped a *federales* machine gun position while riding at a full gallop. Alberto knocked out the machine gun, but was killed when his horse stumbled and fell. He was a war hero and we were all very sad when we heard about him being killed."

Again, Juan stopped to collect his thoughts, "Did you know that your mother Adelina was a school teacher?"

"Yes I do," I answered.

Juan just kept talking while Sam and I listened intently to his every word, "Your mother was a very good teacher and Maria used to help her with the children. But then Maria took seriously ill and became weak. Not too long after, Maria died."

"How long ago was that Juan?"

"It was somewhere near the end of the revolution, 1918 or 1919, I think," Juan tried to remember. "I really don't remember, it was so long ago."

"Do you know if Alberto ever gave Maria a turquoise colored gemstone?" I casually asked. Juan didn't seem surprised by my question, but Sam sure as heck was. I was just thinking that this was a good time to ask, since I may never see Juan again.

However, Juan quickly answered, "I wouldn't know anything about those things. That would've been something personal, but I do know that Alberto was a collector of rocks and stones. Every time Alberto came back from the mountains with *Don* Fredrico, he always had some new rocks to show off. I know that he even had some Indian friends somewhere high in the mountains and they used to exchange items for their collections."

Laura brought over a couple of beers for Sam and I, while Juan continued, "There was one story that I remember very clearly. One day when Alberto was still a young man, he found a pearl handled Spanish knife along one of the mountain trails. The knife was well preserved and may have recently been dropped by some bandits. *Don* Fredrico could never locate the real owner, so he let Alberto keep the knife. One day, Don Fredrico, Alberto and *Don* Luis were in the mountains when they met up with some of their Indian friends that they'd known for many years. One of the Indians was an old medicine man who became so intrigued by Alberto's knife that as token of their friendship, Alberto offered to give it to him. The medicine man was so overwhelmed with Alberto's willingness to give up such a beautiful object that he refused to take it. Instead, he gave Alberto a mystical stone that he had worn around his neck for most of his life. This was a momentous decision for the medicine man to give the stone away. The story goes that somewhere high in the Sierra Madre's there is a sacred snow-capped mountain. This was the mountain where the Indians believed that their gods resided and this was the place where they believed their own spirits would journey one day. They also believe that after dying, their body would enter into the body of an eagle, so that their spirits could be flown to the top of the mountain. However, in order for their spirits to make that flight, they must first be free of all their earthly possessions. Otherwise, the weight would be too much of a burden for the eagle to take them to such heights and this would keep their soul earthbound. Consequently, the giving up of the stone for this old medicine man was more than just a symbolic gesture. It represented the giving up one of his last earthly possessions before passing on to the after life. That's the story as I remember it. I understand that Alberto kept the stone for a very long time. My mother told me that she saw the stone once and that it was blue or green in color. Whatever happened to that particular stone, I would have no idea. I would have hoped that Alberto would have given it away before leaving for the revolution." Suddenly, Juan became quiet.

Somehow Sam and I knew that Juan was done talking. Sam went over to talk to his guests while I sat silently watching the children play only a few feet from me. I wanted to be alone, so I excused myself and went inside the house where I sat down in the living room. I thought about the eagle in flight dream and the soul yearning to be free from the burdens of the physical life. And then there was my mother, whose wish was to be an eagle, even if just for one day. The old Indian's philosophy about life after death wasn't much different than our restless spirit theory.

I suddenly heard Laura shouting from the kitchen and asking, "Hey, Armand. You okay? Can I get you anything?"

"No thanks Laura," I shouted back. "I'm alright. Is it okay if I use your phone to make a collect call?"

"Certainly, help yourself," Laura replied.

I checked the time as I dialed Lynn's phone number. It would be seven o'clock in New York and I wondered if Lynn would be home. The phone rang twice before Lynn answered.

"Hello!"

"Hi Lynn! It's me. How are you?" I greeted.

"This is a surprise, I wasn't expecting to hear from you," Lynn remarked.

"Before I begin Lynn, I want to let you know that I miss you and I wish you were with me right now. It's been five days and I can't wait to see you," I expressed my desire. "However, I've got something very important to share with you and I just couldn't wait to get back to my hotel room."

"I miss you too Armand," Lynn responded. "But you're sounding a bit mysterious, what happened that you're calling?"

"I hope you're sitting down, because you are not going to believe what just happened to me within the last hour," I started. "I'm calling you from my cousin Sam's house here in East Los Angeles. I just met Sam's wife Laura's uncle. His name is Juan Salido and he is an elderly gentleman who knew my family back in

Mexico and he just told me that there were seven sisters in my mother's family. And that the oldest sister wasn't Consuuelo like I had told you, it was Maria! Did you hear me Lynn?"

"Yes, I hear you," Lynn said, sounding a bit surprised, but anxious to hear more.

"Maria died from some unusual illness shortly after the Mexican Revolutionary War. This Juan fellow said that he even had a boyhood crush on Maria," I explained.

Then there was a long pause on the other end of the line before Lynn spoke again,

"I don't believe it," Lynn remarked. "It's one thing to think you're right and it's another when you find out that you are right,"

"There's more Lynn," I continued. "Maria was in love with a man named Alberto, who was a collector of rocks and stones. If Alberto ever gave the stone to Maria, is not known by this gentleman. It's just strange how my family in Mexico overlooked telling me about Maria. I'll have to check this out later. I'll also have to fill you in on the rest of the details."

After I hung up the phone, I couldn't stop thinking about Juan's story. Perhaps my family in San Jeronimo had forgotten about Maria, but one old Juan Salido hadn't and I wasn't going to tell him that Maria was still with us.

*   *   *   *

Early the next morning, I took the shuttle to San Francisco and got to the Little League ball field in time to watch Joseph play in the outfield. I really enjoyed watching the game and got excited when he got his first hit. That night after dinner, we took time to go over the maps of Mexico and plan our trip. We were both looking forward to the trip and I knew that it was going to give me great feeling of pride to introduce Joseph to both Uncle Victor and Aunt Carmen.

CHAPTER 21

▼

MICHELLE'S MISSION

Lynn met me at the airport when I arrived late Sunday afternoon and all the way to my apartment in the taxi, we couldn't stop talking. Once we got to my apartment, I wasted no time finding my address book and dialing Margarita's phone number. Margarita picked up the phone after two rings. We exchanged mutual greetings and made inquiries about everyone's health. I then I asked, "Margarita do you know a man named Juan Salido?"

"Many years ago, the Salido's used to live here in Canatlan. Juan used to stop by and talk to my father. The family moved away some time ago, but if he's alive he must be very old," Margarita commented.

"Well, you are right, he is very old and in good health. I met him in California a few days ago and he mentioned an Aunt Maria that was older than your mother. I don't recall anyone ever speaking about her," I inquired.

"Probably because she died before anyone in our generation had an opportunity to know her. The poor thing was only twenty-five years old when she died," Margarita replied.

"When was that?"

"She died in 1920," Margarita responded.

"Do you know what she died of?"

"No. But I remember my mother telling me how Mama Julia brought down an old Indian medicine woman from the mountains to help cure her. However, her remedies were of no avail. She used to have some kind of attacks that weak-ened her for long periods of time. It seems that they were unable to help her and after a time she withered away and died, so I'm told. Poor thing," Margarita added.

"Do you know if she ever married?"

"No, I'm certain of that," Margarita responded.

"Recently, I had a dream about seven sisters being in my mother's family," I began, without trying to explain Lynn's involvement. "That's why I was so surprised when Juan told me about Maria. Did our grandmother Julia leave any kind of gemstone when she died?"

"That's an unusual question, was that in the dream too?" Margarita questioned.

"Yes it was, but I can't take time to explain it to you now. I will when I come to Canatlan in July," I explained. I then took a few moments to explain what I had been told by Juan Salido in Los Angeles. Margarita was not familiar with any of Maria's suitors or any precious stone. I then asked, "How is Carmela?"

"She's not home now, but she's fine," Margarita answered.

"Do you know if she is having any unusual dreams lately?"

"No, not anything that I know of," Margarita commented. "She finally told me about that night in Detroit. She said that she was extremely ashamed, because she lost control of her emotions. Carmela still doesn't understand what happened and continues to look for a logical explanation. However, it did leave her with one strong emotion."

"What's that?"

"She's filled with so much love that she expresses her affection to everyone that she meets," Margarita explained.

"Well, you tell Carmela that she and I are going to have a long talk when I get there and I will need to talk to Aunt Carmen too," I remarked. "Please let her know that I'm coming with my son Joseph and that I look forward to seeing everyone." After concluding the conversation, I hung up the phone and sat quietly staring a Lynn.

"What are you thinking Armand?" Lynn asked.

"I don't really know where to began," I said. "But it appears that spirits can be called upon to help dying family members to crossover to the other side. Since Maria had already passed away, it's quite probable that she originally came to Detroit in order to help my mother crossover. Therefore, as long as my mother's spirit remained in the house, Maria would have been content. As you can see, it wasn't until a few days after my mother's spirit departed from the house that Maria became restless."

"That's a good logical assumption," Lynn responded.

"I also think we can assume that the man who gave Maria the stone in your dream was Alberto," I continued theorizing. "The stone would have represented an expression of affection from Alberto. Perhaps it's this possessive attachment to the stone that has kept Maria's spirit earthbound."

"The seven sister's dream definitely left me with the impression that she died of a broken heart," Lynn commented

"However, I'm certain that Maria would have had the same desires for family unity, even if she did die in a state of remorse." I remarked.

"But let us not lose sight of the stone Armand," Lynn expressed. "I think there's still a good chance that the stone might still be somewhere in your sister's house, if the thieves haven't gotten to it. Let's also not forget that Michelle has also been having similar basement dreams. Perhaps, Maria has been attempting to contact other members of your family. It's something you might want to look into. Maybe Michelle can help."

All this metaphysical theorizing was fine, but for all this time we were really avoiding the main issue. What were we going to do about Maria? I wondered if I should just phone Marcy and tell her that the spirit of our long lost Aunt Maria is in the basement sending out negative vibrations. Maybe we should just turn the whole thing over to Marcy and let her handle the situation.

There were other options that Lynn and I were prepared to consider. We were willing to contact any of the psychic associations listed in the phone book. The Association of Research and Enlightenment, the New York Spiritual Center and the Metaphysics and Parapsychology Institute where three that were listed. Perhaps someone in one of these organizations could recommend an experienced medium. We would even be willing to pay them. Naturally, we hadn't forgotten about the spirit release specialist that Joanne had spoken about during our Easter Sunday visit. Then, there was Phyllis, the psychic neighbor who I was certain we could count on for assistance.

The last option, and one that we were most reluctant to consider, was that Lynn and I return to Detroit. We could attempt to telepathically communicate with Maria, letting her know that we were now aware of her existence and that we would soon bring help. This might calm her down for awhile until we came up with a better solution. In either case neither Lynn nor I, were anxious to attempt a close spirit encounter. I was uncertain about my ability to deal directly with a spirit. Lynn also felt as though she was being drawn into a situation that could make her feel extremely uncomfortable. Neither of us wanted to conduct some kind of a theatrical séance. At least, not unless we were absolutely sure that it was necessary.

All of these alternatives had possibilities, but none of them included my desire to unit the family spiritually. It appeared that family gatherings somehow caused Maria's spirit to act up and I knew that I would have to include the family in whatever we planned to do. All we needed to do was to let Maria know that we were there for her and for the family to generate enough family love energy to help calm Maria down, and maybe even to help send her on her way.

The one major problem with this particular plan was how I was going to convince my family of Maria's spiritual presence. And even if I did convince them, why should they gather in the suggested manner just to please the spirit of some long forgotten about aunt. For some reason, I was still a bit skeptical about going ahead with anything for the moment. Mainly, because I still hadn't verified the existence of the spirit. For now, all we had were a lot of dreams and theories. I knew there was still more work to be done before I could honestly say that a spirit really existed.

*   *   *   *

The following morning, I phoned Michelle from my office. I spent several moments bringing her up to date on the latest information regarding Maria.

Speaking excitedly, Michelle spoke up, "You know, maybe that precious stone is hidden in my grandmother's old sewing machine or in the old player piano. But aren't there some old stand-up steamer trunks down there too? If I recall correctly, I believe they're all in the storage room. Do you want me to check it out for you Uncle Armand?" Michelle volunteered without my even asking.

"You're reading my mind," I said. "The answer is yes, could you do that for me. All I want is for you to verify that everything we're talking about is actually stored in the storage room. Then see if there is anything else around and don't forget to take a flashlight with you, the light in the room is very dim," I suggested.

Michelle quickly replied, "Heck, I'll be glad to help. I have a key to Marcy's house, but I would never enter the house without her permission. I'll just tell her that my piano is out of tune and that I'd like to practice on her's."

I understood and so I left the timing and manner in which Michelle carried out the assignment in her hands. Two days later, Michelle phoned me at my office. Fortunately, I wasn't busy and was able to speak with her. There was a good deal of excitement in her voice. "Uncle Armand, you'll never guess what jus happened," Michelle began. "First of all, I spoke to Aunt Marcy and asked her if I could practice on her piano while she was at work. Aunt Marcy said 'okay.' So I decided to go over this morning. As a matter of fact, I returned just a few minutes ago. What an experience!"

"Go ahead," I urged.

"Well, as soon as I entered the house, I decided to let Sergeant out into the backyard. But when I started going down the basement steps, I could hear Sergeant outside barking real loud. So I went back upstairs to try and calm him down. Afterwards, I began to descend the stairs one more time, except that Sergeant began that confounded barking again. So again, I went to the back door to try and calm him down. Except that this time when I opened the back door, Sergeant squeezed right through my legs and came running into the house. I thought it was strange when I saw him head straight for the basement. I quickly followed him down the stairs. He ran right for the storage room and started barking as though someone was in there. I had checked the doors and windows before coming into the house, just to make certain that no one had broken-in, so I knew no one was in the house. I did think that Sergeant's behavior was extremely unusual. Anyway, I started talking myself into not being afraid. I took a few deep breaths and with Sergeant still barking, I began to slowly open the door to the storage room. As soon as the door was open, I couldn't believe what I was seeing. There was a white mist hovering directly in front of me. Man, did I freeze. Suddenly, I was struck by something that sent an ugly cold chill up and down my spine. It scared the hell out of me and I immediately knew that it was time for me to get the heck out of there! Man, was I scared!"

"I'm sorry Michelle," I tried to apologize. "Had I been thoroughly convinced that there was a spirit, I would never have asked you to go there. But thanks for doing such a good job. Just do me another favor and phone Phyllis while the experience is still fresh in your mind. Maybe she might offer some good suggestions," I requested, "Oh yes, one other thing, stay out of the basement until we can resolve this situation."

Later that afternoon, Michelle phoned and said, "I just spoke with Phyllis. She said that I was psychically charged with the vibrations from the restless spirit and that she was picking them up right over the phone line. Phyllis said that the psychic vibrations being generated by the restless spirit were harmless. Apparently, the spirit is crying out very loudly and is seeking help from her family." I thanked Michelle and we spoke awhile longer before concluding out conversation.

That evening, I informed Lynn of Michelle's mission and her conversation with Phyllis. We then took time to discuss our alternatives for releasing Maria from the basement. Lynn was empathic about not wanting to deal directly with the spirit. We finally decided to have Michelle contact Phyllis one more time and ask her if she could make arrangements with the spirit expert or medium to release Maria. We had already learned that the medium's name was Sharon. How Phyllis and Sharon went about performing the release didn't matter to us, as long as Maria's spirit was set free and we weren't involved. In other words, we wanted to wash our hands of the entire matter. Family unity would just have to wait until later.

The next day, I phoned Michelle and told her about our decision to allow Maria to be handled by people who knew what they were doing. That we would greatly appreciate it, if she would kindly notify Phyllis of our decision. Perhaps she and Sharon might have some better ideas how to approach this matter and we would be glad to cooperate.

In less than an hour Michelle was back on the phone. However, she sounded a bit puzzled with what she was telling me, "Phyllis said that there was no way anyone from the outside was going to be able to deal with this particular spirit. That neither she nor Sharon could intervene with the spirit on behalf of the family."

"What?"

"Phyllis says that this is 'strictly a family matter' and that the entity only wants to communicate with members of its own family or kind as she says," Michelle related. There was a short pause before Michelle continued, "Does this mean that we're the ones who are going to have to release Maria, Uncle Armand?"

CHAPTER 22

▼

LYNN'S STORY

After having spoken with Michelle, I immediately arranged to meet with Lynn at a Greenwich Village restaurant. Then, as soon as we met we didn't waste any time getting into a lengthy discussion. We concluded that if want we were dealing with was really strictly a family matter, then it meant we wouldn't be able to count on any outside help from any professional mediums. It appeared as though we had reached an impasse and we weren't exactly certain what should be our next course of action. I was aware that the restless spirit needed more that just to be recognized and that trying to avoid any personal contact with the spirit was going to be almost impossible. That in order for the spirit to be released from its earthbound plane it needed the assistance of a physical being, a medium to be exact. The medium will not only need to understand the needs of the spirit, but must also be willing to permit the spirit to actually come in direct contact with their physical body. Psychics who perform spirit releases of this nature are known as physical mediums. With all those distraught spirits crying out for Lynn to help them, I was certain that her gift was that of a physical medium. Although I had not addressed Lynn previously, I was hoping that she might be willing to handle Maria's release herself.

There was a serious tone in my voice when over dessert I asked Lynn, "Do you have any idea what I'm thinking?"

"For some reason I knew that eventually it was going to come to this," Lynn snapped her reply. "I believe you want me to be the one to release Maria, right?"

"That's right," I quickly responded. "I believe that Maria is exclusively yours," I added.

"But I'm not of her kind and if this is supposed to be strictly a family matter then I'm not a member of your family nor am I planning on being one," Lynn answered hastily. "I knew it. Right from the very first moment that I laid eyes upon you in the Wine Press. I knew there was something unusual about our meeting. Yes, I have to admit that I was suspicious right from the beginning. Then my intuition started working overtime. At first, I didn't want to believe it. But I immediately suspected that you were going to get me involved with something that I would be reluctant to do. I have to admit you charmed me into to thinking that you only wanted my body for sex, not for communicating with old spirits. This is one for the books," Lynn expressed, while beginning to display some emotion. "You've been trying to manipulate and seduce me into playing your little psychic detective game. You even took me to Detroit just so you could take me into your dusty old basement. What kind of a date was that? All you were doing was trying to win me over so that I could be your psychic puppet. Well, no thank you mister skimming angel."

"That's not true Lynn," I responded, "I've only been following all the leads by using my intuition too, the same as you. Besides, we just discovered Maria less than two weeks ago," I stated being a bit defensive.

"Armand, on some level you've known exactly what you're doing all the time and you knew that you were going to need some kind of a psychic goat. I'm really disappointed in the way you've used me," Lynn stated annoyingly. She then got up from her chair and nervously began to collect her belongings. "You're just going to have to get someone else to play your ghost hunting games," Lynn said while still displaying some anger. "So goodbye mister angel, I wish you luck in your quest. I just don't like being used," she stated again. Lynn then turned abruptly and I could see tears in her eyes as she headed for the front door.

I made no moves to restrain her instead I sat back and puffed out an exasperating breath. I paid the bill and then while walked towards the subway station I wondered about Lynn's dilemma. However, something told me I was right to have asked her.

*   *   *   *

During my next visit with Diane Evans, I described a few of my recent lucid dreams. I mentioned how the ringing in my ears was beginning to intensify before going to bed. However, I held back on any discussions about Lynn and how much I already missed her.

Back at the office, Rick immediately sensed that something was wrong. "What's up Armand?" he asked.

"I'm having a little difficulty with Lynn. She walked out on me a few nights ago," I responded.

"For good?"

"I really don't know. She sounded pretty serious and may just need some time to think it over. But I'll fill you in on the details on Friday," I commented.

*   *   *   *

That same evening, Michelle who was extremely eager to be part of the Maria release team phoned and said, "Hi Uncle Armand, I'm ready for my next assignment."

"For one thing, I'm planning to go to Detroit in about two or three weeks. I'm going to need your help with organizing a family gathering. I want it to be sort of a last minute thing, but first I'm going to draft up a brief letter to your Dad, Frank, Marcy and Rich. They'll be the main participants during the gathering. First, I'll send them the letter and then I'll follow up with a phone call before leaving for Detroit. I want to make certain that they understand what we're trying to accomplish," I explained.

"What are we trying to accomplish?"

"Since Maria seems to be sensitive to family gatherings, we need to make our presence known directly to her. More importantly, we need to convey our family's love to her," I elaborated.

"What's that going to do?"

"Our first objective was to keep Maria from transmitting those impulsive psychic vibrations to the boys across the street. The second objective, is to muster up as much of the family's love energy as possible, so that maybe we can help to boost Maria's spirit into the next plane of existence, wherever that is," I expanded my thoughts a bit more.

"How do we do that?"

"We open our hearts through prayer and meditation."

"That's going to be pretty hard to do, because none of us even knew Aunt Maria," Michelle stated.

"She's not just any deceased relative to us; she's my mother's sister and an ancestor of our family. The love that we will be sharing with Maria, is out of respect for our family and the afterlife in general," I emphasized.

"Phyllis said that she could probably get Sharon to do a reading on the house before we decide to do anything. She also said that someone in her psychic organization has located a Mexican woman from Chicago. She's also supposed to be from Durango and she might be available, if we need her." Michelle informed me.

Before going to bed that evening, I could hear the Indian flute playing at a very high pitch. I had been wondering how I was going to go about handling the family gathering and the spirit encounter at the same time. It was a rather complicated situation for me to determine. Shortly after I fell off to sleep, I started dreaming about my father. My father was sitting in a large recreation hall filled with people playing cards. Among the players was my brother Frank who was sitting with Aunt Carmen. John, Marcy's late boyfriend, was sitting with Aunt Cleofas on the other side of the room. Pa, who was sitting alone, was waving me over to join him. As I approached him, he held up a small pocket calculator and asked, "How do you use this thing to divide by two?" I told him "it's easy all you have to do is to push this button." I then demonstrated by pressing the divide button and the dream ended.

I awoke with a start and sat on the edge of the bed for several moments while trying to interpret the dream. First, the recreation hall had been divided between people now living and those who were deceased. This interpretation led me to the conclusion that I must conduct the family unity gathering separately from the spirit encounter.

Getting up from the bed, I went over to my desk and was struck with yet another idea. I opened the desk drawer and pulled out the inspirational letter that I had written. After, re-reading the letter very carefully a couple of times, I realized that with only a very few revisions, the letter would be perfect for the family unity gathering.

Then, another strong sense of reality came over me. I recognized that family unity could not be achieved without the support of my brother Rudy. Being the oldest, Rudy knew more about Ma's wants and needs for her family. It was obvious to me that I would have to speak with Rudy sometime prior to the reading of the letter. I also knew that family unity could not be accomplished without some open display of affection. I quickly titled the letter "An Expression of Love" and then added a line about expressing our affection to one another.

The next morning, I took the letter into the office and asked Ann if she wouldn't mind typing a short book report for me. She politely agreed to type the report whenever she could find some free time.

Later in the afternoon, Ann came walking into my office and said excitedly, "Hey this is no book report this is a true story, isn't it?"

"What makes you think that?"

"Because I keep having cold chills go up and down my spine while I'm typing," Ann commented. Then, after turning to leave the office, Ann remarked from over her shoulder, "The whole thing sounds like a lot of old country superstitions to me anyway."

*   *   *   *

It was late Friday afternoon when I left the office and made my way over to Maxwell's. I was heading directly for the bar area when the waitress stopped me and pointed towards the booths. I immediately assumed that Rick was already waiting for me. As I neared the booths, I could see that Rick was speaking to someone. However, I could not see the other person, because they were hidden behind the partition of the booth. Suddenly, Rick caught my eye and within seconds, he was up on his feet smiling and gesturing to me with one hand to whomever he had been sitting with. "Look who we have here," Rick remarked. To my surprise it was Lynn. Rick quickly picked up his drink and tactfully excused himself. "See you later Armand," he said.

Even with a sheepish expression on her face, Lynn looked as beautiful as ever. "How did you two get hooked up?" I quickly asked.

"I'm a psychic detective remember? First, I asked the waitress if you were here and since you weren't, I did the next best thing and asked for Rick. Since you told me so much about him, I was certain that he wouldn't mind keeping me company until you arrived," Lynn explained. "Can we go somewhere where we can talk without all this noise and smoke?"

"Sure, why don't we go into the dining room, it's not very crowded and we can get a table in the corner," I suggested. Lynn ordered her spring water with a twist of lime and I ordered my usual beer. It appeared as though Lynn had a lot on her mind and while appearing a bit uncertain she opened the conversation.

"How's Maria?"

"She's still in the basement, if that's what you're asking," I replied.

"Have you established a plan?"

"I'm planning to go to Detroit in a couple of weeks," I stated. "And since our family spirits seem to be fussy about with whom they communicate, Phyllis has located a Mexican woman who lives in Chicago, but is originally from Durango. The woman is an experienced medium and is available if we need her."

With a bit of disappointment in her voice, Lynn remarked, "I thought you said that Maria was exclusively mine."

Pleased with Lynn's inquiry, I quickly replied, "She is, if you still want her."

"Armand, I admire your persistence. I walk out on you and you just keep plotting right along as though you were on some important mission that has a deadline,"

"I am on a mission," I stated. "It's because of the vortex."

"The vortex? What kind of vortex are you talking about?"

"At the beginning of your seven sisters dream, the old man who did the ushering, said to you, 'this event can only be seen once a year.' From what I've been reading, this may be true throughout the spiritual world. It's only during certain times of the year when the conditions are favorable for spirits to make the transition from one level of existence to another. The vortex is an opening in space that offers little resistance to the spirits wanting to make their transformations. I believe that's the reason why all this metaphysical activity is so heightened at this time. Lynn, this may be the only opportunity, otherwise Maria might be earthbound for a long time," I explained.

"Let me get this straight. You're saying that the time to act is now and that we may not have another opportunity for a long time. Is that right?" Lynn questioned, while still contemplating my remark about the vortex.

"That's right," I replied. "But excuse me Lynn, I interrupted you before and I know you had something that you wanted to say."

"I'm not certain that I know where to begin," Lynn said, while becoming a bit fidgety. She then sat back and took a deep breath. Being relaxed she began, "When I was seven years old, I fell into a pigpen and one of the pigs stepped on my groin, busting a blood vessel. My parents rushed me the hospital and while the doctors and nurses worked on me in the emergency room, my soul began to slowly float up to the ceiling. I could see and hear everything the doctors and nurses were saying and I could see what they were doing. Suddenly, I saw a bright light at the far end of a long tunnel that I was being drawn towards. When I reached the far end, I immediately saw a woman and instinctively knew it was my grandmother, even though I had never met her. Standing next to her was an angel with her face all aglow. She had long white hair and was wearing a white robe of some kind. My grandmother was happy to see me and I felt a great deal of warmth coming from her and I wanted to stay with her. Then the angel spoke directly to me and said, 'you have a gift. You must go back and help others to crossover. Do not be frightened, for you will be guided.' Before I knew it, I was waking up in the recovery room."

"Whoa, what you're saying is that you had a near death experience," I commented.

"Shortly after this experience, I began to hear spirits calling to me," Lynn continued. "As a little girl, I sometimes could even see spirits. That's when my family began to think I was a rather weird kid and that's when my mother took me to see the Indian medicine man. That's when the medicine man confirmed my gift to communicate with the spirit world. It's not uncommon for troubled spirits to make their presence known to me when I'm sleeping. They wake me up and at times I can see a faint shadowy figure standing at the foot of my bed. At times, I can even sense their pain and that's what makes me feel uncomfortable. I've even gotten into the habit of commanding the spirits to leave in the name of Jesus Christ. They always do. I believe these are the spirits who are stuck on the earth-bound plane and who are crying out for someone in the physical plane to help them. They are obviously desperate souls who are attracted to me because of my abilities. All I know is that it's been going on for a long time and I'm beginning to get tired of repressing this energy. It's starting to take its toll on me."

"Have you ever used your ability?" I asked.

"No, I've never even come close. I thought that the term crossover meant helping terminally ill patients when they died. That's why I took the job at the hospital. I was also expecting to be guided as the angel had instructed, but nothing ever happened. I didn't know they meant that I should be helping lost souls who were stuck in limbo."

"So where do you go from here Lynn?"

"A couple of days ago, I was passing a church near the hospital when I saw this beautiful woman standing on the front steps. She had a lovely face and long white hair. I noticed a gleam in her eyes and her smile was a reassuring one. I suddenly realized that I knew her and thought she might work at the hospital. I was about to give her a greeting when she suddenly sent me a telepathic message. 'There is no need for you to be frightened,' she said. She then turned and quickly went inside the church. I went after her, but when I got inside the church she was nowhere to be seen. I quickly realized it was my angel." Lynn paused for a second and said, "So here I am, reporting for duty Mr. Angel!"

CHAPTER 23

▼

THE PLAN

Still sitting in Maxwell's, Lynn and I continued talking when Rick came by carrying his briefcase. He stopped to chat with us for a bit before saying goodnight. Soon after Rick left, Lynn and I ordered dinner.

"As you may have guessed, I've been doing a lot of thinking," Lynn commented. "I've come to the conclusion that by not doing the release I might be jeopardizing my own chances for spiritual growth so I'd like to ask you a favor."

"Certainly, what is it," I replied.

"That no matter how much assurance the angel tried to give me, I still get apprehensive just thinking about giving up my body to some strange spirit," Lynn explained. "You see Armand, I've spent my whole life trying to avoid these encounters. I'm sorry that I took my fear out on you. I didn't mean anything by what I said."

"Apology accepted," I responded smiling.

"But with your help, I'm certain that I can overcome this fear," Lynn stated.

"Listen Lynn," I began. "Please understand that you owe nothing to me, to the Seguera family or even to Maria. You are under no obligation to conduct this release and if at any time you choose not to go any further, just say so. I will understand completely. But if you decide to go ahead, I will support you in anyway that I can."

"I know and thanks," Lynn replied. "But it's not you or your family that I'm thinking about, it's me that I'm thinking of. I feel as though I've been on a collision course with this issue since my childhood. For years now I've been living in fear that some day I may have to face up to the challenge. I remember how I felt when there was even just a hint of a spirit. 'Could this be it' I would say to myself and immediately wondered if my worst fears were going to be realized. I even tried to convince myself that if God gave me this gift then he gave it to me to use and not to keep it hidden in some dark closet. You said it yourself this may be our only opportunity to deal with this issue. But I also have to admit that you did help me with my past life problem. I guess the least I can do is to stick by you with yours."

"I wasn't aware that you were dealing with such a personal problem until you got angry. You didn't call me any bad names so there's no harm done. I guess you were merely questioning my motives. You were pretty accurate, you know," I said jokingly. "Anyway, I'm very glad to see you again," I added.

It wasn't difficult for me to understand why Lynn was so apprehensive about exercising her gift. We were both familiar with the methods that are used by physical mediums when releasing spirits from their earthbound status. The method most commonly used by a physical medium is for the medium to enter into a deep trance state. Being in a trance state makes the medium receptive for the spirit to temporarily take possession of the medium's body. The medium's soul in the meantime takes a short leave of absence or just moves over a little. However, none of this can be accomplished without the medium first giving permission to the spirit. This is left up to the spirit to initially make this telepathic request. Once the possession has taken place the spirit can then begin to channel its emotional issues. These are the same issues that the spirit had taken with them to the other side and they are the issues that hamper their spiritual growth. The most frequent method of channeling that a spirit uses to vent their emotions is the shedding of real tears or it may want to speak through the medium's vocal cords. In some cases it may want to do both. Then, once these emotional issues have been fully vented, the spirit's soul will immediately withdraw from the medium's physical body. Hopefully by then the spirit will be liberated from the emotional bonds that hold it and can be freed to move on into the other realms of existence. At least, that they way it's supposed to work.

However, there were still some things that I needed to know about Lynn's past experiences therefore I decided to make another inquiry. "I know that you went to the other side during your near death experience and again during the past life regression," I asked. "You never had anything extraordinarily bad happen during any of those experiences, did you?" I inquired.

"No," Lynn replied. "It was you who made me secure by protecting my body during the regression experience. That's what I' asking of you now, to please be my protector one more time with Maria," Lynn asked with a serious tone in her voice.

"Of course I will," I quickly responded.

When the medium makes its body available during a release session the physical body becomes vulnerable and therefore in need of a protector. The protector is someone who will watch over the medium's unprotected physical body until the release has been completed. It is also possible that the spirit may want to use the medium's vocal cords to channel its issues and may want to speak. At that time, the protector must be prepared to converse with the spirit. The inherent dangers with a close spirit encounter of this nature are; what if the spirit wants to vent violent emotions or tricked everyone and does not want to leave the medium's body. Of course, the most serious threat of all is the possibility that the spirit might be an evil one. That would have to be left to one's imagination.

"There is still one thing that I fear above all else Armand," Lynn commented.

"What is that?"

"Well, if you recall, your mother's spirit entered Carmel'a body without first requesting permission. At least, from what your niece's told us, it appears that way. It was no wonder that Carmela was so traumatized by the experience. I don't want Maria to do that to me," Lynn stated. "I'll make certain to try and communicate that to her before we do the release. However, there is something else that I need to ask of you."

"Sure, what is it?"

"You must promise me that you'll remain in a state of grace until the release is completed," Lynn requested.

"You have my word," I answered.

I was personally pleased with Lynn's decision and since I said that I would support her and also be her protector, so naturally I agreed to the state of grace. Because of the pending spiritual encounter, it was essential that our bodies and minds remain free of all negative influences. Negativity is something that evil spirits thrive on and Lynn and I didn't want any of those around. Being in state of grace meant no alcoholic beverages, sexual abstinence and no artificial stimulants. It also meant that daily meditation and prayer were also very important. We agreed that the program would begin as soon as we finished drinking our dinner wine. However, after a few affectionate glances we decided to wait one more day before abstaining from sex.

"You know Armand when we first went out, I thought you might be my long awaited prince charming coming to sweep me off my feet. Then, we got around to speaking about spirits right from the start. It was as though you had entered into my private domain without asking my permission. It made me feel uncomfortable that my spirit visitors were no longer exclusively mine. You confused me at first and I almost didn't want to see you anymore. But I must admit that I was attracted to you. That in the short time that we've known one another, we've shared some quite unique experiences together," Lynn reflected.

"Are you trying to tell me that Maria isn't the only reason why you came back," I said chuckling a bit.

"Armand, sometimes I think you're full if it!" Lynn exclaimed, "Besides I still think you're an angel!" Lynn added with a big grin.

*   *   *   *

Our trip to Detroit was scheduled for the weekend of May 16th, which was only ten days away. We planned to leave on Friday morning of the 15th. I phoned Michelle to inform her of our plans and to see if the apartment was still available for our use. Fortunately, it was. I wanted Michelle to arrange for a small family gathering at Marcy's on Friday evening. At that time, we would attempt to communicate with Maria and to see if she might deliver some kind of a signal. If luck was with us, maybe we could even release Maria right on the spot. Saturday night would be the reading of the Expression of Love letter to the entire family. While speaking to Michelle, she suggested that perhaps Phyllis and Sharon should be invited to conduct a psychic reading in Marcy's presence. One of the most important aspects of doing a release is to determine if the spirit is clean and offer no negative threats to the medium. Naturally, this must be accomplished sometime before proceeding any further. Michelle was certain that she could arrange a meeting with the psychics on Thursday evening. This meant that Lynn and I would have to leave for Detroit a day sooner. More importantly, it meant that Marcy would hear about Aunt Maria directly from the experts, thereby making it much more convincing.

Determining how Lynn and I were going to conduct the direct spirit encounter, we decided on a technique used by the famous parapsychologist Hans Holzer. A few years ago there was a television documentary where Hans was called on to investigate a haunting in a Greenwich Village jazz club. An apparition had been appearing to the employees around closing time. During a preliminary study of the property, it was determined that the infamous Aaron Burr had been the original owner of the building.

Aaron Burr had been known to be an extremely ambitious man and that part of his character included a strong possessive quality.

Mr. Holzer then brought in the noted physical medium, Sybil Leek. After completing the preliminary steps, Sybil sat down and immediately went into a trance state. It then appeared that she was giving up her body to the haunting or restless spirit. Almost instantaneously, or appeared that way on the program, Sybil began to utter in some strange sounding voice, not her own, "Get out! Get out! This is not your home."

Hans began to speak softly and compassionately to the spirit's voice. Hans assured the spirit that everything was under control and that the spirit no longer needed to linger in order to protect the house. That is was okay for the spirit to move on and to seek spiritual growth in the higher planes of existence. It was difficult to determine if Hans was really speaking with the spirit of Aaron Burr. In any case, the spirit appeared to have been released, inasmuch as it never made another appearance at the jazz club again.

The plan was for Lynn and I to adopt portions of Hans Holzer's methods and to incorporate a few techniques of are own. I wasn't certain as to what degree of a trance state Lynn might enter. There was also the possibility that Maria may want to use Lynn's vocal cords to express her emotions and that I may even be called upon to converse with her spirit, just like Hans did with Aaron Burr's spirit.

Since Maria was seeking help from her family, it seemed only appropriate that the four brothers, including Marcy, Lynn and Michelle should be the ones present for the Friday night spirit encounter.

I felt a deep sense of responsibility for telling my family about our mother's appearance and about our long forgotten about Aunt Maria. The attendance during the spirit communication session would be extremely crucial. I realized that no matter how the letter that I was going to send them was worded it would still sound unbelievable. But if I could get the letter out of them in a day or two, at least their thinking process would have already begun.

Then, just as I was about to mail the letters, Lynn phoned and asked, "I just received a dream message from Maria. But before I tell you the dream, there's something that I have to ask you."

"Sure, what is it?"

"Does your sister have a box of old family photographs somewhere in her dining room?" Lynn inquired.

"Yes, she does. There's a shoebox just full of old family photographs that Marcy's been putting together for the family. In fact, I saw the box when we were in the house," I replied.

"The dream started with a large group of people preparing to conduct a séance in Marcy's dining room. Then, for some strange reason, everyone quickly heads for the basement, including me. Once in the basement, everyone formed a circle. But for some reason I find myself standing alone outside the circle. Suddenly, I hear a female voice speaking directly to me, 'you must make certain to look at the box of old family photographs that are in the dining room. There must only be one other very important family member present.' At that very instant, I found myself standing next to you on the front porch of the house. That is when the dream ended," Lynn concluded.

Naturally, there was no way of knowing if the message was really from Maria. But we now knew enough about our previous dream experience not to doubt the messages being conveyed, so we decided to drop the plans for a family group session. Instead, we would incorporate the viewing of the photographs. We then assumed that the one important family member referred to in the dream was me. One comforting side effect to the dream was that Lynn had begun to get control of her fear.

"Lynn, are you certain that I didn't point out the box of pictures to you?" I inquired inquisitively.

"No. I don't recall you showing me anything like that," Lynn responded.

"That's funny, because I meant to," I commented.

"Why do you think Maria wants me to look at those photographs?" Lynn asked.

"Those pictures have been lying around the house for many years," I explained. "We really don't know who everyone is in those pictures. I do know however, that there are a number of photographs of my mother and her sisters taken in their youth. Perhaps Maria is in one of those pictures and she may want you to see what she looks like. If you recall, Carmela had viewed those same pictures the night of the Duluth Street incident."

"Are you suggesting that the photographs might be used as a catalyst for putting me into a trance, just like your mother's diamond ring did to Carmela?"

CHAPTER 24

▼

DESPITE THE DEVIL

Between making copies of the letter and getting copies of the cassette made, I was quite busy during the last week of preparations. As the time grew nearer, the outlook for reading the letter to my family was making me a little nervous. Therefore, in order to help myself clam down, I began practicing in the evenings by reading the letter aloud. I couldn't understand my apprehension, because I had given presentations to hundreds of stockbrokers and employees all over the country. I'd even given presentations to the firm's management staff, including the president. Public speaking was one of my strengths and wondered why I was feeling this way. First of all, I was anxious for my family to believe the story and that our mother's love had always been there for us, even after her death. Mainly, I didn't want them to reject the story, because their love energy was badly needed in order to release Maria. Like the voice in the dream, "Family love is the most powerful force in the universe!"

I'd been so busy that I'd forgotten all about Marcy and so I brought it up during my next conversation with Michelle. "Aunt Marcy is coming here for dinner tonight," Michelle started. "I have to go over the arrangements with her, so I have no choice but to tell her about Maria. Besides, we can't do anything without her cooperation anyway. Personally, I think she'll take the news pretty well. She may even go home and run down into the basement and tell Maria to get the heck out of there. I don't think she'll be afraid to stay in the house, one bit! If you remember, she didn't seem to be disturbed after the last incident."

✶   ✶   ✶   ✶

Friday evening I made my first visit to Lynn's apartment in the Bronx. I'd never been there before and can't say that I was looking forward to the special vegetarian meal that Lynn was preparing. She had a much larger apartment than mine and in addition, in the distance there was a view of the Empire State Building. This was going to be our last time being together before our trip to Detroit. It was very important that we carefully go over all the details of our plan.

The plan was for Michelle to pick us up at the airport on Thursday afternoon. That would give us plenty of time to go over the plans with Michelle and Stan. Marcy, Phyllis and Sharon were then due to arrive sometime around seven. Then, Friday evening would be spent at Marcy's, with Lynn scanning through the old photographs. At that time, we would be prepared for anything out of the ordinary, even the appearance of Maria's apparition. Saturday morning, Stan and I would replace Marcy's broken basement windows. Also at that time, we would conduct a thorough search for the brown-colored cigar-box, including the precious stone. Sometime before the reading, I would make an attempt to have a private conversation with Rudy. Saturday evening, the entire family would gather at Marcy's for the reading of the letter. Afterwards, I would distribute copies of the letter and the cassette tapes to each of the senior family members. On Sunday, our flight to New York was scheduled to leave at six o'clock in the afternoon. Hopefully, our mission will have been accomplished.

Saturday morning, we took a long walk around Lynn's neighborhood. However, we continued to thoroughly discuss our contingency plans. It was important that we knew what to do just in case something went wrong.

That evening, Lynn had a private function to attend, so I decided to head back to Brooklyn. It was already late in the afternoon when I boarded the elevated southbound Broadway local subway at 238th Street. The train was relatively empty when I entered the subway car and I had no particular thought on my mind when I sat on the seats facing west. At this time of the day the sun was already low in the western sky. Then, just as the train was pulled out of the station, I closed my eyes to allow the bright rays of the sun to warm my face. I was sill daydreaming when the train approached the bridge that crosses the Harlem River. At this point in the ride, the train was moving slowly and very rhythmically. Suddenly, the sunlight began to flicker repeatedly between the steel girders that support the bridge. Although, my eyes were closed, I was sensitive to the rapidly flickering shadows being made upon my face.

Suddenly, and without any reason, I impulsively opened my eyes into the warm inviting sun. Strangely enough, I was able to stare directly into the sun without having any glare nor did I have to blink. Even the sound of the moving train faded into complete silence. My next impulse was to turn my head and look out the window to see what was behind me. But before I even turned, something told me exactly what I was going to view, even though I had never traveled this southbound line before. What I saw was not unusual. It was a row of red brick apartment buildings that were situated on the high ridge overlooking the river. The buildings were being bathed in the soft orange light from the setting sun. To my surprise, this was the manifestation of a recurring dream that I had been experiencing since my childhood. The scene looked tranquil, just as the dream had always been. For those few precious seconds, it felt as though time had been suspended.

Then, from somewhere behind me, I heard a male voice speaking to me slowly and very distinctly. The voice said, "Despite the devil, we will make it." Just then the train pulled into the next station and the noise returned to normal. I quickly turned to see if anyone was standing behind me, but I saw no one. I was so impressed by the experience that I wanted to get off the train and call Lynn. Instead, I just continued on.

During the remainder of the trip, I kept thinking what kind of collective consciousness was at work here? Could events in our lives be predestined right from birth? Perhaps it was just one of those past life regression experiences, like Lynn had. Whatever it was, no doubt it had been stored somewhere deep inside my unconscious and it was just waiting for the right moment to divulge itself. So what about this devil? Was he lurking about in the shadows, just waiting for an opportunity to strike? However, the inner voice that had spoken to me sounded so reassuring that it gave me the added confidence that I needed to follow through with our plans.

The next morning, I phoned Lynn and immediately related my subway experience to her. Getting excited, she said, "Armand that's your angel talking to you. I think it's wonderful that you're getting some good positive feedback right from the other side. I feel better already just knowing that the angels are around to help."

The following day, I phoned Michelle to ask about the box of photographs. Michelle quickly began, "Uncle Armand, I've got to tell you about the dream that I had last night. The dream started with me standing in Aunt Marcy's dining room. There was a house full of people. Suddenly, everyone started rushing towards the basement. I don't know why, but I was swept right along with everyone. Then, as I was about to go down the basement stairs, something told me not to go any farther and so I ran out the side door. That's the end of the dream. It felt like I was actually in the house and I can still feel my hand turning the door-knob. Maybe it was one of the astral projection type experiences that I've read about."

Michelle's dream was quite similar to Lynn's. To me the dream message was clear and Michelle would have to be excluded from any of the close spirit encounter sessions. She was disappointed but understood that we could not afford to take any unnecessary risks.

Next, Michelle began to fill me in on who would be able to attend the Saturday evening reading and those who could not. Much had to do with the last minute notice. However, I was glad to hear that Rudy, Joanne, Frank and Rich and Debora would be present. So far, there were about seventeen persons committed to attending.

On Tuesday, I had my usual session with Diane. We hadn't discussed my psychic activities very much so I decided that this was as good a time as any. I presented her with the micro-mini version of what had been happening. This included telling her about Lynn and our plans for releasing Maria's spirit. Diane appeared to be concerned as I explained our plans, including the context of the Expression of Love letter.

"Just because you found some new enlightenment in your own life, doesn't mean you can take it upon yourself to impose it upon your family," Diane remarked. "You could come off sounding like some self-appointed TV evangelist and be totally rejected. You are taking a big risk, aren't you concerned about that?" Diane added.

"To be completely honest with you Diane, I am." I answered. "But if my mother thought it was important enough for her spirit to manifest itself, then I have no choice but to follow her example."

Diane then took time to explain the risks involve when dealing with a restless spirit. I explained that Lynn and I were completely aware of them and that we had remained in a state of grace ever since Lynn made the decision. Diane wished me well and then asked if we might need some assistance from some expert mediums that she knew in the field. Thanking her, I said we would rely on the Detroit experts, for this one.

That same afternoon, Michelle phoned again, this time to complain about Ramona. Sounding a bit irritated, she said, "Guess what? Ramona wants to borrow the box of old photographs from Aunt Marcy this coming weekend. Ramona says that for a long time now she's wanted to study them. I can't get over her wanting to take the pictures at such a crucial time," Michelle explained.

"At this point, nothing would surprise me Michelle. Maybe Maria has been trying to communicate with Ramona too," I told her.

The following day, which was Wednesday, Rick and I went for lunch. I had already filled him in on our release plans and didn't waste any time telling him about my Bronx train experience. I also described how my inner voice spoke to me and said, "Despite the devil, we will make it!"

"You don't have to tell me what Lynn said. I already know what she said, angels right?" Rick remarked.

"Right."

"Do you know exactly where you were at the time of the incident," Rick asked.

"Sure, it was just after the train pulled out of the 225th Street station," I responded.

"You were traveling south right?" Rick reiterated. "That means you were just beginning to cross over the Harlem River," he added.

"That's exactly right," I responded.

"Do you have any idea what that part of the river is called?" Rick asked.

"No, I have no idea," was my response.

"It's called, 'Spuyten Duyvil.' In Dutch, it means, 'spit on the devil.' Haven't you ever heard that expression before?" Rick expressed.

"I've heard the expression 'spit on the devil' but I've never heard it associated with that name, Spitting Dievill," I commented with my mispronunciation.

"Spuyten Duyvil," Rick corrected me. "That's the part of the Harlem River where in the sixteen and seventeen hundreds, the Dutch bootleggers used to cross the river in order to smuggle rum onto Manhattan Island. Because of the river's strong currents, it was considered a very dangerous spot to attempt a crossing. Something to do with the tides, I suppose. Apparently, a lot of men died who tried," Rick explained.

I couldn't believe it, despite the devil; spit on the devil it all sounded the same to me. How did my unconscious know? Again, I had no explanation.

Rick then took some time to caution me about the devil and the negative spirit entities that might be hanging around. This was enough to make me think about the gurgling sewer dream and some frightening stories that I'd read. Then, for a moment I allowed my imagination to get the best of me, so after leaving for home that afternoon, I stopped at the local church and poured a bottle of holy water. Back in my apartment, I placed the holy water, a small crucifix, a rosary and a Bible into a brown leather shoulder bag. Since I was also aware that the light was poor in the storage room, I included a flashlight. When or how I would use any of these items, I had no idea. It just made me feel better knowing that I would have backup kit with me. Now the only thing missing was some dramatic background music, I thought humorously to myself.

The following morning I met Lynn at LaGuardia Airport. She looked fresh, well rested and as beautiful as ever. She also looked ready to face the challenge that lay ahead. Then with Lynn at my side and the backup kit slung over my shoulder, we boarded the plane for Detroit.

CHAPTER 25

▼

A CLEAN SPIRIT

During our ride from the airport, Michelle talked about Marcy's skeptical reaction to the news about a spirit being in her basement. However, Marcy had agreed to be present at the family gathering and was looking forward to what the mediums had to say on the subject. She also indicated that she didn't mind everyone coming to her place on Friday or Saturday evening. But because of the late notice, there wasn't sufficient time for her to properly prepare anything. Michelle told her not to worry that she and Ramona would take care of everything and prepare some Nachos. As far as Michelle was concerned everything was now ready for the weekend.

We spent the rest of the afternoon going over our plans, relaxing and then just waiting for our guests. No sooner did my sister enter the house when she immediately remarked, "I understand that I'm supposed to have some kind of a spirit residing in my basement. Well, you can't prove it by me. Everything seems pretty normal and I certainly haven't had anything disturbing me in my sleep."

"Well, we aren't entirely certain yet. That's the reason we're conducting this reading," I stated. "But it's not just any old spirit, it's our Aunt Maria!"

"Aunt who?"

"Maria!"

"I never heard of any Aunt Maria. How is she supposed to be related?" Marcy inquired.

'She was Ma's oldest sister and she died in 1920. That's why we never heard anything about her," I responded.

"How did you find out all this information?" Marcy continued to inquire.

"Through dreams and I also phoned our Cousin Margarita in Canatlan," I answered.

"Dreams? Sounds pretty far fetched to me," Marcy remained skeptical. "So, why does she stay in the basement when there's a whole big house for her to roam around in?"

"Because it's damp down there," I answered. "My research says that spirits need to be around dampness"

"Then she must be awfully uncomfortable, because I'm always running the dehumidifier in the basement," Marcy stated. "But come to think of it, I've often wondered why Tinkerbell never goes down there," she added.

None of what I was saying sounded convincing, not even to me. Just then, there was a knock on the door. It was Phyllis and Sharon coming to my rescue. As they entered the kitchen, everyone exchanged warm greetings and Phyllis introduced Sharon to everyone. Sharon had a serious expression and wore a pair of metal-rimmed glasses. Her hair was swept back into a bun and she reminded me of a substitute schoolteacher. It had been almost two years since I saw Phyllis at Rudy's barbecue and I'm not even certain if she remembered me. It was a pleasure to see that she hadn't.

Michelle immediately invited everyone into the living room where we made ourselves comfortable. Lynn and I sat on the couch and Marcy sat in the large stuffed armchair. Sharon sat on a straight-backed wooden kitchen chair that Stan had brought into the room especially for her.

We spent the next few moments getting acquainted with the medium before getting down to business. Then Phyllis took charge, "First of all, let me explain that I've told Sharon nothing about why she is here, other than that she is going to conduct a reading. Armand, why don't you explain to Sharon what's on your mind."

Naturally, I was happy to oblige. I began with a brief summary of my dream activity along with some key events and some of the reasons why we thought there may be a spirit in the basement. I then began with a series of questions. "What we would like for you to do, is to verify if there really is a restless spirit in the Duluth Street house? And if there is, could you please verify the identity of that spirit. In other words, is the spirit really our Aunt Maria? If not, then who is it? Then, for Lynn's sake, is the spirit a friendly one? And is there some sort of a family heirloom involved in this situation?" I still had a couple of more things on my mind, so I asked, "Can spirits change there place of residence and can they cause a house to be robbed? We're also curious as to the technique you use to release spirits from a house. My last question is, if this really is a family matter, why was Lynn chosen to receive Maria's messages?"

Sharon began by explaining, "Yes, a restless spirit can change their place of residence, especially, if they're of a possessive nature and are attracted to some material object. It's also possible that the spirit can be strongly attracted to someone living in the physical world too. So if the restless spirit is your aunt, she could very well have had a deep attachment to your mother. That's not uncommon in the spirit world and it's not uncommon in our world for that matter. Your mother was no doubt attracted to her children. It is simple, love produces attachments."

"As for thieves," Sharon explained again, "yes, restless spirits are quite capable of attracting negative elements, especially if the house is void of its protective spirits. Restless spirits want attention and will attempt to influence whomever they can. People tend to place demonic connotations on restless spirits when all they want is to depart. Unfortunately, they are grounded by their negative issues."

"Most houses are full of spirits," Sharon continued. "Some spirits protect the house and will help to keep out any negative elements that try to infiltrate the home. There are also spirits who have existed there long before the houses were even built. However, these are usually harmless spirits who mind their own business. Then there are some spirit's who make a fuss and may need to be removed from the premises. All that's needed is to have four people sit around a table holding hands. The circle is used for stimulating the human psychic energy. That energy is needed in order for the medium to communicate with the spirits. As a point for focusing everyone's energy, a lit candle is usually placed in the center of the table. I always begin by reciting the 'Our Father' prayer aloud. Then when we are finished reciting the prayer, I snap my fingers and then command aloud for the spirits to abandon the premises in the name of 'Jesus Christ.' At that time the spirits will quickly depart from the premises. However, please understand that this method only removes the spirits from the premises and does not release them from their earthbound status."

Sharon continued, "After you've released a spirit from the premises in that manner the premises then becomes unprotected. Now, in order to reestablish a new and positive protection shield around the home, a white protective light must be placed over the house. This is accomplished through meditation and by visualizing a protective white light that totally surrounds and engulfs the house."

This all seemed quite simple. However, this method for removing spirits was not going over well with me. We might assume that there could still be the spirits of my Father, uncles and Cousin Paul still lingering in the house. If they weren't disturbing anyone, why bother them, we only wanted Maria, let the others rest in peace.

It was now time for Sharon to begin the reading and so Michelle dimmed the lights. Sharon sat quietly with both feet on the floor and began to meditate. Phyllis then led us in saying the "Our Father" prayer aloud. When we finished the room became very quiet again while Sharon went into her self-hypnotic trance. Everyone waited anxiously while Sharon tried to telepathically get in touch with her spirit guides.

Within just a few minutes, Sharon began to speak, "Yes, there is an active spirit entity in your family's home and yes, it is a deceased relative. The spirit is a clean spirit and therefore you have nothing to fear from the entity. However, the spirit is extremely reluctant to communicate with anyone from outside of her family, making this strictly a family matter. Her name is Maria. She is very sad and is ready to move on. There is also a strong sense of family loyalty here and a strong desire to have the family united. The Maria entity is depending on Armando to help her to take the necessary steps."

After a short pause, Sharon continued, "There is also something of value involved here. It looks like an item of jewelry, maybe a necklace of some kind. Whatever it is, it's something that needs to be passed down from mother to daughter. I'm not getting a clear picture of the item and therefore we are having difficulty describing it. It appears to be blue in color and is somewhere in the lower part of the house." There was another short pause before Sharon spoke again. "We are having a great deal of difficulty locating the object. That's all I'm getting," she added.

Again speaking, "Lynn was selected because she is an old soul companion of the spirit in question. They have been traveling together throughout the cosmos for a very long time. Again that's all I'm getting at this time," Sharon stated.

This time there was a very long pause and then Sharon began to recite poetry from other entities wanting to be heard and who were interfering with the reading. For me the reading was starting to get boring. However, I understood these readings were not meant to be entertaining. Then suddenly, Sharon interrupted her own concentration and said, "Just a moment, just a moment! I've just received an important message for Lynn." Now there was another pause before Sharon spoke again, "The message says to tell Lynn that when she sees the spirit, to direct the spirit towards the light. Again, that's all I'm getting. She then repeated the message several more times and again stated that this was strictly a family matter. It was quiet again for a very long time and there was no more voice activity coming from Sharon. Her spirit guides were no longer communicating and the reading was over.

Everyone sat quietly, each of us with our own thoughts. No one spoke as Michelle brought up the lights. I could sense that there was no point in asking anyone if they wanted to run over to Marcy's. Maria would just have to remain earthbound for another day. I couldn't get over how our family spirits kept refusing to communicate with the mediums. Perhaps they just wanted to keep things private, even on the other side.

On the way to the door, everyone thanked Phyllis and Sharon. Before Marcy left she confirmed our visit for the following evening. Marcy also promised not to look for the piece of jewelry until we were all present. It appeared that Marcy had already begun to become more receptive to our agenda. I was also proud of her, mainly because she didn't seem to have any apprehensions about going home by herself.

Later, I asked Lynn about the message that was directed to her. The one about 'directing the spirit towards the light.' Lynn said she wasn't certain what it meant, but did have some idea. For now she just wanted to give it some thought and take a wait and see approach.

Again my ear started to ring along with the faint sound of the Indian flute playing. Lying in bed, I felt quite confident that everything was under control and going as planned. Except that I was having another one of those unusual dreams. In this dream, I'm a fighter pilot flying my plane over the harbor of a large populated bay area. When suddenly, the plane is badly hit by anti-aircraft shrapnel and the plane begins to spin out of control while also catching fire. Somehow, I manage to miraculously escape the plane and then find myself standing on the shoreline watching my plane trailing smoke as it plummeted towards the water. Then, just as soon as the plane plunges into the bay, it creates a huge plume of water. A few seconds later, there is a second explosion just below the surface in the exact location where the plane had sunk.

Upon awakening, I felt extremely depressed, almost as though I had really been shot down. My first thoughts were, 'what are we doing here?' All I wanted to do was to forget everything, and take Lynn right back to New York. Who did I think I was, trying to impose my new found spiritual beliefs on my family and why I was exposing Lynn to such dangers. Again, I had become apprehensive about reading the letter. How in the world had I let this whole thing get so far out of hand? Maybe there was still enough time for me to put a halt to everything. I'll just leave the letters and tapes with Michelle for her to distribute to everyone.

Later that morning, Michelle took Lynn shopping. I stayed behind and wondered what I was going to do. I had wanted to surprise my brother Rich at his office and I also wanted to speak with Rudy. Being completely undecided, I took a long walk. This was my old childhood neighborhood and as I walked around, I found most of the street names to be quite familiar. It wasn't long before I found myself standing in front of Saint Lawrence church. This was the church where I had received my first communion and where I had sung in the choir. Opening the door, I entered. At this time of day the church was empty and as I made my way down the aisle I couldn't help but notice that the church hadn't changed much over the years. Then, I slipped into one of the pews where I knelt to pray. I prayed that I could fulfill my mother's last wish and unite the family spiritually. I also prayed for Lynn's protection and that she would be able to release Maria without encountering any obstacles. Suddenly, a strong warming sensation came over me. The warm sensation began to drain away like liquid from a bottle, starting from the very top of my head and rippling all the way down through my body to the soles of my feet. By the time I left the church and returned to the house, I felt much better and eager to get on with our task.

CHAPTER 26

▼

A MOMENT TO
REFLECT

Friday evening while Lynn, Michelle and I drove over to Marcy's, I again reminded Michelle that she was not to go into the basement under any circumstances. After we arrived, Marcy greeted us at the door while Sergeant also welcomed us with some of his barking. Marcy immediately ushered everyone into the dining room and on the way I went over and turned on the light to the basement stairs. That was just in case Lynn had to use them in a hurry. We then made ourselves comfortable around the dining room table and I slung my shoulder bag over the back of the chair. Marcy wanted to put Sergeant out into the yard, but we told her to leave him inside. We knew that Sergeant had a good sense for detecting spirits and it would be better if he were close by.

After finishing our dessert, Marcy brought over the box of photographs and placed them directly in front of Lynn. It was no surprise to us that Marcy still remained skeptical and appeared to be challenging Lynn to demonstrate her psychic abilities.

We had decided that no one would attempt to distinguish any of the subjects in the pictures, unless of course if Lynn asked. Because of my trip to Mexico a couple of years ago, I was now able to identify more relatives than before. Certainly, none of us could identify Maria, if in fact she was in any of the photos.

Since Lynn had seen Maria in one of her dreams, she just might be able to identify Maria, if that were possible.

Before commencing, Lynn took a few deep breaths. There was a great deal of
anticipation amongst our small group as Lynn began to slowly scan through the
photos. I alertly watched and listened for Sergeant to bark. I wondered which of
the pictures might throw Lynn into a hypnotic state causing her to scurry towards
the basement. Occasionally, Michelle and I exchanged glances whenever Lynn
paused a little longer than usual with one particular photo.

Suddenly, Lynn began to tremble. In her hand, she was holding the picture of
the group of the young ladies at the outing in San Jeronimo. Still trembling,
Lynn's eyes began to water and even rolled around a little. We held our breaths
and waiting to see what was going to happen next. Then, just as quickly as it
started, it stopped. Lynn sat back in her chair and relaxed for a moment while I
got her a glass of water. She stopped trembling and regained her composure.

"Are you okay?" I asked.

"Yea, I'm okay." Lynn responded, while looking straight ahead. "That's
strange. I was seeing glimpses of a woman's face. She resembled the girls in this
picture," she said, still holding the photograph. "She resembled all the girls in the
seven sisters dreams and I'm certain that it was Maria."

Lynn took a moment to slowly re-examine a number of the other pictures
before placing them aside, but she continued to hold the group photo. Our only
clue as to what Maria may have looked like came from Juan Salido, who said she
had been very beautiful. After a moment, Lynn pointed to one of the girls in the
picture who had the most prominent facial features. It was someone that we
could not identify.

"There was a strong feeling as though something was trying to take possession
of me," Lynn said with shaky voice. "I just kept seeing glimpses of this woman's
face. There was no message just this face and I knew it had to be Maria."

With no more pictures to view, Marcy went upstairs while the rest of us
adjourned into the living room. Within minutes, Marcy was back with a small
beautifully decorated jewelry box. Marcy still appeared to be skeptical even as she
handed the box over to Lynn. Placing the box on her lap, Lynn opened the lid.
To our surprise, Marcy had gotten our mother's jewels out from safekeeping
where they had been stored following the first robbery. Marcy wanted to make
certain that Lynn would be handling the identical objects as those that surrounded Carmela's experience. Lying on top was a small broach, a pendant, a
cameo pin, a diamond ring and an attractive gold bracelet. Lynn began to handle
each item carefully, spending time reading the inscription inside the diamond

ring. It was the very same ring that had jolted Carmela into a hypnotic trance and sent her charging up the stairs. Again, we all waiting anxiously, but nothing happened.

With no reaction to any of the objects, Marcy took the box and went back upstairs. It wasn't long before she was back with two smaller metal art deco boxes. For a moment, I thought one of the boxes might be from my dream. The boxes were filled with more old heirlooms, such as letters, more photographs, and a few pieces of inexpensive jewelry and some old style writing pens. Still, there were no vibrations. Marcy was running out of small boxes and I was running out of ideas. Our agenda for the evening had come to an end and it was time to thank Marcy and to say goodnight.

In the car, Michelle asked, "Why didn't you just go into the basement?"

Because we didn't receive any message from Maria," I replied. "But I'm not disappointed about this evening's attempt. After all, we were only following what we thought were Maria's instructions. Besides, Lynn did get a glimpse of Maria's face and that might play some significant role later. When Maria's ready, I'm certain she'll give us a sign."

"For two people who have no experience at this sort of thing, you certainly act and talk like you know what you're doing," Michelle commented.

"We're just following the messages given to us in through our dreams. One of my dreams demonstrated that the spirit might need a boost before it can be released. That was the dream with the jet spray of water pushing the light through the lamp and hitting the ceiling. Aunt Carmen told Carmela that a white light in a dream represents a spirit. Both Carmela and I dreamt of a white light prior to my mother's appearance. So if Maria needs some energy, then we may have to wait until after the family's love energy has been generated from the gathering tomorrow night. Let's not forget that she acted up after every family gathering," I explained.

"You certainly have a lot of faith in those dreams," Michelle remarked. Although Michelle was in complete support of what we were doing, she just didn't seem too confident in the way we were going about it.

*   *   *   *

Saturday morning, Lynn, Stan and I along with the two boys, Bobby and Raymond returned to Marcy's. After entering the house, Stan and I went straight to the storage room. Leaning up against the wall was a ladder and some garden tools. The first thing we did was carry out the old Singer sewing machine and placed it under the light. We opened the cover and carefully examined each drawer looking for some secret compartments. There were none. Next, we inspected the old player piano. The old leather sacks on the piano were all dried out and again there were no secret hiding places or precious blue stone. The last items that we examined were the two steamer stand-up trunks. We opened each of the small drawers that were designed for storing valuables. Again, we found nothing. On the shelves in the storage room were some vases and dusty dishes. Stacked on the floor were some recently packed boxes, so we ignored them.

With that part of the plan carried out we started to replace the broken windows.

Marcy went back to her house cleaning leaving Lynn alone in the basement. Stan took Raymond and began to replace the storage room window from the outside. I took Bobby and we started replacing the window over the washtub. I wanted to be in a position to observe Lynn, who was standing in front of storage room. She was attempting to communicate with Maria by speaking aloud in a meditative manner. "Please give us a sign Maria. Armando and I are here to offer you love and support. We know that you need our love and understanding. Tonight, the entire Seguera family will be gathering upstairs in order to generate the love energy that's needed to help release you. Please do not be afraid. And should you need to shed tears, I am prepared to share my physical body with you in order for you to do that. All that I ask is for you to request my permission. Your time has come to embark on a new journey and to ascend up into the higher levels of existence. Just please give us a sign whenever you're ready."

Wanting to be receptive to any of Maria's messages, Lynn paused and calmly waited meditatively from time to time.

I found it a little difficult trying to put in a new pane of glass, answering Raymond's inquisitive questions and watching Lynn all at the same time. I was also somewhat uncomfortable because I had left the backup kit in the car.

Lynn was having little or no success with her attempts to make contact, but continued trying until the repairs were completed.

Afterwards, we went upstairs and Stan went to the refrigerator to get a couple of cold beers. As soon as he handed me one, I said, "Sorry Stan, I'm still in a state of grace." Stan looked at me funny and put the beer back in the refrigerator.

Then, as we were about to leave, Marcy asked, "What are you going to be reading to the family tonight?"

"I think that it's time to share the secret of our mother's appearance with the rest of the family," I answered.

"Do you think the others are ready for this revelation? I don't pretend to understand what happened that night, do you?" Marcy questioned.

"I don't pretend to know either," I responded. "But ready or not, I'm going to tell them, only because they have a right to know. What I've been trying to do for the last two years is to come up with some rational explanation and in all that time, I haven't been able to come up with anything. So the most important thing here is to be truthful. What I'm giving them is my perception of the events that led up to the incident. I also want to share some of my own personal thoughts. However, I'm going to hold off on Maria until I'm totally certain that her spirit really exists. It's going to be hard enough for them to try and comprehend one family spirit, let alone two."

*   *   *   *

Later that evening when I returned to Marcy's, Rudy was in the kitchen having a snack. There was still time before the others would begin to arrive and so I quickly seized upon the opportunity to speak with Rudy privately. We went out to the yard and made ourselves comfortable on a couple of lawn chairs. I then asked Rudy, "Do you remember if Ma ever talked about any of our relatives in Mexico?"

"Sure, all the time. She used to talk about her mother and father and was looking forward to the day we would meet them. Apparently, she was very close to her mother," Rudy explained.

"Do you recall if she ever mentioned a sister named Maria?"

"She talked about her sisters, but that was a long time ago and for other than Consuelo, Carmen and Cleofas, I don't recall any Maria. Ma was constantly reminding us that we would be meeting everyone of them very soon," Rudy recalled. "I remember Ma as being a very proud woman and she loved music. That was why Pa bought her the player piano," he added.

As Rudy continued speaking, I realized that my impressions of my mother were now becoming clearer. For the first time in my life, my mother was now becoming a living person. No longer was she just a cold stone slab lying in the grass. No longer was she, just a few articles of jewelry that I had rarely ever seen or touched. No longer was she just a stack of old photographs that never spoke or smiled. No longer was she just that mysterious woman from my childhood that no one ever spoke about or pretended as though she had never existed.

There was pride in Rudy's voice as he spoke, just as I heard him speak a few years ago. Suddenly, Frank arrived and joined us to add support to what Rudy had already said. All I had to do was to listen. They were in fact passing on to me the confidence that I needed in order for me to read the letter. It had been those repressed memories of my mother that had awakened me from some deep sleep in the first place. Ever since that evening in January of 1979, I had sought to understand the meaning behind her manifestation. The answer was now simple. All she wanted was for us not to forget the love that she had passed onto us, nor did she want us to forget the goals that she wanted us to achieve. She had never abandoned us.

Next, Michelle came out onto the back deck and announced that everyone was ready. As I walked towards the house, Rudy stopped me and said, "Oh Yea, one other thing. I finally remembered why those pictures of Ma had been put away."

"You remember?" I asked.

"It was because of you," Rudy remarked. "You missed Ma so much that you had a temper tantrum every time you saw one of her pictures. Pa and Aunt Yolanda didn't have much choice but to hide the pictures from you. I hope that answers your question."

"Sure does, thanks for remembering. Makes sense," I replied. "Guess I was a bit of a problem child."

"No, you just wanted Ma, we all did."

CHAPTER 27

▼

THE GATHERING

Before entering the house, Lynn took a hold of my hand and gently squeezed it. "I'll be at your side Armand and I know everything is going to be just fine," Lynn whispered.

Folding chairs had been carefully arranged around the living room with a few of them being placed half way into the dining room. I sat on a kitchen chair that had been placed in one corner of the living room. Sitting directly to my left, was Lynn, Rudy and then Frank. To my right, were Stan, Michelle and Rich. Marcy and my sister-in-laws Joanne and Debora made themselves comfortable on the couch. Ramona and Holly sat on the floor at everyone's feet. Patty, Paula and Freddie sat in the back. It appeared as though there were thirteen or fourteen family members present.

The humorous remarks being exchanged by the family helped to relax me. I had been thinking about using some humor to help loosen everyone up, but I found that the family was one step ahead of me. Not really knowing where to begin, I decided to get their attention by blurting out, "Did you know that our mother's spirit appeared in this house a little over two years ago?"

Instantly, the room became quiet. Then, within seconds the room came alive with questions, "You're kidding! When did this happen? Where? Who saw her? Why didn't anyone tell us?" With such and overwhelming response, all I could say, "I'm glad you asked, because that's the purpose of this gathering. To the best of my knowledge, I hope that I can explain when and how all this occurred.

However, my explanation comes in the form of a letter. I could've just mailed it to you, but then I decided it would be better if I came here in person and read it to you. So please allow me to read the letter in its unedited form. I've titled it, 'An Expression of Love.' Let me begin."

After crossing my legs, I cleared my throat and began reading aloud. "To my family, I write this letter with the inspiration that I received from our mother's spirit and I write it with the express purpose of fulfilling her dreams. It is written in order to enlighten you, to answer any questions that you may have regarding the Duluth Street incident and to dispel any rumors that you may have already heard. In effect, this story is yours as much as it is mine. Therefore, it is our mother's wish that this story be told."

"I have formalized this story in order to keep the important events and details in their proper sequential order and for you to have written documentation for your families. I am also attempting to illustrate the series of coincidences that began months before the Duluth Street incident. In some ways, I'm certain that you too may have your own pieces of this puzzle to add to the story. Your pieces of the story are those that I am not aware of and perhaps you will share them with us after the reading is complete."

"I do not ask that you believe any part of what I'm about to tell you, I can only wish it. The story is about a journey. A journey from our hearts into the twilight sector and then back again. It is a trip full of far more love than we have ever imagined. This story represents my thoughts and my opinions as to how I perceived these events and the reasons for there occurrence."

As I continued to read, I thought about how long I had anticipated this moment. It was something that had been on my mind for over two years. How the family would perceive this unusual incident had crossed my mind hundreds of times. Soon—I would know.

The first part of the letter describes how Ramona asked me to extend an invitation on her behalf and mainly because of the family urgency dream. I then covered my trip to Mexico and the way in which the invitation was received by our relatives. Of course, there was Carmela's strange premonition about going to Detroit, her visa and the cemetery dream. Then, there was my own passenger jet dream, including my compulsive remarks at the Dallas airport. Next, came Carmela's encounter with Phyllis at the bowling alley and then I slowly read my second hand account of the apparition and the circumstances surrounding the event.

Besides the sound of my voice the only other sound was that of the slow churning tape-recorder. On occasion, someone would glance over to Marcy,

Ramona or Michelle. Perhaps they were looking for some kind of a reaction. The three women listened very carefully knowing quite well that they would be the center of attention as soon as the reading was completed. Since we were in Marcy's house, there were even those who looked around trying to visualize the incident as it was being described.

Upon completing the detailed portion of the letter, I immediately began reading my interpretation of the events and why I thought that they had occurred. My aloud reading of the letter continues, —"During my last visit to San Jeronimo, Aunt Carmen showed me two tear stained letters written by our mother to her mother Julia. The letters were written just prior to her passing. Our mother had written that she was totally aware of her imminent passing and that it had been her desire to have us taken to Mexico, so that we could be raised by her mother and her sisters. Unfortunately, due to her illness, she was unable to obtain the necessary legal documentation for leaving the country. I have included copies of these letters in the packages that I have prepared for each of you and so that you may read those letters in the privacy of your homes. However, let me read the last letter that she wrote to her mother Julia,"

To My Beloved Mother,

I hope that this letter finds you and the rest of the family in good health, thanks be to God.

If only I could become an eagle for one day. I would fly to San Jeromino so I could spend that day with the family. I want nothing more than to hug and embrace you all for one last time. Only then would I return to my family in Detroit, so that I can die in peace with my children at my side.

I have been so proud for having had you as my mother. My love and my spirit will be with you always.

Your Loving Daughter

Adelina Rivera Seguera

"I'm totally certain now that our mother cried for us, embraced us and gave each of us very important last minutes instructions. She then poured her heart out and gave us all the love that we would need for our future survival. It is a love that can be shared with others and it is a love that can be passed onto our children. There is no doubt in my mind or in my heart that that expression of our mother's love is still within us."

"After our mother passed on, her desire to stay and protect her children was obsessively strong and so her spirit remained in the house. Having died at such a young age, she knew that the job of rearing her five children had not been completed according to her wishes and her expectations."

"In the spirit world, it is sometimes necessary for spirits, when attempting to help other spirits, to call on their earthly relatives when extreme measures are required. It is also well known that when people are in a near death situation, they begin to see or sense the presence of relatives who have since passed on. Therefore, it is logical to assume that our mother's spirit should be called upon to help her sister Cleofas spirit to cross over to the other side."

"And since the purpose of our mother's manifestation was to unify the family, she needed to leave a sign. This was an extreme measure on her part and signifies the importance of the manifestation."

"At this time, we do not know if Carmela ever actually saw the spirit or if she was in some kind of hypnotic state. This is something we will not know until she is ready to relate the experience."

"Naturally, I began to ask myself what does this mean. For one thing, I had learned that we are a sensitive people, inheriting a spirituality that has been passed down to us from our Indian ancestors. That was long before the first house of worship was ever built. It means that spirituality is something that exists at all levels of existence and that it knows no boundaries. It is the kind of spiritual energy that nurtures our creative abilities."

"Therefore, we should look for these abilities within ourselves and in our children. Those abilities may be what are needed for them to communicate their own expressions of love to others. Many of these expressions may appear simple or as insignificant achievements. But no matter how small the achievement, they are all important to the total expression of love. For one of our greatest gifts is the freedom to explore any or all avenues of expression. Another is to love without fear, so that we may share this love with others in whatever manner we so desire. Remember we must first respect ourselves before we can respect others. Try to understand that it is the unification of the family that generates the bonding love, mainly because it knows no boundaries and therefore it remains unconditional."

"We have a family where many of our children still seek self-identity and still crave neglected childhood attention. We have a family full of broken and unhappy marriages. In essence, we have somewhat of a love-starved family, both emotionally and spiritually. Our own spiritual growth may also be stagnated.

Each one of our children would love to have a close intimate conversation with his or her parents and to speak openly and freely with us."

"Now, although our mother's spirit has moved from the Duluth Street house, the job is still far from complete. It gives me great joy to know that her spirit was in the house. But by remaining, she affected her own spiritual growth and she may not be able to rest in peace until her wishes are fulfilled. So let us learn to live in peace and in harmony."

"Although we were all thrown into an emotional stupor on that bleak day in October of 1936, I know with all my heart that we have always loved one another. Therefore, we have not gathered here to judge our past actions, but to forgive our ignorance of them."

"There is no doubt in my mind that at this very moment, the spirits of our mother and father have gathered here with us to share in this joyous occasion. Therefore, and with all due forgiveness and in order to free the spirits of our parents for further spiritual growth and for the spiritual growth of our children and their children, I propose that in the name of God, our mother and father and in the spirit of our family's heritage and traditions, that we exhibit an open display of our love and affection for one another from this day forth. Let us no longer harbor our expressions of love, but convey that love with warmth and embraces."

After completing the reading I immediately stood and everyone followed my example. With tears in many of our eyes, everyone started to exchange embraces. I embraced Rudy first. Next, I embraced Marcy, then Frank and Rich. It was a wonderful moment and I could feel the energy circulating throughout the room. Hopefully, we had fulfilled our mother's wishes and that we had also generated sufficient enough love energy for releasing Maria.

After the rounds of embraces had been completed, Rudy began by asking Marcy, Michelle and Ramona to tell the family their first hand accounts of what had happened. Now after two years of keeping the incident a secret, it was their turn to speak. First, Ramona gave her eyewitness account of what transpired and what Carmela spoke while in the trance. She also described Carmela's immediate response and how withdrawn Carmela became following the incident. Next, Michelle supported what Ramona had said and took her time describing the actual materialization of the apparition. She also said how certain she was that it was her grandmother. However, Marcy continued to remain a bit reserved regarding the incident. And she acted as though she still wasn't convinced that anything had happened. The girls had everyone's complete attention and afterwards they were more than happy to answer any and all questions.

Reactions to the story were mixed amongst the family members. Some showed signs of extreme skepticism while others were quick to believe the story. A few like Rudy wanted to keep an open mind on the subject and wanted to make this a new beginning for the family's bonding. I couldn't ask for anything more. It was now up to each individual to try and comprehend the story in their own way

Then Paula spoke up and said, "You know, Uncle Armand, I've been dreaming about this house a lot lately. As a matter of fact, I just had a dream about three nights ago. I dreamt that there was this long ladder extended upward into a blue sky. Then there was a woman dressed in a white blouse and a long black skirt climbing the ladder. I couldn't make out who it was. Anyway it was a weird dream."

Next Holly spoke up, "About a month ago, I also dreamt of this house. I was standing on the roof and there was this beautiful bald eagle circling overhead. What I remember the most is how blue the sky was."

Not knowing if the word had gotten out, I assumed that Paula and Holly knew nothing about Maria. And if they did know, it didn't matter. Both dreams fit within the main theme. Michelle also had her basement dream experiences to share, but omitted her storage room search. Ramona hadn't said anything, except that she also had had a strong urge to see the photographs again.

Then Frank accidentally slipped off his chair and exclaimed, "Someone just pushed me." Not everyone laughed, thinking that it may not have been an accident. Could Maria's spirit be in the room?

I then distributed the copies of the "Expression Love' letter plus copies of the Carmela psychic reading tape. There was still an air of excitement as the gathering broke up and people began to leave. Lynn, Michelle, Stan and I stayed after everyone had left. Marcy seemed to be overwhelmed by the show of emotions that we had all shared. We then had some coffee while Lynn took another look through the photographs. When she got to the group picture she held it a while, but nothing happened. We said goodnight to Marcy and left feeling pretty good about what we had just accomplished.

Upon our arrival at Michelle's home, she immediately gave me an embrace and said, "Thank you Uncle Armand that was one of the nicest evenings of my life. I got to hug everyone including my parents and I even went around the room twice just to make certain that I didn't miss anyone." She then asked, "Any sign from Maria?"

"No, I'm afraid not," I answered disappointedly.

CHAPTER 28

▼

CRYSTAL TEARS

Back at the apartment, Lynn and I stayed up late as usual to recap the events of the day. We were extremely happy with the success of the reading and mainly with the sharing of affection. But tomorrow we would be returning to New York and Maria had somehow still eluded us. Perhaps this proved that the whole thing was just a hoax and that our imaginations had fooled us and the psychic experts into thinking that there really was a spirit. Disappointed because we hadn't heard from Maria, I found it difficult to get to sleep. My ears were now buzzing instead of the usual loud ringing and for a brief moment I even heard the flute. Still restless, I tossed and turned in order to find a comfortable position.

Just then, Lynn asked, "Are you still awake?"

"Yes, I'm still awake. Wide awake in fact," I responded

"Maria was just here!" Lynn remarked in her usual soft manner. "I just needed a moment to think about it before I told you," she added.

"Maria was just here!" I exclaimed as though in disbelief.

"I was just lying here on my side facing the wall when something told me to open my eyes," Lynn explained. "Then when I did, Maria was right there staring at me from just a few feet away. It was a little spooky, but I knew it was her. It was the same face that I had seen glimpses of when I was looking at the photos. She had dark eyes and her dark hair was brushed back. Then, without moving her lips, she sent me a telepathic message. She indicated to me that she was extremely pleased with the family gathering and that she was now ready. Simultaneously, she slowly blinked her eyes as an acknowledgement of our mutual understanding. Her face then faded away into the darkness!" When Lynn finished describing the incident, she calmly said, "Tomorrow we've got to go back to Marcy's."

In the morning, Lynn and I enjoyed breakfast at Michelle's while Stan played the "Expression of Love" tape recorded from the previous evening. It sounded as though the reading went smoothly, but I was slightly uncomfortable at the amount of emotion that I had expressed. Suddenly, the phone rang, it was Rich wanting to drive Lynn and me out the airport. I agreed and told him to meet us at Marcy's around three o'clock.

After packing our bags, we said goodbye to Stan and the boys. Michelle then chauffeured Lynn and I over to Marcy's. But before leaving, Michelle got out of the car so that she could hug and kiss the both of us. She also wished us luck and asked if I would call her before we left for the airport.

Even from outside on the porch we could hear Marcy playing the piano. After hearing the doorbell, she stopped to answer the door. Once inside the house, we just dropped our luggage off in the foyer. Since there was no barking, I assumed Sergeant was apparently out in the yard. Then while we enjoyed a cup of hot tea, I informed Marcy about Maria's midnight visit. I then told her that we were going to go into the basement. She then asked if there was anything she could do. We thanked her and told her that we would be just fine.

Once Lynn and I were in the basement, I turned on some lights and opened the storage room door. Meanwhile Lynn found two folding chairs and placed them several feet in front of the door and ironically it was directly above the drain. It was dark inside the room except for a small amount of light that was filtering in through the newly installed windowpane. I stared into the room and could see nothing unusual. Upstairs, Marcy surprised us by beginning to play a medley of old traditional Mexican ballads. We now had the background music that we needed in order to assist us with the release. However, in my excitement I had forgotten the backup kit, but then again, I knew we weren't going to need it.

Lynn sat down while I sat to her left, almost facing her just a few feet away. We immediately began to recite the "Our Father" prayer aloud. Afterwards, Lynn put herself into a mediating position with both feet flat on the floor. She then sat back and rested her hands on her lap with the palms turned upward. Then, after taking a deep breath, Lynn began to silently meditate and induce herself into a self-hypnotic state.

Only a few moments had passed when, suddenly, Lynn began to shed tears silently and without sobbing. The tears were the size of large pearls and had somewhat of a yellow tint to them. They rapidly popped out of Lynn's lower lid, one tear quickly followed by another. The tears dripped onto Lynn's bare arms and flowed down to her wrists, whereupon they dripped to the floor. I could clearly hear the pitter-patter of the first tears as they hit some old dried newspapers that were beneath her feet.

My assumption was that Maria's spirit had already entered Lynn's body and that Maria was in the process of releasing her remorseful emotions. I waited with a great deal of anticipation for Maria to speak through Lynn's vocal cords. However, no spoken words came forth; instead Lynn began to hum aloud in a distorted harmony with the music that Marcy was playing upstairs. I also noticed that the tears had lost there unusual yellow tint and had now become crystal clear. Lynn's eyelids had remained partially closed throughout this entire session.

Upstairs, I heard the doorbell ring. Marcy stopped playing and I could hear her walking overhead to the front door. At the same time Lynn stopped humming and so did the flow of tears. It was Rich and Debora, who had arrived to take us to the airport. I immediately overheard Rich ask, "Where's Armand?" Marcy told him I was in the basement. I could then hear him walking in the direction of the basement stairs. My immediate concern was what if Rich decides to come down the stairs? Being Lynn's protector, I could not leave her side and had no choice but to wait and see if I had to intercept him. Instead, he walked past the stairs and went into the kitchen to get a beer out of the refrigerator. A cold beer was something that I would appreciate about now too. I thanked God when I heard Rich walking back into the living room. But before I realized it, Lynn was out of her trance and shivering. I quickly found a sweater in one of the clothing baskets and placed it over her shoulders.

Lynn's first words were, "She's gone! Maria's gone and she's okay!"

Lynn stopped crying and dried her eyes with the handkerchief that I handed her. "Oh my God! What an experience!" Lynn repeated a few times. She then got up from the chair and exclaimed again, "I can't believe what I just went though! It was such an unbelievable experience!" she repeated again. "What I've got to do is take a break and get myself back together."

"Why don't you go up to the bathroom on the second floor." I suggested. I'll bring you a glass of water," I offered. Then, without any hesitation, Lynn quickly made her way up the stairs.

I was about to close the storage room door when I decided to make one final inspection. On the shelves were those vases and dishes and then for some reason, I just moved them aside and saw a brown wooden box that was about the size of a shoebox. The box was covered with dust and after taking it off the shelf I took it out into the light to clean it off. This was no ordinary box and I wondered why it had been in the storage room when it should have been on display in the living room. It was a beautiful wooden oak antique music box. Thinking back, I recalled that as children, we were never allowed to play with this box. I lifted the cover that exposed a pronged brass cylinder that was housed inside the box. Situated beneath the box was a small metal knob that I reached for and gently turned. It was the lid to a small compartment and no sooner did it open when suddenly a black object fell to the floor. I bent down to pick up it up and discovered that it was small black velvet pouch. The pouch was quite heavy considering its size. My heart began to pound like an explorer about to make a major discovery. Opening the pouch, I reached in with my fingers and brought out a beautiful blue beaded rosary with a small ornate silver cross. The chain was also made of silver. It was a very exquisite looking rosary and I couldn't believe my eyes.

I couldn't help but stare at this beautiful object. I then kissed the rosary and made the sign of the cross. This rosary represented the only physical piece of evidence that connected all the dreams and our mysterious coincidences together. Returning the rosary to the pouch, I quickly turned off the lights and headed for the staircase. But then, just as I was about to go up the stairs, I couldn't help but notice Tinkerbell casually sitting on the steps and making his visual inspection of the basement.

Upstairs, Marcy was just entering the kitchen when I made my way to the refrigerator to get some ice water for Lynn. Then while pouring the water, I casually whispered to Marcy, "Maria's gone!"

"Gone, what do you mean by gone?" Marcy exclaimed.

"She's been released from the storage room and is on her way to the higher levels of existence," I answered. "If you want the details, why don't you go upstairs and get them directly from Lynn. You can take this glass of water up to her while you're at it and why don't you take this pouch with you?" I believe it's something that belongs to you," I said while I confidently handed her the pouch.

"What's this?"

"I think it might be a turquoise beaded rosary," I remarked. "Remember what Sharon said at the reading? That the piece of jewelry in the house was something that was to have been passed down from mother to daughter—and so I guess that's you!"

After removing the rosary from the pouch, Marcy stared at it in awe. "Where did you find this?" Marcy asked.

"It was in the music box. Why don't you take it with you to show Lynn," I suggested. "Lynn doesn't know that it's been found. I'm certain that she'll be very surprised."

Still acting bewildered by the entire situation, Marcy took the pouch and the glass of water and went upstairs. I then got myself a cold beer and joined Rich and Debora in the living room.

Coming down the stairs, Lynn had to step over Sergeant who was resting quietly on the bottom step and who made no attempt to move. Lynn's eyes were still a bit watery, but her expression was absolutely beautiful and she even looked angelic. She had a gleam in her eyes and appeared to be at peace with herself.

I then went upstairs to phone Michelle so I could give her the good news. Michelle was so excited that the only thing she could say was," I don't believe it. But I knew you guys could do it. This is really going to be something for me to tell my grandchildren." She then added, "I love you Uncle Armand and thank you again."

"I love you too, Michelle."

Since Rich was already heading out the door with our luggage, there wasn't time for any further comments.

*   *   *   *

On the flight back, I leaned over and gently kissed Lynn on the cheek. Lynn returned a weak smile and quickly returned to staring straight ahead. It appeared that she was deeply engrossed with her own personal thoughts. Out of respect for her privacy, I decided not to disturb her anymore.

It was difficult to try and comprehend where this whole thing had started or ended, if in fact, it had ended. There really was no rational explanation and my concept of reality had come to include an invisible dimension of existence. How the unseen world of spirits and angels could silently weave themselves in and out of our lives was totally incomprehensible. Most amazing was how our dreams could be influenced.

The energy that Lynn and I had used during this entire course of events was remarkable. We hardly slept because of our long conversations that lasted until all hours and even into the morning. Then to have our sleep interrupted by dreams on a regular basis was incredible. We spent hours trying to interpret each dream and because they were coming at such a rapid pace we hardly finished with one interpretation before there was another. It even took time to jot down all these dreams into a dream logbook. Not only were there dreams, but what about all those unexpected events that came into our lives without any warning. We spent time discussing each event, plus our theories and more importantly we were constantly going over our plans. Then each evening, we spent time summarizing all the events that had occurred during the day. Yet, we were never tired, even after a few hours sleep. Somehow, I was able to do my job, handle my studies and hang out with my friends once in awhile. The best part to all this was the sharing of affection with my family and the feeling I had for having fulfilled my mother's last wish. And because of this experience, I learned that there is no shame to cry and that it doesn't hurt to embrace and to tell a family member that you love them.

Astonishingly though, I had never prayed for so much guidance in my entire life. This made me aware that none of what had happened could have been accomplished without some divine intervention. Therefore, I am totally grateful to God and his Angels for their guidance and protection.

Surprisingly, we also learned how easy it was to generate the families love energy. All that was needed was for us to have an open mind and an open heart.

CHAPTER 29

▼

THANKS FOR THE LOVE

As soon as we entered my apartment, we immediately decided to take walk. Outside, the air was fresh and the sky clear as we headed in the direction of the bay. After reaching the park that overlooked the promenade, we sat on one of the benches. Lynn then stated, "Before we discuss what happened this afternoon, I want you to know that I could never have accomplished any of this without your support. You helped me to conquer my fear and I want to thank you for being my protector. It was absolutely a beautiful experience! I have never felt so close to God as I was there on the other side. It made my work so much easier, but I'm glad it's over."

"I'm glad it's over too," I said.

"I'm so happy that you found the rosary, it was so beautiful. Marcy said you found it inside a music box, is that right?" Lynn asked.

"That's right, it was right in front of us, only we never bothered to look behind the vases that were on the shelves. I don't know if those beads are actually turquoise or agate. But then, we don't know if the stone in your dream was turquoise and it really doesn't matter, our main goal wasn't the piece of jewelry, anyway" I explained.

"You're right, what we were dealing with went far beyond anything material," Lynn commented.

"But if you want to take some time and tell me what happened later, I can wait," I remarked.

"Absolutely not, it wouldn't be fair to you and I suppose it would be best to tell you while the experience is still fresh on my mind," Lynn commented while pausing a moment to contemplate. She then took a deep breath before beginning. "It happened so fast. First I was sitting in the chair and before I knew it, I was on the other side. I immediately saw two booths situated on a platform. They both had arched doorways. There was complete darkness in each of the booths. One booth was to my right and the other booth was situated just a little beyond. I immediately sensed Maria's presence only I couldn't see her. It took me a moment before I realized that she was in the booth to my right. So I began to direct my thoughts in her direction telling her that I was there for her. I also told her that there was no reason for her to be frightened. I tried to make it clear that I was there with the abundance of love energy that had been generated during the family gathering. I told her that the love had been given openly and freely."

"Maria then sent me a telepathic message, saying that she wanted to communicate something important before she left. I understood and told her to express whatever it was she wanted. Suddenly, I could see a shadowy figure of a woman standing in front of the booth to my right. Maria seemed friendly, but also appeared to be a bit shy. Maria then said, that what she wanted to express could only be done through the physical form. Then without any hesitation, I gave Maria permission to enter my body. But for some reason, Maria still appeared to be hesitant and didn't want to leave the protection of the booth. I had to continue coaxing her a bit more before she decided to come forward."

"When Maria finally stepped towards me, she instantly transformed herself into a white spiral cloud. The spiral was rotating slowly and had appeared to have a yellowish tint or hew to it. The spiral remained hovering several feet from me before it began to move closer. It was heading directly for my solar plexus and that is where it began to immerse itself into my body. I was obviously apprehensive since this was my first experience, but I was not frightened. I then began to feel myself welling-up and I wanted to cry. And then while Maria was still inside of me, she said that she loved Marcy's music and I sensed myself trying to hum in harmony with what was being played on the piano. It amused me to think that Maria had taken some additional liberties to express her joy."

"I knew then that Maria's sadness had been completely dissipated and that she had resolved her issue. Maria was still in the form of a spiral as she withdrew. Except that now, the yellowish tint had also disappeared and the spiral was pure white. Again, the spiral remained hovering a few feet directly in front of me. But now there was a whole bunch of white like tubes loosely attached to the spiral. The tubes extended in every direction. I couldn't see where they went, except I knew one of them was attached to you. My impression was that the tubes were attached to everyone who had attended the family gathering."

"Then, just like a spacecraft being launched, the tubes began to slowly detach themselves from the spiral, one at a time. The last tube to withdraw was the one that was attached to you and that was when Maria quickly materialized into spirit form again."

Lynn then stopped for a moment so she could recall the emotions that she had experienced during those precious moments. She started again, "I could see Maria dressed in turn of the century clothing. She had on a long dark skirt that reached to her ankles and she had a ruffled white blouse that had a high collar and leg of mutton sleeves. Her long dark hair was combed back and flowed down her back almost to her waist. And yes, she was beautiful. I could see that she was happy and eager to express her joy. Except that now she appeared confused and didn't seem to know what she was supposed to do next."

"However, still situated on the platform was the second booth and in it I could see a small bright light in the entrance. Instantly, I remembered Sharon's message. So I immediately followed her instructions and told Maria to 'go towards the light.' Maria, then turned saw the light and then remained motionless staring at it for a moment. It was as though she didn't want to go, so I urged her again, 'go into the light!' But now the light was getting brighter and appeared to be beckoning to her from some other dimension. Then Maria began to slowly walk towards the light, except that she stopped, as though having forgotten something. She then turned in my direction and said, 'Please give my thanks to the family for the love that they have given me—and to them—I give my love in return. I also thank you—and I also give you my love—and to all I say farewell.'"

"Again, Maria turned and this time without hesitating, she walked directly into the bright light. No sooner did she enter the light and the light began to lift off. As the booth slowly ascended, the sky suddenly became clear blue and I saw an eagle circling overhead. I could see that Maria was still smiling and even waved to me for one last time. But as the white light gained speed, it quickly faded away into a faint glimmer and then blinked out. When I opened my eyes there was nothing for me to see but the washtub."

Tears had been in Lynn's eyes all the time that she had been describing the details regarding the release procedures. She was now staring at me and looking for my reaction. I was speechless and I got up and went over to the park rail. Looking out across the bay, I could see the lights from the planes that were descending to land at Newark Airport. There was also a brightly-lit ferryboat slowly heading for Staten Island and the lights from the bridge brightened up the bay not far from where we were sitting. I thought about how someday, I would have to deliver Maria's 'farewell message' to the family. Only this time, I wasn't going to wait two years. Then while I glanced straight upwards into the starlight sky, I tried to visualize Maria's ascent. Maybe she was heading for the seven sisters star cluster or to some other galaxy. Maria had asked and Maria had received. Her spirit was now free to wander among the stars and to learn all the secrets of the universe. Tears had now filled my eyes when I walked over to Lynn and kissed her. "Thank you so much for everything, I will never forget it." I said.

On the way back to the apartment we walked down the street until we came to the foot of the pedestrian staircase. We discovered that the streetlight at the foot of the staircase was out, so Lynn said, "Look Armand, the streetlight is out. We didn't do that, did we?" Lynn questioned.

"No, we didn't come this way," I responded.

"Do you think we could put it on?" Lynn challenged.

"Sure watch this!" I said. I then took a hold of one of Lynn's hands and confidently walked over to the light pole and then placed our hands on it. Instantly, the streetlight came on just as though we had flicked a light switch. I quickly grabbed Lynn and while we were both laughing and giggling, I gave her a big hug.

"Do you know Lynn, we just experienced a miracle and I know that no one is going to believe us! But that doesn't matter. It's what we know and feel in our hearts that counts!" I exclaimed.

"I know!" Lynn responded proudly

I then took Lynn by the hand and we proceeded to bound up the stairs two at a time, laughing all the way. Upon reaching the top we stopped to kiss and embrace.

"I can't wait to see Carmela and Aunt Carmen," I said. "Only this time, I will have become the new family storyteller," I added

Suddenly I was reminded of the flying eagle's dream and the wink that he had given me. Just as the eagle had indicated everything turned out just fine and with our state of grace having ended, Lynn and I went to bed feeling fulfilled. Lynn was no longer depressed and it was my first night of uninterrupted sleep that I hadn't had in a long time, no ringing of the ears, no Indian flute, and no—vivid dreams!

MARIA

0-595-33660-4

Printed in the United Kingdom
by Lightning Source UK Ltd.
R678300001B/R6783PG119889UKX46B/41}